Sketch Map of
POWD[ER]
COUN[TY]

POWDER RIVER

N
S

BLACK HILLS

DAKOTA

CHEYENNE RIVER

RENO STATION

[P]ORTUGEE'S [R]OUTE

The Blizzard

The Passage of The Mountains

NORTH PLATTE RIVER

NEBRASKA

[L]ARAMIE MOUNTAINS

FORT LARAMIE

NORTH AGAINST THE SIOUX

BY KENNETH ULYATT

PRENTICE-HALL, INC.
ENGLEWOOD CLIFFS, N.J.

Copyright © 1965 by K. R. Ulyatt

Published in Great Britain by Wm. Collins Sons & Co. Ltd.

First American Edition published by
Prentice-Hall, Inc., 1967.

Library of Congress Catalog Card Number: 67-16393

Printed in the United States of America

T 62374

Prentice-Hall International, Inc., London
Prentice-Hall of Australia, Pty. Ltd., Sydney
Prentice-Hall of Canada, Ltd., Toronto
Prentice-Hall of India Private Ltd., New Delhi
Prentice-Hall of Japan, Inc., Tokyo

CONTENTS

BOOK ONE

THE
EPIC RIDE

1
THE FIRST BLOW

Loud and unmistakable above the ringing of the axes, a rifle shot echoed across the clearing and brought work to a halt. There was no hesitation, not even a shouted command among those who heard it; this was Indian country and every man in the work party knew that only seconds lay between him and a desperate fight for life. The axes dropped among the wood chips at the foot of the big trees. Rifles were snatched from where they rested, propped against the grey trunks, and down the hillside to the wagons below streamed some fifteen to twenty men. Many were stripped to the waist; a few caught up jackets and shirts as they ran but most of them did not bother. They had one objective: to get back to the wagons before the attack began.

From the shelter of the trees a little higher up the valley burst a compact group of mounted Indians. As they rode at breakneck speed towards the horses tethered beyond the wagons they split up and began a high-pitched, ceaseless screaming. A tattered blanket streamed in the air, swooping from side to side like some large bird of prey and, as if this were a signal, from the hillside above the hidden guns of the Sioux began to speak. Behind the thick boards and heavy wheels the wagoners replied with two or three solitary shots, until a sharp command told them to "hold fire."

By now, the group of galloping Indians had almost reached the horses who were beginning to neigh loudly at the noise and tug at their tether ropes. Two guards crouched down behind the scanty cover of the bushes, waiting with rifles leveled until the very last moment, determined to make their shots

pay. The wagon horses grew more restless as the clamor of the
Indians and the wild thud of hooves swept nearer.

"Fire!"

From the circles of wagons came the sharp volley of a dozen
rifles. At the same time the two horse guards let fly. The
Indian with the blanket fell forward over his horse's neck, hung
for a moment as if steadying himself, then tumbled to the
ground, rolling over and over in the dust. The guards broke
cover, running back as they struggled to reload their rifles.
Then the Indians were on them—and ignored them! This was
no time for counting coup, the braves had one single task to
accomplish swiftly. A slash from a knife and the first horse-
line broke. An Indian mount reared, its forelegs threshing the
air as its rider, one foot hooked over its back, the other in a
rawhide noose under the horse's neck, leaned almost to the
ground to cut at the second rope. Another line of wagon
horses was loose! The din rose to a howling climax and dust
almost completely obliterated the swirling mass of shouting
Indians and frightened horses. Then, like sparks from a cath-
erine wheel, the horses began to rush out in all directions from
the churning center, until at last, the whole mêlée of tossing
manes, gaudy feathers and brandished lances was gone in a
ragged stampede down the valley.

Shots pursued them, but hanging low over their mounts
and protected by the dust and the glare of the July sun at
noon, the Sioux were safe. The noise of the hoofbeats died
away; the dust drifted across the valley, cloaking down upon
the motionless soldiers and half-clad woodmen, spreading
white and even on the flatboard bottoms of the wagons. Unshaven faces peered grimly over the barrels of the rifles; here
and there a man moved to wipe sweat out of his eyes with his
forearm. Complete silence settled over the scene.

Presently, as nothing further happend, the tension eased.

"Aw, why don't they come on and get it over with?" The
speaker was a young soldier, tanned brown by the wind and
sun but still new to the plains.

"They'll come soon enough, son." An old man, white streaks
showing in the untidy, dark hair that straggled from under a

battered hat, spoke from the shelter of an upturned box nearby. He was one of the civilian scouts who had joined the detail of soldiers on the wood-cutting expedition. "The Sioux never ducked a fight yet, to my knowledge."

A movement in the bush on the left caught his eye and he slid his rifle silently forward. The young soldier cocked his rifle and the click of the hammer coming back echoed across the clearing.

"Hold your fire," shouted a lieutenant from where he was kneeling in the center of the circle. The movement in the bushes ceased. There was nothing to be seen in the valley. The dust of the stampede had settled completely.

"Think that was all they was after, the horses?" Another trooper spoke from the old man's left.

"I dunno." The scout moved his rifle slightly, resting it more comfortably in the crook of his arm. "I dunno. It ain't usual, this quiet. They always come before in one mighty rush, stampedin' the horses is just part of it. It ain't usual at all! But then Red Cloud ain't no ordinary Indian."

The lieutenant, who had moved closer to the wagons and was peering out across the valley, nodded a silent agreement and turned to survey the nearby hills. He called across the circle:

"Sergeant!"

A tough, stumpy figure came at a crouching run across the open space, straightened up as he reached the lieutenant and saluted.

"Sergeant! Take four men and reconnoiter beyond that ridge." The lieutenant pointed to a rise in the floor of the valley about five hundred yards away. It rose higher as it crossed the level ground until it joined the trees where the woodmen had been busy such a short time before. The view beyond, the route back to the fort and safety, was blocked from the circle of wagons.

"Move up to the top and you'll get a look down the whole valley. Signal back what you see. Don't go beyond the ridge, or into the trees."

The sergeant and men clambered over the wagons and disappeared into the stunted bushes.

The sun beat down. The young trooper spoke again. "Do you think they know, back at the fort, that we've been attacked?" he asked.

"Can't tell, son," the old scout answered him. "We're a mite farther out than usual . . ." He broke off and looked keenly at the trees which stirred slightly in the fitful breeze. "Nope." He shook his head. "Don't reckon they'd hear. And you wouldn't see nothin' from Pilot Hill, neither."

All round the circle the men stirred as the information was passed on. Rifles rattled as they shifted position, stretching to cure a cramped muscle or to get a better view over the wagon boards. There was no hope of the lookout on Pilot Hill either having heard or seen the fighting then. Time alone would bring their plight to the notice of Colonel Carrington in the fort, and it seemed that they were in for a long wait before help could reach them.

The men settled down. The desultory conversation died away. Lieutenant Mallory perched himself up on a wheel. Down the valley he could see the sergeant and his men beginning to climb the ridge.

Two hours later there was still silence over the valley—but it was the silence of death. Even the crackle and roar of the burning wagons had subsided.

That was how Portugee Philips found them. The scouting party, warned early by the nonappearance of the wood train that something was wrong, came cautiously up the valley. The first thing they noticed was the smell of burning that still hung in the air. Then the scattered tracks of many horses told them the beginning of the tale.

They came next upon the bodies of the sergeant and his men, lying in an irregular line, stripped of their uniforms, scalped and mutilated. The terrible trail pointed up the valley and, as they rode on, the evidence of the fight multiplied until they drew rein before what was left of the wood train.

In silence they looked at the heap of ashes, the iron hoops and stays of the wagons sticking up from the still-smoldering remains, at the scattered equipment and clothing, at the terrible heap of bodies.

Red Cloud had struck his first blow at Fort Phil Kearny.

2
THE FIGHT
FOR THE PLAINS

There had been war in the south between the red man and the white for a long time. The fierce tribes of the southern plains, the Kiowas and the Cheyennes, had watched the wagons of the palefaces roll westward across their land in ever-increasing numbers, pushing along the Santa Fe and the Platte River trails towards California and Oregon. Why did they come? the Indians asked. What did these strange people want from the lands that had always belonged to the Indian?

These questions were not easy to answer. The red man, in fact, could find no answer to them that made sense. From the times when the Great Spirit had given the lands to his children, the Indians had lived in peace. True, the tribes fought among themselves, but to the red man war was a glorious and honorable game. If he did not fight, how else was a warrior to show his courage? How else could he gain the coveted emblems of bravery, the tufted feathers, the battle scars and markings of a man to parade proudly before the squaws of his village?

But although they fought each other persistently, the Indians' form of warfare could really be called a deadly sport in which certain rules were scrupulously observed by all and brave deeds counted more than the extermination of the enemy; a sport that could be compared more easily with the chivalrous battles of the knights of the Middle Ages than anything else. War was a testing ground for the courage of the individual and often it was more important to "count coup"—to touch an enemy before the eyes of the other warriors in the heat of the skirmish—than to kill. The barbaric war of the white man, where all possible means were used against soldiers and civilians alike to bring defeat to the enemy was unknown to the Indian. And so was the white man's hunger for land and his love of the strange yellow metal for which he dug so patiently in the hills.

When the Great Spirit had given the land to the Indians long, long ago, he had given in plenty. The rivers teemed with fish, the mountain slopes were alive with game. Fruit and berries grew in abundance and the plains were black with buffalo. Why, the Indians asked, should a man want to fence the land or call a certain portion of it his own when it all belonged to the Great Spirit who, in his wisdom, had provided enough for all the tribes as they wandered and hunted at will?

With these thoughts at the back of his mind, with centuries of good hunting and roaming free across one of the most beautiful lands in the world behind him, the Indian watched the advance of the white man with some curiosity, but little fear.

For the white man's part the land was a challenge, something to be conquered at all costs, something that offered a richer, better living and perhaps the treasure trove of gold. If the Indian stood in the way so much the worse for him. Who cared, anyway?

The Cheyennes and the Kiowas and the great Indian nations of the plains were being forced to care as the tide of the white man's civilization flowed relentlessly westward. The white man had conquered the great woodlands of the east; he had tamed the forest, farmed the broad valleys. From the Great Lakes to the swamps of Florida, he had built towns and villages and industries. Now, ever hungry for the land beyond, he looked avidly over the wide Missouri River towards the rich, warm, gold-filled lands of California and Oregon beyond the Rocky Mountains.

But to reach that land he first had to conquer the plains. They stretched westward from the wide river—a vast, rolling, seemingly-empty expanse that nevertheless teemed with life. Black herds of buffalo wandered across them, dark masses which, from the distance, looked like slow, creeping cloud shadows moving over the waving grass. And the Indians of the

plains lived by the buffalo. Food, clothing, housing, even their
weapons were all provided by the body and hide of this shaggy,
ungainly beast. In summer they followed him, hunting and
feasting. In winter they moved to the shelter of the canyons
and there, in their tepees made from the hides of the buffalo, in
their great buffalo robes and buffalo sleeping bags, they lived
on the dried buffalo meat, or pemmican as they called it, until
the snows had gone and the spring weather tempted them out
to the plains again, into the next round of life that the Great
Spirit had ordained for his tribes.

Perhaps it was the disturbing of the buffalo that first aroused
the Southern Indians against the white man. With creaking
wheels and bellowing cattle, with shouts and shots and cracking of whips the fighting caravans rolled on to the plains,
frightening the buffalo from the country, ruining the hunting
grounds.

The red braves had further reasons for complaint. As the
flow of immigration to the west grew bigger, staging-posts
sprang up on the prairie, places where the traveler could find
food and shelter and a rest on his long journey. The Indian
watched and gradually he began to understand that the white
man was no mere traveler across his hunting grounds. Where-
ever his wagon wheels were allowed to bite into the grass of
the great plains they ate the land away from under the Indian's
feet. And, like many a proud race, the red man took up arms,
before it was too late to call a halt to the advance of civilization.

The story behind the Indian wars of the eighteen-sixties
and seventies is a long and complicated one, a story of shame
and dishonor for the white man who was bent on conquering
the west at all costs. As the Indian bands swept down on the
wagon trains, the travelers called out loudly for protection.
The Government sent the Army out in answer and along the
trails to the west they began to build a line of forts. Treaties
were concluded with the tribes to grant safe passage to the
white man through their country and to mark the limits of the
Indian lands. Boundaries were agreed, over which no white
man was to cross.

But such treaties were doomed before they were signed, for no sooner did the Indian relax on what he believed to be the safety of his own hunting grounds, than one daring white man would cross into the forbidden territory, discover a cache of gold or rich land to farm and then hundreds would follow, sweeping aside all Indians who stood in their way, eating up up the land for themselves.

In the medicine lodges of the Great Plains tribes, the plan to strike back at the white man was born, and soon the traffic across the prairie was brought to a standstill as the Indians swooped on the isolated trading posts and any wagon train that dared to try the journey.

In the north the Sioux watched. Treaties had given them all the lands beyond the Platte River. For some time there had been peace—and then gold had been discovered in the distant territory of Montana. Within weeks a trail—the Bozeman Trail—had been blazed through the Sioux hunting grounds and the white stream again began to pour westward into the red man's land.

Red Cloud, Chief of the Sioux, knew that the beginning of the end had come. If the white man was allowed to set foot firmly in this great territory he knew that disaster would follow for his people. He urged the young Sioux warriors to action. Savage attacks on all who attempted the Bozeman Trail began, until in 1866 the Government called a great council to settle the matter at Fort Laramie on the Platte River.

3
THE GREAT COUNCIL
AT LARAMIE

From afar off Portugee Phillips could see the tepees pitched beside Laramie Creek. There were some half a dozen of them set a little way from the fort, and as the Cavalry rode nearer he could distinguish the bright color patterns painted on the sides and see the squaws busy over the cooking fires. Thin lines of smoke crept up into the clear June sky.

It was a brilliant sunny morning and Phillips was riding towards Fort Laramie with a detachment of the United States Army. He had taken the job, with his friend Jim Bridger, the famous frontiersman and scout, of guide to a secret expedition which Colonel Henry B. Carrington was leading into the northern hills. After weeks of hard going, the weary column of horses, wagons and footsore Twenty-Seventh Infantry was approaching its destination. Laramie was their last stop before they set out into the wilderness.

There appeared to be little activity around the fort on this warm summer's morning. On the slender palisades which surmounted the perpendicular walls of mud-brick, a few men could be seen grouped together watching their approach. Behind the fort, desolate ridges of barren country receded into the distance where grey, jagged and forbidding, the Black Hills rose seven thousand feet into the clear blue sky. Cattle and horses roamed the corrals that straggled out across the meadow running down to the river. But the usual bustle and activity, the coming and going that normally went on around each little prairie township was entirely absent. Even Jim Bridger, who had ridden ahead earlier in the morning, was not there to greet them.

Portugee urged his horse forward at a signal from the group of officers riding ahead of him. He cantered up the side of the column of cavalry and reined back beside Colonel Carrington.

"What do you make of it, Mr. Phillips?" asked the Colonel, pointing a white gauntlet towards the tepees. Phillips answered without hesitation.

"Red Cloud," he said. "Seen those lodges before. He's in the fort, I reckon."

Colonel Carrington nodded. "Then the council is still in session. We're a little early." He turned to the lieutenant riding on his left and gave an order. The lieutenant wheeled his horse away and flung up an arm. Immediately the column behind clattered to a halt, the horses stretching their necks down towards the short, burnt grass at the edge of the trail, the troopers relaxing in the saddles or leaning forward to pat the necks of their mounts. A thin cloud of dust drifted away to the east. The Colonel and his aides rode on. Portugee Phillips kept pace with them, a little to one side.

"Mr. Phillips," called the Colonel, "you and I will ride on in. The column will halt here until we see what's doing."

Phillips raised his hand to his wide-brimmed hat in acknowledgment and the Colonel turned to consult his officers. They rode on in conference for a few minutes, then pulled away, saluting, and galloping back towards the column. The Colonel kept Sergeant Haggerty with him; motioned to Phillips to ride closer and urged his horse into a canter. Phillips swung alongside and, out of the corner of his eye, he caught sight of the wagons and the two howitzers moving out from the rear into a position of readiness. He's taking no chances, he thought to himself as they rode forward.

The water swirled and boiled round the horses' legs as they forded the creek. Climbing the opposite bank they turned their mounts towards the fort and galloped up to the gates. The guard saluted as they thundered under the blockhouse which spanned the entrance. Portugee caught a glimpse of faces at the high window between the double gates, which was used to parley with suspicious visitors to the fort in times of trouble—then they were out of shadow into sunshine once

more, pulling the horses to a walk to pass through the buildings inside the walls and riding into the big square in the center.

Abruptly they reined in. The square was packed with people. The Colonel dismounted, tossed his reins to Sergeant
Haggerty and strode forward. A lieutenant, pushing through
the throng of troops and civilians who were grouped in a great
semicircle, stopped and saluted him.

"Colonel Carrington, sir? General's compliments and would
you please come and meet the Commission, sir?"

Carrington returned the salute, nodded and followed the
lieutenant through the crowd until they reached the open
space in the center.

The entire population of the fort seemed to be assembled
there and were watching the council which was in progress on
the far side of the square. Dogs whined and scurried about,
a few children played idly together behind their elders and
there was some shuffling and talking, but for the most part the
crowd was silent and attentive. Phillips, quietly sitting on his
horse near the buildings that lay huddled against the inside
walls of the fort, could see beyond the heads of the crowd.
There were large trestle tables set up on the opposite side of
the square. The General and the Commissioners from Washington were grouped round them and appeared to be in
earnest debate. The tall figure of Jim Bridger, Portugee's
friend, could be seen among the General's staff behind the
tables. To the left, sitting in a compact group on blankets
spread on the dusty ground, were the Indians. Between the
two, from which position he had been addressing both groups,
stood a tall, solitary figure, a blanket round his waist, his hair
in heavy plaits down the side of his gaunt face, the sun shining
on the beads of his jacket and on the decorated staff he held in
his hand.

"Red Cloud."

Phillips turned at the words and an old man who had been
leaning back in the shadows of a nearby shack came slowly
along the raised balcony towards him. He gestured with the
stem of a pipe and leaned forward over the railing, his bearded
face just above Portugee's.

"Red Cloud and the General are goin' it, like a couple of prairie dogs." The old man grinned. "Started off all peaceful this mornin', but it's been workin' up ever since. Reckon the Indians ain't in no mood for bargainin'."

Phillips nodded, his keen eyes once more turned towards the tall figure of Red Cloud. He had ceased speaking and was watching Colonel Carrington striding towards the table.

"What's the trouble?" asked Phillips.

"We-ell," began the old-timer. "They've had just about much as they can stand. Yep. I don't reckon you can ask any man to take more'n what them durned Sioux have taken over the past two, three years."

Phillips looked up with awakening interest. This was something new; any attitude that showed sympathy towards the Indians was rare in this raw country. Exaggerated tales of massacre and treachery spread back in the east by people who had probably never seen a plains Indian caused many pioneers to regard them with dread, fiends to be avoided or beaten off at all costs. The men who were settling on the edge of the plains or making a living on the trails that crossed them regarded the Indians in much the same way as they regarded the wild prairie dogs—as pests to be exterminated on every occasion.

The only people who had a good word for them were a few of the old trappers and traders who had lived with the Indians and appreciated their way of life. The old man must be one of them, reflected Phillips as he looked into the clear grey eyes with their network of wrinkles around them and the slightly "unfocused" look that comes of gazing too long at the far horizons. The old man went on:

"Why, two years ago, Government made a treaty with old Spotted Tail. Actually give them all land north of here from the Platte River for their hunting grounds. Good land it was, I'll say that; but Indians got to live somewhere like any other folk. Now," he paused and spat in the sand, and Phillips, glancing across the heads of the crowd, saw that Carrington had reached the table and was being introduced to the officers now standing behind it, "what happens? There's a new gold

strike up in Montana and before you know it folks are pourin'
through the Sioux country. Not peaceable like, mind you, but
shootin' anythin' they can see and drivin' the Sioux out of
what Government give them two years back. Can't wonder
the medicine men are tellin' them that the White Eagle—a
great chief—is comin' out of the east to eat up their lands and
. . . why, what's that? What's goin' on now?"

It had happened so quickly that Phillips thought for a moment that Red Cloud had attacked Colonel Carrington. The
Colonel had turned from the table and taken two or three steps
when the Sioux Chief leaped forward. Carrington made an
involuntary movement to one side as Red Cloud's hand flew
out. But it carried no weapon. A rigid arm and forefinger
pointed at Carrington's shoulder. The Colonel glanced down
at the silver emblem of his Army authority. Red Cloud was
speaking in ringing tones, his eyes blazing. Behind him, his
chiefs had also leaped to their feet and were crowding forward. There was a stir among the army officers around the
table.

Red Cloud's arm swung round like a scythe. He paused for
a moment and not a soul moved in the tense and hushed
crowd. He dropped his arm and, grasping his ceremonial lance
with both hands, drew it across the ground before him leaving
a ragged line in the dust, plain for all to see. Looking up, Red
Cloud addressed Carrington in the white man's language.

"This," Red Cloud indicated the line with the hilt of his
lance, "Crazy Woman River."

"This," he jabbed the ground nearest Carrington's feet,
"belong white man. This," another jab on his own side of the
drawn line, "belong Indian. He drew himself erect, the lance
now balanced easily in his right hand, his men close and menacing behind him. His next words rang out like the crack of a
bullwhip across the square.

"If white man walk in Sioux land . . ." he made a swift
gesture with his free hand towards his own head, the long forefinger traced a savage scalping circle in the air. There was no
mistaking the deadly meaning. At the same instant he raised
his right arm and flung the lance downwards. It stuck quiv-

ering in the line he had drawn across the sand. The Indians gave a hoarse shout of assent.

In the silence that followed, Red Cloud wheeled and strode from the council.

Portugee Phillips watched him come across the circle.

The familiar features, the piercing black eyes, hawk nose and resolute mouth, were stern and unrelenting. The crowd parted in silence, the children pulled hurriedly away, the dogs slinking back, to allow the Indian a clear passage. Phillips eased his horse sideways—he had spoken with Red Cloud perhaps three times before. He raised his hand in greeting. The Chief gave no sign. Aloof, he strode past, his men following at a little distance. They disappeared round the corner of the buildings and went out through the gates of the fort, under the empty blockhouse upon which the old red running horse painted there nearly twenty years before by the early fur traders still beat a pattern of defiance with its stamping hooves.

The crowd broke into an instant uproar. Pushing through the throng, Colonel Carrington came striding back towards his horse.

"Haggerty!"

The sergeant spurred forward. "Sir!"

"Ride back to the column. Tell Captain Peters that the Indians are leaving in peace. The column is to remain where it is now at a state of readiness—but on no account are the Indians to be molested. Understand?"

The sergeant wheeled and saluted in one movement. "Yessir!" He put his spur to the horse and cantered out of the fort. Phillips dismounted and hitched his horse to the rail in front of the shack. The crowd was breaking up—many were moving back to their work in the fort, others stood around in noisy groups.

"What was it?" Phillips asked. "What sparked him off?"

The old man's eyes glinted with suppressed excitement. He took his pipe out of his mouth. "What I told you," he said. "The White Eagle, the legend: Red Cloud says it's the Army come to take away the Indian lands."

"Yes, but why pick out Carrington?" mused Phillips.

"His badges; you know what an army colonel wears on his shoulder!"

Suddenly Phillips understood. An army colonel's emblem was the silver eagle of the United States. Red Cloud had seen the eagle on the shoulders of Carrington's uniform and had seized the opportunity to conclude his argument on a note of indignation. He had identified the U.S. Army with the White Eagle of Indian legend—the eagle that was to cut up the Indian lands.

Phillips looked across the square. The officers had moved away from the tables. Before them a knot of idle spectators stood gazing at the ground. Red Cloud's lance swayed there, the June sun glinting on the feathered ornaments and metal tip. It was a sign of death to all who dared cross the river into the Sioux lands.

And Colonel Carrington's instructions were to proceed north and build two forts in the Powder River country, two hundred and fifty miles inside Indian territory!

4

THE BUILDING
OF THE FORT

The first stake that was driven into the ground at Piney Creek was tantamount to a declaration of war. One after another the stakes went in until the projected fort was outlined and the sweating soldiers began to dig the first foundations of the stockade. Fort Phil Kearny, it was to be called, named after the great American soldier and explorer.

In very defiance of the treaties signed at the peace councils the Government of the United States was staking a claim to territory which it had already given to the Indian. Colonel Carrington had orders to restock and repair the old Fort Reno just north of Laramie, then to move on and build two new forts to protect the Bozeman Trail. He selected the first site with care, on a small branch of the Powder River, some two hundred and fifty miles north of Fort Laramie. But although the site was good, the construction of the fort presented many problems. The surrounding countryside was bare of trees, and wood for every inch of the great stockade, together with the many buildings inside, had to be fetched from the forests on the edge of the meadows over seven miles away.

Portugee Phillips, who was helping to plan the layout of the fort, looked up from the drawings before him and gazed round at the low hills. To the northeast lay the river; beyond, a conical hill rose up, from the summit of which was gained a clear view of the winding stream and distant woodlands. Colonel Carrington had already stationed three men at the top as lookouts and Phillips could see them erecting some sort of shelter on the grassy summit.

His gaze swept onwards, over the contours of the countryside and the irregular blue-grey hills on the horizon. He frowned, and Lieutenant Mallory, coming quietly up behind him, saw that worried look as Phillips turned to greet him.

At this time, Portugee John Phillips was a youngish man of medium build with the loose, easy grace that spoke of a life of action spent largely on horseback in the forest and on the plains. His brown eyes were set wide apart in his smooth, dark face and the trace of a distant Spanish ancestry shone in the black hair and eyebrows, and the thin tracing of stubble on his upper lip and chin. His frown accentuated the piercing quality of his gaze and the lieutenant felt a touch of apprehension as he joined the scout.

"Anything wrong?" asked the lieutenant.

Phillips shook his head. His eyes searched the hills behind the lieutenant's shoulder. "Nope," he finally answered, "nothing wrong here." He looked abruptly back to the lieutenant's young, open face. He liked the man. He was new to the Indian country but he was cheerful and enthusiastic and he seemed anxious to learn.

"How's the timber to be organized?" Phillips asked.

"The Colonel has got the report now," Mallory answered. "Two or three teams working in relays most likely. It'll be slow going at first because there'll only be a few spare troopers and the foresters who are coming up to work with the wagons tomorrow. But once the stockade's up, Colonel plans to bring in more folks. Maybe families—you know, storekeepers, blacksmiths and the like. It'll be a sort of trading station, too, I reckon."

Phillips shook his head. "There'll be no trading here."

Lieutenant Mallory looked at him, puzzled, but said nothing for a while. Then he volunteered a little more information.

"First woodcutting party moves off after noon," he remarked. "They aim to mark enough timber for the stockade in the valley over there. Then, when the lumbermen come in, they can go straight to work without delay. I'd sure like to go with them," he added reflectively.

Phillips looked at him again, a trace of a smile on his lips.

"Don't worry," he said, "you'll see enough of them before we're through here."

The lieutenant flashed him a quick look. "Indians?" and Phillips nodded. "Is that what you meant about no trading?" Mallory asked. Phillips thought a while before answering; when he did, all trace of banter had gone out of his voice. He made his statement with the assurance and certainty of one who knows what he's talking about.

"You were at Laramie. You saw Red Cloud. The Sioux never had a Chief like him before. Indians," he took a deep breath and went on, "have fought us and fought each other up till now. It's their way of life. Fightin's a sort of sport with them. Oh, it's savage enough, according to our standards. Yet, I don't know. There's a sort of, of . . ." he sought for the right word and then continued, "chivalry about it. The warriors fight, they leave the squaw and papoose alone. Then there's some tribes who are just natural enemies. The Crow and the Sioux, now. And there's the Cheyenne—they're so busy fighting each other, we've been able to move right in on them. And before they've knowed it, they've been pushed off land that's been theirs since time began." He broke off and his eyes ranged the blue hills. Mallory watched him in silence until he went on again.

"Red Cloud's altered all that. He's the biggest thinkin' Chief they've every had. Not only the Sioux. I hear tell that over Little Goose River he's got Sioux and Cheyenne and maybe Oglala as well. Sure must take some doin' to weld a bunch like that together."

"Why's he doing all this now?" questioned Mallory.

"The Bozeman Trail's the last stand, I reckon," said Phillips. "It cuts right across territory we gave the Sioux by treaty more than a year ago. Red Cloud knows no Government Treaty ain't worth more than the paper it's writ on. I'm not saying the Government don't want to keep the peace, mind, it's just that they can't. Out west here there ain't much law and order. A few wild spirits move in and shoot up Indians like it's fun and you've a first-class war on your hands. That's what happened

in the south. That's what I reckon it's comin' to here. Red
Cloud's getting ready for us. He knows that once we set foot
in the Big Horns we're here to stay. You might say Red Cloud's
determined to stop the white man comin' any farther west.
And he's organizin' the whole Indian nation to do this."

"And that means a war to drive us clean out of the territory?
He'll never do it!"

Phillips nodded agreement. "He can't win. In the long run,
whatever the rights and wrongs of it, he can't win as I see it.
But he's going to try!" And he turned towards Pilot Hill
where the lookouts were still working on the shelter.

"It must be here," he continued. "Once this fort's built the
land south as far as the Platte River will be as good as lost to the
Sioux. Red Cloud will do his durndest to stop it."

"Well, that means we can expect a heap of trouble." Mallory hitched up his belt slightly his hand brushing his holster.

Phillips nodded.

"That's what we're here for, I guess." The lieutenant
waved his hand in a gesture of parting and strode away, his
head bent in thought. Yes, that's what they were here for.

And Mallory had his fill of fighting the next day, when he
went out with the first wood train. The work party was wiped
out to a man among the overturned and burning wagons five
miles west of Piney Creek. Red Cloud had struck his first blow
against Fort Phil Kearney.

But the building went on. After that first disaster they
learned that they needed as many guards as workers on the
wood trains. Red Cloud laid siege to the fort from the moment
the first poles were driven in. Scouting parties of Indians surrounded the fort in a circle of death. They watched the long
stockade go up—one thousand, six hundred feet long by six
hundred feet wide. They saw the tower by the gateway take
shape, the corrals and the buildings begin to grow. And never
for a moment did they leave the white man in peace. Parties of
workmen, wives and few children came through to the fort—
in wagon trains armed to the teeth and heavily guarded by
soldiers. Equipment came in to help the building: saws, a

blacksmith's forge, stoves, baking ovens, and other items. But once inside, the men were confined to the fort, under the protection of the thick wall and the silent, squatting howitzer guns. Each man who left did so knowing that he might never see it again.

Soldiers accompanied the wood trains that set out to get the timber. Men worked with their rifles close at hand for five hard months. Attacks occurred like the first one—and were repulsed. Sometimes the wood train was cut off, surrounded, until violent signals from the lookouts on Pilot Hill brought troops galloping from the fort to rescue them. Eventually, Red Cloud's attacks grew so persistent that no force of less than one hundred and fifty armed men dared venture out. Even then, many men were cut off from the main party and killed. Sometimes they just disappeared, which was worse, for that meant that they had been captured and carried away for torture.

Fort Phil Kearny was surrounded by a ring of death from July 15th, 1866. Portugee Phillips's forebodings were proved tragically true, and in December, when the sky was heavy with snow about to fall and the fort was virtually finished, Red Cloud struck the heaviest blow of all.

5

THE FIRE-EATER

"Give me eighty men and I'll ride through the whole Sioux nation!" If Red Cloud had heard of the boast his eyes would have glinted with savage amusement. Certainly it caused Portugee Phillips, leaning against the rail before the Colonel's headquarters, to look long and hard at the speaker as he strode angrily through the door and across the parade ground. He was followed by a second officer who hurried rapidly after him and began an animated conversation. They disappeared on the far side of the parade ground into the officers' quarters.

Jim Bridger, leaning against the hitching post alongside Phillips, pulled himself upright and spat reflectively in the dust.

"Durned stupid fire-eater!" he muttered.

The phrase stirred something in Phillips's memory. "Fire-eater Fetterman." The words echoed through his head as he looked in the direction in which the officer had gone. Yes, that was it. Two days ago when they had been talking about the new additions to the fort's already strong garrison he had heard somebody refer to one of the new officers as "Fire-eater Fetterman."

"Well, he'll learn." Jim Bridger, frontiersman born and bred, had little time for such tactics. "He'll get all the Indian fightin' he wants before long if my hunch is right. I only hope he don't kill off some poor unfortunate devil in doin' it."

Phillips nodded in agreement. He, too, had seen many men come from the east, so anxious to have a stab at the redskins that they endangered the lives of others. Such men, especially if they were in command of an army unit, spelled more trouble to an already harassed fort than a wagon load of trading muskets.

Colonel Fetterman was new to the west, but he arrived at Fort Phil Kearny trailing a cloud of glory behind him in the shape of an outstanding military reputation gained during the American Civil War. Promotion had quickly followed his exploits, and now he was a brevet lieutenant-colonel, addressed as "Colonel" in common courtesy. He regarded Indian fighting as something of an adventure and, from the very first days of his arrival, disagreed with the conduct of the campaign against Red Cloud.

"Carrington," he said to his brother officers in the mess, "is over-cautious. What those varmints need," he had thumped the table to emphasize his points, "is a lesson they are not likely to forget, and sitting back behind these stockades is not going to give it to them."

There was much more in the same strain, for Fetterman had a reputation for rapid and decisive action and was determined to strike a blow at the Indians as soon as the occasion arose —or before, if he could find the means of manufacturing an incident which would give him the opportunity to ride out at the head of his troop. He was listened to with interest and enthusiasm by some of the others. A few courageous officers who had seen something of the fight for the plains and had a healthy respect for the red foe, and especially Red Cloud's warriors, disagreed with him and said so openly.

Fetterman treated their opinions with scant respect and his fire-eating policy found an enthusiastic ally in Captain Brown —another young officer who was soon due to return to the east and was determined "to get Red Cloud's scalp to take back with him as a souvenir."

Fetterman had had one brush with the Chief since he joined the garrison at the fort. Half a dozen men had been killed in a clever ambush when the wood train had been attacked some weeks ago, and Fetterman had literally scoured the plains for miles with the hope of picking up the silent band who had struck the blow and disappeared as soon as help had rushed out from the fort. The Indians' refusal to engage in a fight had lent strength to Fetterman's poor opinion of the Sioux. "They just won't fight an adequately armed and trained force," he declared, and he appealed to Colonel Carrington to let him lead a detachment against the Sioux as the start of an offensive from Fort Phil Kearny.

But Colonel Carrington was a soldier who knew the plains and the tactics of the plains Indians as well as he knew the back of his hand. Moreover, he had a healthy respect for Red Cloud, a respect which had deepened as he saw the determined and persistent opposition that the fighting Chief of the Sioux offered to the white army's efforts to strengthen the outposts along the Bozeman Trail. And that was Carrington's job—his orders were first and foremost to provide the bases from which the Indian wars could be finally halted. Fort Phil Kearny was the first. Plans were already afoot to begin work on Fort C. Smith, many miles to the north. To step aside from this main task and engage in an offensive against the Sioux armies might well cost him the rest of the winter—and the lives of hundreds of men into the bargain.

"You must remember, Fetterman," Colonel Carrington faced the heated young officer across his desk, "that Indian warfare demands, above all, perfect coolness, steadiness and judgment. Red Cloud is fighting for his best and almost his last hunting grounds. He can't be whipped and punished by some little dash after a handful of braves. He must be made to respect and fear the authority of the United States Army."

"But, sir, that's just what I'm saying," broke in Fetterman, eagerly. "Give me eighty men, just . . ."

"No, sir!" Colonel Carrington was cautious as ever, and rigid in his determination to oppose Fetterman's wild plan. "That's not our task. As long as I am in command of this garrison, Colonel, we will stick to the main purpose of building and arming these forts. When that is completed, and not before, you will get your chance of engaging Red Cloud. And I may add, with due respect to your fighting reputation and ability of which I have not the slightest doubt, that when the time comes you will find Red Cloud as able an adversary as you would wish for."

Angrily, Fetterman left the office, followed by Captain Brown, who had supported the appeal for a force of eighty

men to ride through the Sioux nation. Jim Bridger and Portugee Phillips watched them go. Bridger raised his eyes to the
greying sky and dug his fingers into the pocket of a thick
jacket in search of tobacco.

"There's snow in the air." He sniffed keenly at the breath of
wind that sighed gently between the poles of the only unfinished building in the fort—the hospital. "Maybe a good
norther will cool that fire-eater off for a bit," and as Phillips
grinned in agreement Jim Bridger turned and stumped into the
outer office.

Yes, there certainly was snow in the air, despite the brightness of the wintry sun. It would come down off the hills,
whose tops were already white, quite suddenly in a day or
two, thought Phillips. And then work on the building would
have to stop. Maybe they would get the roof on the hospital
first. He glanced at the sky as hammering broke out anew from
the unfinished building and a group of men began to lay the
long rafter at one end. They'd have to hurry, if he knew anything about the weather signs. "Snow will be here before
tomorrow night," he murmured to himself as he turned up his
collar and walked back to the bunkhouse.

"Come on, men, the wood train's been attacked again!"
It was just after eleven o'clock when Portugee Phillips saw
frantic signals from the lookout on Pilot Hill. The wood train
which had started out a short time before was being attacked
by a party of Red Cloud's braves, behind the hill, several miles
to the west of the fort. A bugler ran from Colonel Carrington's
office as Phillips hurried towards the building and the army call
to action, "Boots and Saddles," rang out briskly on the clean
air. Almost immediately the fort burst into life. Men ran from
the barrack blocks buckling on their equipment. From the
corrals came a sudden flurry and neighing of horses as the
cavalry mounts were saddled.

In his office Colonel Carrington was already giving his
orders to Major Powell; Lieutenant Grummond stood in the
background listening keenly to the instructions, which involved taking a company of cavalry to drive off the attack,

when Colonel Fetterman strode through the door. Phillips, waiting in the outer office with Jim Bridger, could hear every word of the conversation.

"Sir!" exclaimed Fetterman as he brought up smartly before the desk and saluted. "I wish to be put in charge of the party going to the relief of the wood train. My rank, sir, of brevet lieutenant-colonel entitles me to the duty, with all respect to Major Powell." Fetterman nodded to his colleague and turned back to Colonel Carrington; there was a glint of excitement in his eyes.

Carrington looked steadily at him. He was perfectly right, of course, the rank of lieutenant-colonel, albeit an acting one, entitled him to the command before a mere major, but the Colonel hesitated. Fetterman was spoiling for a fight and Carrington knew that he could not afford to engage Red Cloud's men in great numbers without exposing the fort to considerable danger. Nevertheless, it would be a deliberate insult to give Major Powell the command over Fetterman's head. Could he trust Fetterman to relieve the wood train and return to the fort?

He made up his mind swiftly.

"Very well, then." Carrington stood up and faced the fire-eating Colonel across his desk. "Colonel Fetterman, you will take charge of the detachment. Take your own duty men, and Lieutenant Grummond will accompany you. You are to support the wood train, relieve it and report to me. And I want to make this quite clear. You are not to engage or pursue the Indians at the expense of leaving the wood train exposed. Under no circumstances are you to pursue beyond Lodge Trail Ridge. We are fighting a brave and desperate enemy. I do not doubt your own courage or that of the men under your command, but Red Cloud is out to harry us to the extreme and this may well be a cunningly laid trick. Remember my instructions, Colonel, and obey them implicitly. That is all."

The officers saluted, turned and hurried from the room, their booted feet clattering down the wooden steps to the parade ground. Across the square a detachment was already assembled, the December sun glinting and flashing on their equipment as they adjusted a girth here or a rifle scabbard there. As Colonel Carrington moved through the outer office, two bearded, buckskin-clad men came running up, carrying long, new-looking rifles. They were old hands on the frontier—hardened Indian fighters acting as messengers for the fort—a lonely and dangerous job. The guns which they carried were the new, sixteen-shot Henry repeaters, which had just arrived from back east, and they were anxious to try them out against the Indians.

"Colonel, may we go with them?" called one as they approached the steps. "We want to try out these new rifles!"

"Very well, then," replied the Colonel, his eyes on the officers now mounting in front of their men. "But remember, as civilians you go at your own risk. Don't run into unnecessary trouble."

"Thanks, Colonel," replied the first of the two, Fisher by name. "C'mon, Lucky," and the two comrades doubled in the direction of the stables.

Portugee Phillips and Jim Bridger were watching the detachments wheel round towards the gates of the fort which were already swinging back to let the men through. The two figures holding the big gates back, straightened in salute as the column, headed by Colonel Fetterman, began to pass.

Jim Bridger shook his grizzled head slowly. "I don't like it," he muttered, "that fire-eatin' fool and . . ." He broke off as the three horses rounded the corner into the parade ground and cantered after the column.

"Well, there go Fisher and Wheatley," broke in Portugee Phillips. "They should be a big help if those new shooting irons are all they're claimed to be. Wonder who that is going with them," he muttered to himself in an afterthought, as he watched the third figure, in an officer's uniform, disappear through the gateway.

Colonel Carrington was gazing after the detachment, doubt clouding his fine grey eyes. He glanced round at the two scouts, and seeing Jim Bridger still shaking his head seemed to help him reach a decision of his own.

"I don't think Fetterman really understood . . ." he said,

and, jumping down the steps, strode off across the square towards the parapet south of the gate. Reaching the ladder he climbed up and advanced to the edge of the stockage just as the gates banged shut and the guards began to slide the huge bars into place. The column was below him as he stood there, a tall, commanding figure against the clear sky. He cupped his hands to his mouth.

"Colonel Fetterman!" he called.

Fetterman raised his hand and the column drew to a halt. The Colonel wheeled his horse under the stockade and drew up respectfully, if a little impatiently. In the distance a mutter of shots could be heard above the stamp of the horses and jingle of equipment.

"Colonel Fetterman!" called Carrington again from the sentry platform. "Remember my instructions. Under no circumstances are you to pursue beyond Lodge Trail Ridge. When the wood train is relieved, you are to report back to me. Do you understand?"

Fetterman did not reply. He nodded, brought his hand up to the brim of his Stetson in salute and wheeled his horse to the head of the column. His hand went up, high in the air, and then forward. The column broke into movement and streamed northwestward away from the fort.

6

WAITING

Carrington watched them go. Fetterman had obviously decided to go round the Sullivant Hills and come upon the Indians from the rear. The road to the west was the shorter route, but these were reasonable tactics, thought the Colonel, and anyway if Fetterman came on them from behind and drove the Indians to the west he would not be tempted to take up pursuit towards the dangerous pine-clad slopes beyond the creek called Lodge Trail Ridge.

"Colonel, sir! Hostiles down by the bridge!" the sentry's voice brought the Colonel's attention back from the column setting out to relieve the wood train and caused him to think of the immediate problems of the fort's defense.

He turned and looked in the direction of the creek as Bridger and Phillips climbed up to the platform behind him. Bridger was carrying a long telescope which he carefully adjusted, and began to sweep the country in the direction of the river crossing. Through the glass he could see the new bridge which the Colonel had ordered to be built over the river and just beyond, moving cautiously towards the approaches of the bridge, he saw about five or six redskins.

"How many there, Bridger?" Carrington asked, a note of anxiety in his voice. With a total of over a hundred men, soldiers and civilians, now away from the fort he was not anxious to fight off another attack from Red Cloud's warriors.

"About half a dozen I can see," replied Bridger, moving the telescope slightly upwards, "but I reckon there's more in the trees."

Carrington strode to the edge of the platform.

"Lieutenant Martin!" he called.

"Sir?"

"There's a group of hostiles at the bridge. I want you to see if you can discover any more in the trees beyond. One shot should do it, I think." "Hostiles"—the Colonel had used the official army term for an enemy. Hostile the Indians certainly were. A few scattered rifle shots whined towards the fort.

"Right, sir!" The Gunnery Officer hurried to the south wall where his men were waiting, grouped round one of the howitzers already in position in case the stockade itself should be attacked. In a few moments he reappeared.

"Now, sir?"

Carrington nodded, and in response to the signal from Lieutenant Martin the Gunnery Sergeant yelled "Fire!" Almost simultaneously the cannon thundered out. A blast of smoke rolled out from the stockade and the watchers on the platform strained their eyes in the direction of the bridge.

"There they are, sir, look!" Portugee Phillips flung out an arm and Bridger, still peering through the telescope, added, "Yeah, up to left of the bridge, near them ponies."

The cannon shot, scattering through the trees, had caused about thirty Sioux to break cover and join the others on the roadway in a straggling retreat up the hill. The disappeared into the wood as the lieutenant returned to the platform.

Carrington glanced down. "Excellent shooting, Lieutenant, I think that will do!" Martin saluted and turned away, passing the Colonel's orderly, who climbed to the platform and handed the Colonel his field glasses. Carrington trained the powerful lenses in the direction of the hills. Fetterman's column had disappeared behind the shoulder of the hill, moving in good order along the foot of Lodge Trail Ridge.

The men on the platform stood watching in the bright sun. Bridger was the first to break the silence. "I dunno." He shook his head slowly, thoughtfully, and Carrington, knowing the scout of old and sensing that something was troubling him, said quietly, "Well, Jim?"

Bridger gave a grunt. "Huh!" He cleared his throat and spat over the side of the parapet. "I don't like it, Colonel.

Grummond's a good, steady officer, but Fetterman . . . and Brown . . ."

"Brown?" interrupted the Colonel. "I gave no orders to Brown to accompany them!"

"No, sir, but he's gone, nevertheless. They're certain to take a crack at Red Cloud, those boys, and I wouldn't put it past that fire-eater . . ."

"But this is in flagrant disregard of my orders," broke in the Colonel again. "I had no intention of letting those hotheads pair up. Fetterman on his own can be trusted to carry out his orders; especially after the caution I gave him outside the fort, but put the two together . . .! By heaven, Brown will have some explaining to do when he gets back!" He looked out again across the hills. There was a desultory burst of firing from the direction of the corralled wagon train which died away into silence. "They should be all right, though . . ." mused Carrington almost to himself, " a large force like that."

Portugee and Jim Bridger exchanged glances.

"How many?" asked Bridger.

"Eighty-one," replied Portugee, and as the old frontier scout whistled quietly, he added, "One more than he wanted."

"Wanted? What for?" asked the Colonel sharply.

"To ride through the whole Sioux nation!"

Once again an ominous silence settled over the waiting group.

Suddenly there was a cry from the sentry. "Lookout signaling, sir, from Pilot Hill."

Portugee swung round. Yes, the lookout was signaling urgently from his vantage point above them on the rocky hill. Portugee caught the gist of the message and turned to the Colonel.

"The wagon train's beginnin' to move off, sir," he said. "Colonel Fetterman must have come round the hill and up behind them—though I didn't hear no shootin'," he added reflectively.

The Colonel looked from Portugee's puzzled face to Jim Bridger and then turned his field glasses to the north, to Lodge Trail Ridge, where Colonel Fetterman's column had last been seen. Slowly he traversed the slope with his glasses, and then back again. Nothing. Nothing was visible at all. No soldiers, no Indians . . . yes, there were! The colonel gave an involuntary exclamation as his glasses picked up the dark forms of two Sioux who were running, crouched low, along the top of the ridge. They seemed to be anxious to keep out of the sight of something behind the ridge, something shielded from those in the fort by the humped shoulder of the Sullivant Hills.

"I don't like it," the Colonel said abruptly as he lowered his glasses. "Bridger, there are Indians on the ridge. Where's Fetterman? If he's gone round the hill and driven off the Sioux as we think, why isn't he coming back according to his orders? And how's he driven them off from the wagon train without firing? Is it possible we wouldn't hear firing on the other side of the hill?"

Phillips shook his head. "Nope. If there was shootin' we'd have heard it. The Indians have drawed off and left the wagon train. But it couldn't have been because of Colonel Fetterman's action, sir. If he's relieved the wagon train the lookout would have seen it. Nope—something else's driven them off . . . or maybe they weren't driven."

"What do you mean, Phillips?" snapped the Colonel. "If they weren't driven off, why should they just stop attacking the wagon train?"

"Maybe they'd caught something bigger," chimed in Bridger. "Maybe Fetterman didn't go right round the hill."

"By thunder, it's a trap!" the Colonel almost shouted the words. "If Fetterman had obeyed orders he'd have been in sight by now down the valley. He's gone the other way, along the Lodge Trail Ridge."

"Or maybe over it." The words were hardly out of Bridger's mouth when a sudden roar of distant rifles rolled across the valley. All the men turned in the direction from which it came, beyond the dark bulk of the Sullivant Hills, beyond the Lodge Trail Ridge.

Colonel Carrington leaped into action. From the high platform he could see men and women—yes, and a few children —pouring from the fort's buildings into the square, drawn out by the noise of the shooting. Two officers came running from their quarters, buckling on their holsters as they ran.

"Soldier!" snapped Carrington to the man on duty in front of the gatehouse. The man looked up. "Sir?" "Tell the Corporal of the Guard to get his men in position. Sergeant Peters!" Another soldier ran forward and looked up at the stern figure on the platform. "Sir?" he saluted.

"Call out every man in the fort. Have them report to the magazine for arms and ammunition."

The note of a bugle rang out loud and harsh across the fort.

"And, Sergeant, get the women and children into the main buildings—this may be an emergency. I want every man and woman in position within ten minutes!" He raised his eyes from the figure of the running sergeant and watched the two officers who came panting to the steps below.

"Captain Ten Eyck," he called without waiting for the officers to salute. "Take your company and be ready to move off without delay. I feel Colonel Fetterman has been ambushed. Major Powell, organize a support force to follow Captain Ten Eyck, three wagons and as many men as you can muster. Tell them to fill their pockers with ammunition. This may be a major fight once it starts. I'll come down right away and give you further instructions."

Both officers saluted and, turning away, broke into a run towards their quarters, calling for their men.

"Bridger." The Colonel was already at the top of the ladder. "You remain here and try to locate the firing. I want to know the latest position when Captain Ten Eyck is ready to move off."

He clambered down the rungs, Portugee following him.

"Sir, permission to accompany Captain Ten Eyck?" Portugee asked as they reached the Colonel's office.

Carrington looked at him keenly.

"All right, Phillips. I don't have to tell you that as a civilian you need not go." Phillips grinned and shook his head. "All right. Tell Captain Ten Eyck I give you authority to accompany him as messenger." He turned abruptly into his office which was already crowded with men, and Portugee ran out

of the house on to the parade ground. Behind him he could
hear the Colonel issuing orders which would bring the whole
fort to a state of complete readiness to repel an attack.

Two minutes later Portugee leaped into the saddle and
urged his horse skillfully out of the corral towards the parade
ground where Captain Ten Eyck's men were already formed
up and preparing to move off. Out of the corner of his eye,
Portugee could see the whole fort alive with activity. Men
were running towards the magazine, leaving the ovens and
the preparation of the midday meal as they hastened for arms.
A small group of women moved across the road in front of
him and he reined in to let them pass. Behind the group, shep-
herding three lagging small children, Portugee saw a tall,
pretty young woman, her hand on the shoulder of the smallest
boy. Grummond's wife, he thought grimly, as the party
moved under the impatient, tossing head of his horse. Where's
her husband now? What's happening to Fetterman?

At last the road was clear and he urged the big-boned
prairie horse across the square. Captain Ten Eyck's column
was already wheeling round and the gates of the fort swung
open. Portugee cantered to the captain's side. "Colonel's leave
to place myself at your disposal, sir," he called.

Ten Eyck answered briefly. "Good, we're going to need
every man. Stick behind me," and he spurred his horse to a
gallop that took them to the head of the column.

They were going fast when they went through the fort
gates and out, to wheel right on the open ground beyond,
following the same trail as Colonel Fetterman had taken, hoofs
pounding on the hard earth, dust and stones scattering before
them. Portugee caught a glimpse of the sentry waving from
the platform above the gates and then they were through,
thundering down the bright valley, and the fort, with its blue
haze of smoke rising in the clear morning sky, was dropping
swiftly behind.

The watchers on the platform could hear the firing as the
noise of Captain Ten Eyck's column died away. Volley after
volley rolled across the valley and, in between, scattered shots.
Old Jim Bridger swept the ridge to the north with his tele-

scope, the ridge over which Fetterman had disappeared in defiance of orders. What was going on beyond the scrub-covered slopes? Bridger turned as the Colonel climbed out on to the platform behind him.

"What do you see, Jim?" he asked.

"Nothin!" said Jim, resuming his sweep of the hills with the telescope. "Maybe a trace of smoke behind Lodge Trail Ridge—but I can't tell." Another burst of firing came echoing to the fort. "But there sure is all hell breaking loose over there somewheres."

"The whole fort is standing to arms," said the Colonel. "Major Powell is taking five wagons and the infantry out to support Ten Eyck. It doesn't leave us much of a force if Red Cloud attacks here. I know that . . ." he hesitated, "something's got to be done to help that fool Fetterman."

Bridger glanced at him. It was the first time he had heard the Colonel criticize an officer before anyone else; a just and firm man, he was also strictly military. Fetterman's disobedience of orders had shocked him deeply.

"I've sent a messenger to recall the wood train," continued the Colonel. "Timber or no timber we must be at full strength here in case the devils attack the fort."

There was a fresh burst of firing in the direction of the ridge. It reached a crescendo as the two on the roof saw Captain Ten Eyck's column, tiny now, far down the valley, cross the river by the Virginia City Road and being to climb the hill beyond.

"Trust God they'll be in time," muttered the Colonel, more to himself than to Bridger.

The noise of the firing died suddenly away. Below, in the fort, the men paused in their duties, heads cocked, eyes turned to the northwest, listening, listening. . . .

The silence spread like mist across the valley. Faintly, faintly, came a thin roar of what seemed like a thousand wild voices.

7

MASSACRE!

Portugee Phillips cursed beneath his breath as he urged his horse up the slope. The captain was a few paces in front of him, his horse straining as the rider forced it to leap upwards towards the crest of the hill over which had come that strange, bloodcurdling sound. Behind, some fifty troopers crashed through the scrub in extended order—all riding like furies for the top of the ridge.

What was happening beyond? Portugee asked himself. Why had the firing stopped?

They'd know soon enough. It was obvious now that the attack on the wood train had been a ruse to draw soldiers away from the fort. The sudden retreat from the corralled wagons, too, had all been part of the plan. And it seemed as though Fetterman had fallen for it—had pursued the fleeing Indians up the hill and over the ridge into what could only be the biggest ambush Red Cloud's combined forces had ever laid. Phillips wiped the sweat from his face with one buckskin sleeve and loosened his rifle in the scabbard. Captain Ten Eyck was making a wide, sweeping gesture with his right arm. The whole column of troopers bunched together as the leader reined in momentarily and then spread out into a single deadly line, which, at the given signal, began to advance to the summit of the ridge.

Nearer and nearer came the skyline. The bushes crashed apart before the slipping, scrabbling hooves of the horses. Pebbles flew back in Phillips's face as the captain urged his horse up the last sharp incline, his pistol already out, his eyes searching the topmost ridge for the least sign of movement.

Upwards, upwards, the last few yards now . . . and then with a final, panting, mad rush they were there . . . reining back, silhouetted on the skyline, sweating, steaming, as they sat on the heaving flanks of the horses and at last looked down into the valley beyond.

The sight which met their gaze held them glued to their saddles with horror.

The valley was filled with a yelling, whooping horde of Indians. Never in his entire life on the plains had Portugee Phillips seen such a gigantic war party. Sioux, Cheyenne, Arapaho, with war bonnets flying, horses wheeling and circling and raising clouds of dust in the weak, wintry sunshine. There must have been nearly two thousand howling red men below them.

Captain Ten Eyck and the troopers remained motionless as the seething throng drifted and swayed beneath them. Several braves began to wheel their horses and twirl their lances, making short rushes towards the ridge and then turning back again, yelling taunts at the unmoving soldiers and inviting them, in pidgin English, to come down and fight. One party of braves on foot scrambled upwards to a pile of rocks and, drawing their bows, let loose a flight of arrows towards the troopers.

Captain Ten Eyck gave a sharp order and the men began to edge their mounts slowly back down the ridge. The derisive yelling and jeering of the Indians rose to a fever-pitch as they saw the while soldiers begin to retreat. More braves rushed towards the ridge, but the main throng of hostiles remained in the valley, surging and shouting round a group of boulders to the south.

Ten Eyck shouted to Portugee: "What do you make of it, there, down in the valley?" He gestured towards the thickest cluster of Indians and the boulders.

"I don't know." Portugee had to yell above the war whoops. "Couldn't see nothin', no sign of Fetterman, dead or alive."

They dropped out of sight and halted—a dazed, stupefied group of men, fingering their weapons, each moment expect-

ing the horde of Indians to pour over the ridge and engulf
them.

"Hold your fire, men," called Ten Eyck. "Sangle!" His
orderly rode forward and saluted. "Sir?" Ten Eyck was scrib-
bling furiously on a field message pad. He tore off a page of
paper and thrust it towards Orderly Sangle. "Take this back
to the fort. We'll return below and await Major Powell's
column. We can't go down there without support. I'm asking
for a howitzer. Phillips, you go with him."

He whirled away towards his men. Phillips and Sangle
swung their mounts round and, without a second look at the
little column bunched below the ridge, spurred back towards
the fort.

Back at Fort Phil Kearny, Colonel Carrington, watching
through his field glasses, saw them sweep down on to the plain,
splash through the shallow creek where Major Powell was
struggling onwards with his loaded wagons and, without
stopping, stretch out in a long gallop to the fort. He lowered
his glasses and, with Jim Bridger following close behind, hurried down the ladder and strode back to his office, where he
waited on the step.

Shortly afterwards the gates of the fort swung open and, in
a flurry of dust, Portugee and the orderly thundered through
and flung themselves from the saddle. Sangle drew himself up,
saluted and thrust his message at the Colonel.

"Report from Captain Ten Eyck, sir," he panted.

Carrington read it at a glance.

"Howitzer?" he barked. "What for, what's going on behind
the ridge?" Where's Fetterman?"

"There's no sign of Colonel Fetterman, sir," replied the
orderly, "but there's plenty of Indians: the biggest war party
I've ever seen, sir, in the valley beyond Lodge Trail Ridge. God
knows what's happened, sir, but . . ."

"Thank you, Sangle," broke in the Colonel. "Phillips,
what's your opinion?"

"Orderly's right, sir," Portugee replied. "I reckon about
two thousand of them—Cheyenne, Sioux, Arapaho . . . they

ain't moving at yet . . . soon as they saw us, wanted us to
come down into the valley and fight, but they're too occu-
pied with something else lower down the trail, sir."

"Fetterman?"

"Can't say, Colonel. No shootin', no sign of the Colonel's
party, sir . . . but there's Indians all round the valley, I
reckon."

"Colonel," Jim Bridger broke in. "I don't like to be pessi-
mistic, sir, but I reckon that fire-eating soldier has just about
got all the Indian trouble he wanted!"

While they had been talking, a group of men had gathered
round them. They were armed and anxious . . . waiting for
news of Fetterman and the fate of the fort.

"Right, gentlemen." Colonel Carrington made up his mind
swiftly. "We've no spare horses to take a howitzer. I've recalled the wood train, that will give us fifty more men: Captain Arnold, what is the state of your garrison?"

"Soldiers and civilians, sir, one hundred and nineteen, including the guard," replied the post adjutant.

"Right! Release all prisoners from the guardhouse, arm
them and place them on duty. Every man will hold himself in
readiness for immediate action—all work will be suspended—
all arms stacked before quarters."

"Right, sir!" the adjutant saluted and withdrew on the
double.

Carrington turned towards the office, the others accom-
panying him, breaking through the group who had gathered
to hear the news and were now busily talking among themselves.

"Sangle, you'll return to Captain Ten Eyck with this message," he strode up the steps into his office. A soldier jumped
to his feet and grabbed a message pad in answer to the
Colonel's gesture.

"Captain," he dictated, "I have recalled the wood train and
will send fifty men as soon as they arrive. No horses can be
spared for a howitzer. Major Powell should have joined up
with you by now, giving you a further forty armed men and
three thousand rounds of ammunition in wagons. As soon as

you feel you have enough strength under your command, proceed into the valley and try to locate and unite with Colonel Fetterman. On no account are you to risk any action which will jeopardize the defense of the fort. Your mission is to unite with Fetterman and return at all speed."

There was a moment's silence as the soldier finished writing and sealed the message. Sangle took it, and saluted. Portugee Phillips followed him out, they crossed the square, mounted their lathered horses and, yelling at the guard to open the gate, galloped out once more into the valley.

Bridger and the Colonel watched them go.

"Where in God's name can Fetterman be, do you suppose?" said the Colonel quietly.

Bridger didn't answer. He shook his grizzled old head slowly and felt in the pocket of his buckskin coat for a wad of tobacco. In silence the two men turned, walked towards the gatehouse and began to climb to the sentry platform to watch again the drama that was being enacted on the distant ridge.

Their horses were spattered with flecks of foam when Phillips and the orderly reached the ridge once more. Major Powell's party had joined up with Captain Ten Eyck and the whole column was drawn up into a position to advance when the two messengers arrived. Captain Ten Eyck read the Colonel's message in silence and then threw it towards Major Powell.

Powell read it and looked up. "Shall we go, Captain?" Ten Eyck nodded. "I reckon we're strong enough anyway, without waiting for any more men. Sergeant, we'll advance when I give the order. Keep your men together, fire slowly when you have to. We'll move into the valley from the north and drive them down towards the creek. Major Powell, your wagons will follow in close support. Understood?"

"Right, sir!" Both men saluted and turned away. The column tensed, adjusted their equipment, and despite the danger the men seemed relieved at the prospect of action after the long, anxious waiting. Moving to the head of the column, with a wave of his hand Captain Ten Eyck led them forward and over the ridge.

There was no need for words as they moved slowly down the valley. Everywhere the ground was churned and scattered by the hooves of hundreds of horses. Soon there were odd items of equipment to be seen lying casually in the grass, as if dropped from a horse by a tired and unthinking trooper . . . until they looked closer and saw amidst them trampled earth the darker stains of blood. The jingle of harness, the thud of hoofs and the sudden snort of a frightened horse were the only sounds as they moved forward. Portugee leaned over and patted his horse's neck, murmuring soothing, wordless sounds as the great ears twitched and trembled. Even their mounts sensed that something was wrong and moved, as it were, on tip-hoof, ready to shy at the slightest sound. But there was no sound . . . even the animals had fled.

In front of Ten Eyck a trooper reined in his mount suddenly and pointed. The rump of a dead horse bulged through the bushes, and beyond were the stiffened forelegs of another, lying on its back with something . . . something white and horrible beside it.

They were the first of the dead and their position told part of the tragic tale. It was the story of the young lieutenant with the wood train all over again . . . but this time it had happened to an older and more experienced officer and perhaps four times as many men. Happened needlessly, too, thought Phillips, as he urged his horse forward once more. If only Fetterman had obeyed orders!

They found him, with Brown, behind the boulders. The bodies of his men were grouped around him. A little way off lay the two old plainsmen surrounded by neat piles of empty shells. Both had been shot in the head, suggesting suicide rather than submission to capture and torture. All weapons had vanished—taken by the hostiles. Only the dead were left. The pincushion arrows, the torn clothing, the torn limbs and other derisive gestures of mutilation that the savage claimed as his right over a beaten adversary—he would do it to any enemy tribesman as well as to the white man—filled in the details of their ghastly end.

Much later, as his men finished the sad task of gathering the dead together—men with whom they had laughed and joked a mere twenty-four hours before—Captain Ten Eyck spoke for them all:

"Fire-eater they called him. Sure, he was brave, but he didn't have to kill all his company to prove it!"

But of the eighty-one men who set out, only forty were to be found. Where are the others, the men asked, looking anxiously round the valley, quiet, still and eerie now as dusk began to creep up the slopes. Where's Grummond and the others? There was no sign of them and it was too late by this time to search farther. The ammunition wagons had reached the ridge and were silhouetted there against the reddening sky. In the east a great, grey bank of cloud was piling up. A long column of bowed figures silently began to carry as many of the bodies as they could up the hillside.

8

THE RING OF DEATH

As Captain Ten Eyck's troop clattered over the now freezing ground into the fort at dusk there was not a sound from the waiting crowd. Then, when the wagons with their pitiful burdens came into sight, a muffled sob went up from many throats and a procession fell in as the wagons moved across the square. Women with children began to run behind and to cling to the tailboards in an effort to see if their loved ones were among the dead. The troopers, dismounting before the stables, tightened their lips or muttered savage threats against Red Cloud's warriors as they heard the distressed cries from the crowd.

"There was no sign, then, of Grummond?" asked the Colonel when Captain Ten Eyck came to the end of his report.

"No, sir, not a trace . . . but I don't think there's any hope for them, sir. Anyone who had survived would have reached us or at least given some sign that they were alive. I would have searched farther down the valley, sir, but the light was fading and . . . and . . ."

"Quite right, Captain," Carrington answered as Ten Eyck's speech broke at the thought of the terrible task he had just performed. "You acted rightly. Tomorrow we must search further. Now our immediate concern is for the safety of the fort."

With nearly a quarter of their small force killed or missing, the thought uppermost in every man's mind was "would Red Cloud press home his advantage and attack?"

"It's my guess he won't," said Phillips to Jim Bridger as they stood guard upon the lookout tower at the gate and gazed

towards Lodge Trail Ridge, where the mystery of Grummond
and his men still lay concealed. "Not because he doesn't want
to, it's the obvious thing to you and me . . . but he's got a
mixed bunch there: Sioux, Arapaho, Cheyenne . . ."

"I never seen the likes of it before," broke in the old scout.
"How's he keepin' them together? It's a mystery to me."

"That's just it," replied Portugee, "Red Cloud's got enough
on his hands without pressing his luck. He's won a big victory
and his braves will want to celebrate. They'll go it all night,
feasting and scalp dancin', and my guess is Red Cloud will let
them get on with it. Tomorrow they'll pow-pow and then
we'll have to watch out."

The plainsman's words proved right, for although every
man—soldier and civilian alike, from the officers down to the
storekeepers—took his turn on guard throughout the long, cold
night, and although signal lights burned in the hope that any
survivor would see them from the hills and be guided to the
fort, dawn found the little garrison tired but untried. No
night attack had materialized and the plains were empty and
grey as the sun began to pierce the winter mists. The sun's
appearance was brief, however, for the clouds of the previous
night had spread to cover the greater part of the sky and as the
day advanced the dull, leaden layers told everyone that winter
was at last on its way and snow would not be long in coming.

In the Colonel's office, Carrington faced a grave company.

"Gentlemen," he said, "we are still uncertain as to the fate
of Lieutenant Grummond and his detachment and I have
called this meeting to seek your opinion on the advisability of
sending out a further search party. I propose taking command
of it myself."

A silence followed his words and each man thought of the
danger they were in. More than a quarter of the garrison was
already missing. Was it wise to deplete the little force still
further in an effort to find Grummond and his men? God
knows they were probably beyond help anyway! And while
the search party was out, who would defend the fort in the
event of an Indian attack?

Jim Bridger, sitting hunched at the back of the room—for

the Colonel had called the old experienced scouts in as well as his officers—spoke the thoughts that were uppermost in every man's mind.

"Colonel," he said, "there ain't much doubt that the lieutenant and his men are beyond any help we can offer. If any of them boys was alive we'd have heard something by now. You can't do any good by going after them . . . and you may do a lot of harm. You must take fifty men or more for your own safety—and what does that leave the fort if we're attacked?"

They were blunt words, as anyone would expect from the old scout, but there were grunts of approval as he finished. Colonel Carrington let his eyes sweep over the assembled officers before he answered.

"Mr. Bridger," he began, "what you say is quite correct. With a depleted force the fort would be exposed to the greatest danger. But it's my belief that Red Cloud won't attack yet. He's won a great victory—much to our cost—and his braves and the braves of all the tribes who took part will want to return to their lodges with their trophies of war and spread the news of their success. Red Cloud will have a job to hold them at the moment. Later I think he will tempt them to come against us again for greater glory, but not yet. The second and more important point, however," the Colonel continued, "is one of custom which I'm sure you'll agree the Indians well appreciate. You all know how the hostiles carry off their dead from the field of battle, whatever the risk? Well, what of our dead boys? . . . and I can think of them in no other way," he added quietly. "What if we leave them wherever they are? Apart from feelings of ordinary decency and the need to give them the Christian burial they deserve, won't the Indians think it a sign of weakness on our part if we don't venture out? In such a case, won't they be tempted to press home their attack with even more recklessness when they do come?"

There was a dead silence. Every man present felt that the Colonel was right. Even Bridger nodded in agreement.

"I've my own wife and child here," continued the Colonel. "I'm not asking anyone to perform any act or risk that I wouldn't consider undertaking myself. That's why I'm calling

for volunteers to accompany me on a search party within
the hour."

There was a stamp of feet as those present, to a man, rose
and signified their assent.

Later, much later, that day, with the hours he had spent on
the Lodge Trail Ridge weighing on his mind like years, Colonel Carrington led his force of volunteers back into the fort.
Lights were burning on the flagstaff to guide them back and as
the men slid to the ground, stiff and cold from many hours in
the saddle and saddened and angry from the task they had had
to perform, a light snow began to fall.

Slowly, the Colonel walked to his office. The rough furni-
ture, the printed notices and the rifle racks . . . his eyes ran
over the familiar things but did not notice them. Wearily he
dropped his hat, unbuckled his belt and let the pistol and
holster thud to the table. Then he sat down, still staring before
him with eyes that did not see the maps on the wall opposite.
Slowly he lowered his head into his hands and, as the sounds
of the fort crept out of his consciousness, he thought of what
they had found.

Grummond was indeed dead . . . so horribly killed that he
had given orders to bury him on the ridge along with the other
victims of Red Cloud's warriors, so that Mrs. Grummond
should be spared the sight of her mutilated husband. The
search party had brought news of their widowhood to other
wives, too. All of Grummond's party had been overwhelmed
in the final surging rush of the Indians down the valley as they
fought desperately to link up with Fetterman's surrounded
company.

Fetterman . . . for a moment the Colonel's mind blazed
up. What wild idea had prompted him to disobey orders?
Eight-one men in all had fought their last fight on Lodge
Trail Ridge and Fetterman was to blame. But would they
think that in Washington when he made his report? He had
misjudged Fetterman's ability to carry out specific orders and
ultimately, he was responsible; they were men under *his* command who had died. But they gave a good account of them-

selves, thought Carrington grimly as he raised his head and pictured again the scene in the Peno Valley.

He could see it vividly in his mind . . . the Indians massing on all sides, the incredible noise and war whoops as they prepared for the final charge. The men grimly loading their rifles knowing what was coming. Then the rush itself. . . . They had counted sixty-five bloody patches where Indian dead had lain before their tribes dragged them off. It had been almost a life for a life: the trapped party had fought valiantly before they were overwhelmed.

But what good was this terrible strife; who would profit from the bitter warfare that was now sweeping the plains . . . ? He pushed the thoughts abruptly from his mind and straightened up as the door opened and Sergeant Haggerty came in.

"Coffee, sir, and food. I've been keeping it hot for you, sir."

"I can't eat . . ." began Carrington; then, seeing the hurt look that came into the old soldier's eyes, he softened his tone. "Well, yes, perhaps I will. The coffee certainly is welcome." He poured out a cup of the black, steaming liquid and began to sip. After a moment, as though the coffee was giving him strength, he stood up, moved from his chair and went over to the window, where he remained motionless for a long time, sipping the coffee and watching the activity outside.

Against the rapidly darkening sky he could just see the bare poles of the unfinished hospital away to the right. A red pool of firelight splashed out on the far side of the square where the men in the armory tended the forge, overhauling every weapon as they prepared for the attack that they felt certain was to come. Beyond the armory, grouped solidly along the west wall of the fort, were the stoutest of the log buildings. Yellow lights flickered in the windows as the women and children settled into their new quarters. Shadows crossed the squares of yellow light; men passed and repassed on hurried errands about the fort. Somewhere a tired child cried. Smoke climbed from the oven chimneys as the bakers hastened to bake the bread that could not be baked when they stood to arms. While he watched, the Colonel noticed that the snow

was already lying white on the cold ground and trails of
footprints mingled together to form regular paths across the
open space.

Without turning round, Carrington spoke.

"Sergeant, tell Captain Arnold and Major Powell I want
to see them, will you?"

Sergeant Haggerty came to attention. "Yes, sir," he said
and turned towards the door. He hesitated before he went
out. "Sir," he ventured, "the food's getting cold, sir."

Carrington nodded and turned to the table as the sergeant
closed the door and clumped down the steps.

When Major Powell and Captain Arnold came in, the
Colonel was sitting on the edge of the table eating from his
plate. He waved their salutes aside and motioned them to
chairs.

"Gentlemen," he began as he put down his empty plate
and took the coffee pot off the stove, pushing it towards
them. "I want to know the position down to the last detail."

The position was indeed a grim one. The nearest neighbor-
ing fort lay over two hundred miles away at Laramie. The
garrison had lost nearly a quarter of its complement in the
disaster in the Peno Valley. Including civilians and children
about three hundred people remained in the fort, and of these
perhaps only two hundred could be counted on to take an
active part in its defense. Two officers had been killed, leaving
only five to take on the onerous duties of command, helped by
trusted N.C.O.s, who had suffered their own losses with the
Fetterman column. Morale, too, was low; the death of so
many comrades, the sudden onset of winter threatening to
cut off all help and the obvious imminence of an Indian attack
combined to depress even the oldest hands at frontier life. The
stores of arms, ammunition and food were adequate for the
moment, but barely enough for a sustained siege. The building
of the fort was virtually complete and a stock of wood for
firing was piled high against the east wall. They could hold
out well enough if they could hold off Red Cloud! There was
still no sign of the Indian warriors and several officers had
voiced surprise earlier at this inactivity.

"Could be he's having trouble with his rival chiefs," volunteered Major Powell. "There's no love lost between Sioux and Cheyenne. And when you throw in a few more besides it may lead to old quarrels flaring up . . . perhaps he can't hold them together any longer."

"Don't underestimate Red Cloud," Colonel Carrington shook his head. "This battle will bring him enormous prestige and even to the most rebellious Indian it is going to be clear that by uniting one tribe with another they can push the white man back over the Platte. No, it's my guess they're still feasting . . . and the snow might keep them in the tepees a little longer. But make no mistake. Red Cloud's authority is complete out there. Maybe he thinks he can come and take the fort at leisure after yesterday's massacre . . . maybe he's playing a waiting game and means to starve us out. That'd be unusual for Indians, but it's what any general would do in their place.

"But whatever Red Cloud does decide to do, we've got to be ready for him. Now Major, listen carefully. From your report, and that of Captain Arnold here . . ."

The three men leaned over the table long into the night, planning the defense of the fort. They went over each section of the buildings, over each possibility and each answer to the threat time and time again. All night long the lights burned in the fort. Stores were checked, stockades inspected; guard routines for each section were planned and put into operation. Messengers came and went, each bringing in a swirl of snow and freezing wind, until the office floor was wet with slush and all three officers huddled in their greatcoats to keep out the cold. At last it seemed that every loophole had been blocked, that the "hated fort on the little Piney" as the hostiles called it, was completely prepared against surprise attack.

And then, in the early hours of the morning, another and unexpected enemy struck.

The snow had been getting thicker as the night progressed. The thermometer which had been dropping all day, now stood at 25° below freezing point, and a strong wind began to moan through the buildings. Up on the stockades the guards stamped ceaselessly up and down and shivered. Almost unrecognizable as soldiers, they were wrapped in buffalo robes, blankets, and still desperately slapped their sides and blew into their gloves in an attempt to keep out the cold.

The wind increased to blizzard force, bringing only one consolation with each icy blast. No Indian would venture out in such weather. For the moment, the fort could afford to relax. At least, they thought they could. Whether it was a deer or moose blundering through the snow or whether it really was one of Red Cloud's warriors no one knew, but a guard heard and saw movements in the trees beyond the northeast stockade and in leaning out to locate the noise found the snowdrifts!

Sweeping down from the hills above the creek, the wind was bringing with it an extraordinary fall of snow; driven over the smooth plain it piled up against the walls of the fort, climbing steadily up the stout timbers until the guards could reach out and brush the top of the drifts with their rifle butts. Soft, deep and treacherous, it was a danger to the defense of the fort, for with the temperature so low and still falling, morning would find it a solid frozen mound over which a man could run and leap for the top of the stockade.

"It's a royal invitation for maraudin' braves to pay us a visit," grunted old Jim Bridger as he leaned over the stockade and prodded deep into the drifts with a long pole. "Gotta shift this stuff now, before it freezes. Does the Colonel know?" he called, turning his back to the wind and driving snow, and hunching his hands deep into the pockets of an old buffalo robe that made him seem more like a bear than a man. He had drawn a woolen scarf tightly round his hat and down over his ears, tying it under his chin. The effect was like an old lady's ludicrous bonnet, but it seemed to keep the snow out and many of the soldiers on the wall were following suit.

"All right, granny," jibed one of the guards. "Colonel's been told. Sergeant's gone for shovels . . . before you came up."

Bridger grunted and pushed his hands farther down into the comfortable fur. Below, lanterns flickered in the wind and a party struggled to open a small side gate and move out into the snow. The drift before the door was almost head-high and they had to dig their way out. Bridger, leaning over the stockade, saw them file out into the darkness, and presently, during a lull in the wind, he could hear the noise of shovels striking against each other as the work party fought to clear the drifts.

At fifteen-minute intervals, more men came out to take over. In the bitter cold few could work longer without the risk of frostbite. The wind dropped for a little while, the snow held off, then began to fall again—a steady fall, but vertically this time, without the straying wind to drive it across the plains and up against the fort. For hours the struggle went on as the cold, grey light of dawn crept into the east and the guards redoubled their watchful scrutiny of the hills and woods in case of a dawn attack by the hostiles. At last the drifts were cleared and once more the wall stood strong, tall and formidable against the white plain.

All over the fort fresh lights began to flare and smoke began to rise as breakfast was prepared and the digging party attempted to thaw out their frozen hands and feet before almost red-hot stoves.

Colonel Carrington came out of his office, gazed across the lightening square and looked up at the sky. The snow stopped suddenly. The light grew stronger and Jim Bridger, sleepy, cold and weary after his part in the night's vigil, was preparing to go down the ladder and join Portugee Phillips, coming to relieve him, when a cry echoed down from one of the watch-towers.

"Smoke to the east, sir," and almost immediately another call, "Smoke to the west, sir, by the Sullivant Hills."

Bridger turned and gazed southwards; he could hear Portugee climbing up behind him and, as his friend reached the platform, he shouted, "Cookin' fires, and to the north. That only leaves one side and you can bet your last dollar they're there too!"

Fort Phil Kearny was indeed surrounded. Red Cloud had not been idle during the snowstorm. His warriors were spread all round the fort—beyond howitzer range, in deep cover out of sight—but the smoke of their fires, and other signs which grew more obvious as the morning wore on—a glimpse of horses in the distance, half-seen figures dark against the distant snow or sky—told of the ring of death that had locked round "the hated fort on the little Piney."

The defenders lined the walls and watched for their enemy. The Indians sat still and seemed content to wait—unusual Indian tactics, perhaps—but not a soldier there could but admit how cruelly effective they were. Red Cloud was calling the tune and the defenders of Fort Phil Kearny could do nothing but dance on the battlements in an effort to keep out the killing cold.

9

THE VOLUNTEER

Late that day, Colonel Carrington called a council of war. The defense of the fort was well organized. Officers, men and civilians were all too well aware of the hazards of frontier life to question the rigorous discipline imposed in the face of the threatening danger from Red Cloud. But Carrington had thought long and deeply about their position and knew in his heart that despite the determination of every man to resist the redskins, there was one game they could not play for long— and that was to stand up to a prolonged siege. And indeed it seemed as if this was to be Red Cloud's main stratagem against the whites: to keep the ring of death tightly closed about the fort through the long winter weeks, months if need be, to see the white soldiers weakened by lack of food and their defenses made vulnerable by the gradual drain on their ammunition as they answered small skirmishing attacks with precious bullets —and then to overwhelm the hated fort with one wild, vengeful attack, which could only culminate in fire and death.

Could the dismal prospect be avoided? Colonel Carrington thought it could and, while Red Cloud's warriors waited with strange patience, he called his council of war in the largest building the fort possessed, a long, high barn, planned for winter storage, behind the stables.

When Colonel Carrington entered the barn, the noise and talking stopped immediately, and leaving his officers the Colonel climbed on a great bale of straw and looked around him.

The air was tense and expectancy showed in each face. Every man who could be spared from his duties had crowded in. Veterans ranged side by side with youthful soldiers who were experiencing their first taste of frontier war. The men were packed together, some sitting, some standing; others had climbed on to the stacks of hay and were leaning against the walls of the barn or the great timbers of the pines that supported the roof in a colonnade down the center. One man had even mounted one of a group of five horses at the north end of the barn, in order to see better. Lanterns illuminated the corners made dark by the waning afternoon. A cloud of tobacco smoke hung in the air among the rafters and despite the zero temperature there was an atmosphere almost of warmth emanating from the press of men.

The Colonel and his officers were in the center of the gathering where all could see them. There was complete silence and, as the Colonel climbed up to address the men, it seemed that even the horses stopped champing and stamping the better to hear him.

"I don't need to tell you," began the Colonel in a quiet but clear voice that carried to the far corners of the barn, "how serious our position is. You all know that we have lost a quarter of our force in tragic circumstances. You have a good idea of our condition with regard to stores and ammunition. You know the enemy and what to expect when he comes. Some of you have seen comrades die out there on the plains and there's not a man here, I know, who would not welcome a chance to strike a blow back in repayment. But in our present state that is going to be impossible."

He paused, and the stillness indicated only too clearly how closely the men were listening to his words; words which he now used, bluntly and forcefully, to tell them the exact position.

"We have food in plenty to withstand a siege until help reaches us." The Colonel began to speak again in his clear, confident voice. "As long as we ration it carefully, we have no immediate worry on that score. The hay here," gestured to the bales on which the men were standing, "would have lasted our horses the winter through anyway. And enough fuel has been gathered already to see us over the worst of the bad weather." He paused, then went on. "That's the good side of the picture. Enough to eat, enough to keep warm. Water, of course, we can draw from the creek or even dig wells within the fort. But the bad points are: one, lack of arms and an adequate supply of ammunition; two, the weather—we've already over a dozen men in hospital with frostbite; and three, our inability to provide a force large enough to break through Red Cloud's warriors and still leave enough people to man the fort while they ride for help. Fort Laramie is over two hundred miles away to the south. That's twenty-four hours' hard riding under good conditions, and God knows, men, what the weather has in store for us. So you see it's at least three days before we could expect help to arrive, and that's only if we can get word to Laramie without delay. There's a wagon train due in about the middle of next month, but there's no knowing whether they'll continue the journey if the weather worsens. We might rely on trappers and scouts in the vicinity giving news to Laramie that Red Cloud's out—but you know as well as I do that that's a remote hope."

He broke off, and a weary movement ran through the assembly as they shuffled from one foot to another. There were few comments, for Colonel Carrington had told the men nothing that they had not realized for themselves during the anxious hours that had succeeded the Fetterman tragedy. What they were waiting for was the Colonel's plan of action. How did he propose to beat Red Cloud's ring of death? His answer to their unspoken question came promptly.

"Your officers and I have considered practically every possibility and come to the conclusion that an attempt must be made to reach Laramie. From there we can expect immediate help—from there the telegraph runs east and regiments can be brought rapidly to assist us. How to reach Laramie is the burning question. A large force could possibly fight their way out, but you know how short in number would be those left to face an attack. It's impossible with all the women and children to evacuate the fort. Two scouts went out this morning and have since reported that Red Cloud's warriors encircle the fort—but not so efficiently that one determined man could not slip through, unknown, at night and be clear away before it was

light enough for his tracks to be discovered and for the braves
to get after him. One man, well-provisioned and well-mounted,
could get through. It's no easy task. There are hostiles to face
and a dangerous journey in what may prove to be worsening
conditions of weather. It's our only chance, however; the only
real chance of rescue for the women and children with us, for
the safety of the fort, for all of us gathered here."

Colonel Carrington stopped speaking. He looked down at
the damp floor and then suddenly up at the men nearest him.
For a moment they could see the dilemma in his eyes, the slight
wavering of his glance as he was forced to choose between love
for the soldiers under his command and the relentless course
that he knew to be his duty. Then he looked high up, at the
back of the barn, and said, quietly:

"I must call for volunteers."

Not a sound was heard. Men looked down; turned away as
they faced what was probably the hardest decision of their
lives. Danger from a hundred sources, death in all probability,
lay in wait for whoever undertook this terrible journey. Men
could picture the dark Indians racing in silent pursuit, see the
gaping chasms in the high ground, the impenetrable trees. They
could almost feel the deep drifts in which a man and his horse
might disappear without trace. Visibility down to fifty or a
dozen yards closed darkly in on them. Frozen, broken ground,
swarming with Indians . . . they could see all this in the mind's
eye and shuddered as they contemplated it. Grey heads were
shaken slowly as they considered the courier's chances of success and rated it a hundred to one against.

The silence lengthened. Carrington did not look at his men.
Eyes high on the smoky roof of the barn he waited.

Presently a quiet voice said, "I'll go, Colonel."

It was Portugee Phillips.

Once the decision had been made to send a courier to Fort
Laramie there was no time to be lost. Late into the night preparations went on. Phillips's sole request once his offer to ride
for help had been made was for the swiftest horse in the post.
Colonel Carrington himself had taken Phillips to the stables

where the officers' mounts were kept and shown him his own thoroughbred stallion. Phillips ran a keen, frontiersman's eye over the mount. Tall, strongly built, with a barrel-like chest and fine forelegs—it was the ideal horse for the country, an unusual combination of fleetness and strength. Nevertheless, the task facing it was going to be a hard one for even the best of horses.

Phillips ran a hand over his neck and the horse lowered his great, grey head and shook it two or three times. Portugee tore down a handful of feed and pressed it gently into his muzzle, nodding with satisfaction as he stroked the flank and felt the muscles ripple beneath his hand.

"What do you call him, Colonel?" he asked.

"Fortune," replied Carrington. "You like him?"

Portugee nodded and straightened up. The flickering lantern carried by an orderly cast their shadows, man and horse, big and bold, on the stable wall. "Let's hope your name's an omen," he murmured, stroking the horse again. "We're going to need all the fortune we can get, you and I."

A hand shook Portugee's shoulder about an hour before dawn. For nearly five hours he had slept in the sergeant's bunkhouse while the final preparations for his ride had been made by the Colonel in person and Sergeant Tom Haggerty. The Colonel looked tired and drawn in the guttering candle-light and he reached out for the inevitable cup of coffee as Portugee rolled over and sat up.

"There's hot food ready, John," said the sergeant, addressing the scout by his little-used first name. "You've got about half an hour before you start," and as Portugee pulled on his boots and settled down to the table where a royal meal was waiting for him—eggs, ham, molasses and brown-baked biscuits, a royal spread considering conditions at the fort—he once more ran over the equipment for the journey.

Rifle . . . ("Pity it isn't one of those new repeaters poor Fisher had with him," muttered the sergeant to himself) . . . food for man and horse that with care would last four or five days . . . a bottle of French brandy, again supplied by the Colonel . . . the leather wallet containing the dispatch to the

Officer Commanding Fort Laramie . . . knife, rope, ammunition, all the indispensable kit of a frontiersman, but pared down to a minimum weight . . . every item had been checked and rechecked in the last few hours while Portugee snatched precious sleep.

From a peg in the wall Sergeant Haggerty took down the scout's hand gun. He slid it from the holster and spun the smooth cylinder. It was a Navy Colt, .36 caliber; a six-shot revolver weighing two pounds ten ounces and thirteen inches long from the barrel tip to the end of the carved ivory butt. Made in 1861, to take powder and ball, it was now loaded with the new, self-contained cartridges which had percussion cap, powder and bullet in one container. Haggerty checked each chamber, ran his finger along the finely-decorated barrel and put the gun back into the holster. He hung the belt over the back of Portugee's chair as his friend finished his meal.

A short while later Portugee and the Colonel crossed to the stable where Fortune was waiting. A rifle, wrapped in oily rag, already hung in a cavalry scabbard. The saddlebags were both firmly packed and balanced on either flank. The rolled blanket and waterproof were tied high behind the saddle and, behind that again, the tight pack of feed for the journey, open at one end so that Portugee could pull handfuls out with the minimum delay. There would be little enough food under the ice for his mount, he thought grimly.

The snow was still falling steadily.

"Wind's dropped, thank heaven," said Sergeant Haggerty, straightening up as they entered. He had been tying rags round Fortune's hooves to muffle the noise as they left the fort.

"And the snow will cover your tracks quick-like," said Jim Bridger, who was waiting in the shadows with a few friends to bid Portugee "Good luck!"

The good-byes were brief and silent. The men shook hands with Portugee. Their presence conveyed more than they could put into words and Portugee felt a tightness in his jaw as he looked at one and then another of these friends of the frontier whom he might well be seeing for the last time. He turned away and drew on his mittens, catching Fortune's reins and slipping them off the hitching rail. As he did so, there was a sudden interruption and two women entered from the small door at the back of the stable. One was unknown to Portugee but the other he recognized as Mrs. Grummond, the widow of the lieutenant who had accompanied Fetterman and who had died in the ambush on Lodge Trail Ridge.

The Colonel removed his hat. Portugee stood waiting, not knowing whether this lady wanted to speak to the Colonel or perhaps to the frontiersmen. She stepped forward, her face pretty and yet drawn and tired with the ordeal of the last few days.

"Mr. Phillips," she began a little hesitantly. "Mr. Phillips, we, that is all the women in the fort, we want you to know that we all appreciate more than we can say what you are about to do for us." She paused and then held out her hand, palm upwards. In the lamplight something glittered. "Take this," she said, "my husband gave it to me when I came to join him out here . . . it will bring you good fortune."

Portugee reached out slowly and took the little gold locket and, without taking his eyes off her face, thrust it deep inside his jacket.

"Thank you, ma'am," he said a little hoarsely, "thank you. It will be a great comfort."

Mrs. Grummond's face relaxed, the anxious eyes smiled a little and with a slight nod she turned away.

Portugee pulled down his fur cap; the sergeant swung open the stable door and, with the scouts and Colonel Carrington following close behind, the little party moved outside. Fortune turned his head and snorted at the snow.

Quickly they reached the wall of the fort where two troopers were waiting with darkened lanterns. Not a word was spoken. The lamps were extinguished and the side gate unbarred. It swung noiselessly inwards on greased hinges, revealing the dark forest some way off and the silent swirling snow.

Horse and man passed through the door into the waiting wilderness and in a moment were shut from sight.

10
GETAWAY!

Portugee felt rather than heard the heavy timber door shut behind him. He stood quite still, one hand holding the reins, the other gently stroking Fortune's long jaw. Nothing stirred in the white empty space of the clearing. The wind had dropped and the snow came down, silent and straight. Great flakes drifted onto his face and eyes, and a white cover began to form on the horse's mane and saddle, and on the butt of the rifle sticking from its saddle holster. The mechanism was tightly wrapped in oiled rag to keep out the snow; he would have no need of a gun out there in the clearing. Trusted eyes watched through the loopholes behind him; many rifles were ready to speak in his defense should Red Cloud's warriors be waiting in the snow. But although the white expanse of the clearing remained empty it hinted at hidden danger and the dark shape of the trees on the other side seemed a long, long way off. A man and horse was going to look awful big and black against the snow even though it was the dark hour before dawn, thought Portugee as he stood there in silence.

Fortune's flanks heaved as the horse drew a deep breath, preparing to snort the tickling snowflakes from his nostrils. Portugee clapped a hand over his muzzle and gently rubbed his fur mittens along the soft upper lip.

"Steady, fella, steady." He talked a quiet, senseless commentary to the horse, and presently Fortune relaxed and thumped the ground once with his forefoot as if to say, "All right, I won't make a noise, but let's get going!"

Portugee scanned the open space as far as the dim light would permit. Behind him other eyes peered out silently, too, striving to pierce the gloom, and their owners prayed that the heavy snow and searing cold was keeping the savages huddled in their wigwams and that the way would be clear for their last-hope messenger to make his getaway.

At last Portugee pulled the reins gently and stepped forward. Like a ghost horse, Fortune thrust into the snow, his grey color and the dusting of white on his mane and head combined with the rags on his feet to make him a dimly seen, scarcely heard phantom. Once in the center of the clearing he put his head down and, freed from Portugee's restraining hand, blew softly through his nostrils; then, having made his protest at the cold and the senselessness of the man who wanted to leave the warmth of a good stable on such a wild expedition, he followed the floundering figure of the frontier scout towards the trees.

The snow in the open was quite deep and the watchers in the fort felt an agonizing impatience at the slow progress of the two, man and horse, as they struggled onwards. Now, perhaps more than at any other time on the journey, was the moment of extreme danger. Wild weather and darkness would normally drive the toughest Indians to shelter. Brave as they were, the warriors preferred to do their fighting in the light of day, withdrawing from battle as darkness fell, resuming the fight again as the sun came up. But with Red Cloud's warriors you could never tell. If warriors had been posted close to the fort, Portugee's chances of escape were slim, unless the exceptional blizzard had driven them into shelter and sleep.

By now, they were halfway across the clearing, naked and exposed between the shelter of the fort walls and the safety of the trees, a sitting target for the silent arrow or the sudden, unexpected bullet.

Nearer and nearer to the gloomy bank of the forest crept the two figures, now separated by a patch of white, now huddled together in one grey block. And all the time the snow drifted down like a curtain, continuously falling between the lonely man and his friends in the fort.

Twenty-five yards from the trees, Portugee halted and brushed a hand across his brow. Wet trickled down his temples and neck. Beneath the fur cap he was sweating despite the be-

low zero temperature. Not a thing moved. Dimly he could
make out the snow-laden branches bending towards the ground
under the weight of the fall. In the fort, Carrington lifted a
hand towards the bar of the door as the faintly seen figures
stayed motionless before the trees.

"What's he waiting for? What's he seen?"

The questions hammered into the Colonel's brain as he
peered towards the distant scout.

But Portugee was about to move on, satisfied that nothing
lurked in the trees, that his way out was clear.

Suddenly a sharp crack echoed out. He looked swiftly in the
direction of the sound and saw a broken branch whip upwards,
freed of the weight of snow which slid in a white heap to the
ground beneath. Portugee breathed again, grunted to his horse
and moved forward. Step by step the stunted trees approached,
looming out of the darkness. Low branches brushed his face and
whipped along the horse's back, springing over the saddle with
little scratching noises. Every bush seemed to contain a shadow;
every shadowy tree hide an enemy. Portugee fingered the knife
in his belt. There would be no protecting volley from the fort
now if anyone was waiting for him among the trees. His own
rifle would be a handicap and a shot would bring other braves
to the spot. Far better to trust to the silence of a good knife
thrust . . .

Suddenly he heard a cry, faint and indistinct but a cry certainly, and stopped in his tracks. Fortune bumped into his
back, halted with ears pricked, but although they strained and
the minutes dragged past, it was not repeated, and after a while
he moved on. Perhaps it was an animal, although what moved
abroad in such a snow he could not guess.

Under the trees the snow was less deep, the steady fall broken
by the branches. They wound their way through the scrub,
feeling the ground slope down to the Little Piney, hearing the
steady trickle of water through the ice before they reached the
frozen stream. It was still dark, but eastward a faint dawn
change in the sky could be discerned by the sentry on the fort
tower. In the scrub-covered valley it was still deep gloom, and
Portugee had to press on to make good his escape before day-

light came. One good thing: the falling snow was already filling his tracks across the clearing, covering up the tale of his getaway from any scouting warriors.

He had left the fort on the south side, moving parallel to the stream and keeping it on his left. Now, as he worked his way silently through the thick scrub, he began to ease a little southeast, making for an old Indian trail that would lead him away across the high ground south of the fort, past the stone ruins of an earlier settlement and then away to the open country and the two hundred and sixty-eight miles to Fort Laramie.

At the foot of the ravine he found a stream, a tiny tributary of the Piney, frozen solid in the shallows, but with dark holes and a faint sound of trickling water in the sheltered spots beneath the banks. The darkness in the valley had increased and the snow which had fallen so steadily during his escape from the fort now began to swirl and eddy up the ravine, driving into his face and bringing with it a keen flurry of wind that moaned cruelly in the branches.

Although it made the going more difficult, Portugee welcomed the storm. The dark snow clouds would delay the cold grey light of dawn and the wind would obliterate his tracks all the more quickly.

Horse and man crossed the stream and climbed up the slope. Once over this rise and on his left, if he was not mistaken, Portugee hoped to find the main watercourse and, farther on, the hard going of the old Indian trail. If he could gain that and make it over the ridge to the south, the light could come as soon as it liked. He would be beyond the iron ring of Red Cloud's warriors and the way would be open before him.

The ground began to slope down and, encouraged by the increasing noise of the wind, Portugee pushed more swiftly ahead with Fortune crashing through the brush behind him. Then, during a lull in the gathering storm and through the shadowy trees, he caught a glimpse of something that made his heart freeze. A dull red glow was coming from behind a rock not more than fifty yards away. He turned to place a cautionary hand over Fortune's mouth and a renewed gust of wind hurled more snow upon them. When he turned the fire was gone, or at least he had lost the position of it in the cloaking blackness. Quietly he dropped back alongside the horse and, reaching up, slipped the rifle from its scabbard. It was the work of a moment to unwrap the oiled rag and slip it into the mouth of the holster. Then, looping Fortune's reins round a branch, he moved forward in the direction they had been going. A few yards and he turned to the left, scrambled over a crop of rock and lay peering into the blackness. Dimly something flickered, and there down below him was the spark and swirl of a fire freshened up by the wind until it leaped and eddied in the tiny crevice between the rocks where someone had cunningly placed it. Portugee crawled forward, brushing the snow carefully from the branches, avoiding all possibility of noise and praying that Fortune would not neigh back there behind him. He had to know who had lit the fire and what they were doing.

Then he made out a rude shelter leaning against the rocks beyond the fire, covered with snow but dark and inviting beneath the poles that held up a scrub-wood roof. It was an improvised Indian hut, the fire made almost in its door-way for warmth and light. Wood lay in a pile beyond the fire and the snow hissed and sputtered as it fell on the embers.

So Red Cloud had his guards posted round the fort even in this blizzard. Were they asleep? How many of them were there? Not more than two or three in a shelter that size— and if Portugee summarized rightly, not more than one there now—while the others kept watch on the trail about a quarter-mile down the river, where it crossed the ford on its way to the fort.

But even one was a danger. Within half an hour or so, even in this blizzard, it would be light enough to see his tracks and not long enough for the snow to fill them. He must tackle the occupant of the hut and trust to luck that it would be an hour or more before his companions returned.

Inch by inch he moved nearer, until he could feel the warmth of the flames. He placed his rifle on the rocks. Drawing his knife he slid quietly over the edge and moved like a shadow to the door of the hut. Inside a long, dark shape . . . a rug that seemed to move. A flame leaped up in the wind, and in answer the shadow jumped in the hut. Portugee flung himself forward, crashed through the doorway, and with one sweeping movement plunged the knife downwards—into the dark heap of a brushwood bed and an old, stinking blanket! The hut was empty. For a second or two Portugee lay there, the oily smell of Indian war paint in his nostrils, then he rolled over and sprang up in one quick movement. Advancing to the fire, he kicked snow over it, dulling the embers. He looked round. Nothing moved. No one came. He caught up the rifle and went quickly and silently back to the place where he had left the horse.

Fortune stirred at his approach, raising his head in greeting. Portugee patted his wet muzzle and unlooped the reins, then, still carrying his rifle, started swiftly on up the valley. His one aim now was to put as much distance between himself and the Indian guard-post by the stream as he could before daylight revealed his tracks. No scout on earth could conceal his movements across a carpet of snow like this; only time would erase the trail and there was little enough of that left before the light of day penetrated the storm clouds.

The snow began to thin a little as he pressed upwards, but the wind increased steadily in volume and by the time he reached the old Indian trail it was whipping with increased fury around him. An unprecedented storm this, almost disastrous for the small band of defenders in the fort, but a helpful cloak for Portugee in his escape—without it Red Cloud's braves would have made any getaway impossible. As it was, even in the light of the blizzard, he had almost met disaster in the valley as he stumbled on the guards' fire. But where were they? Why was the hut empty? Portugee could visualize at least three braves there—two to guard the trail while one slept, later to relieve the watchers. But no one had been sleeping in the hut—were they all abroad in the snow-swept valley at the dark hour before dawn which Indians fear most, for it is then the spirits of the forest walk?

Where they were when he crept into the hut Portugee never knew. Where they were an hour later he found out, suddenly, savagely and almost fatally.

The trail took him across the Piney once more and then up

towards the crest of the ridge of hills to the south of the fort.
Daylight was just breaking as he pulled Fortune towards the
top of the rocky pass. What was left of the snowfall was driving horizontally over the hill and whirling into his eyes as he
struggled upwards. A little below the crest of the hill Portugee
stopped and wrapped the rag round the breech of his rifle. He
pushed it into the holster, pulled the one remaining rag from
Fortune's left foreleg and swung himself up into the saddle. The
going was easier now that he was out of the deep snow in the
valley and at all costs he must press on.

He tightened his knees, lifted the reins, and at that moment a
violent blow struck him on his right shoulder and the side of his
head, almost knocking him from his horse. He swayed forward
and as he did so saw the great arrowhead hanging two inches
from his face. It had taken him in the shoulder, miraculously
missing the flesh, and now hung from his furs like some barbaric ornament.

Fortune spun sideways. Portugee, pulling the rifle from its
holster, flung himself from the saddle as another arrow whistled
viciously in the wind through the space where he was sitting
a moment before. He hit the snow and rolled over and over
into the brush at the side of the trail. As he came up on one
knee he brought the rifle forward, tearing the rag from the
breech. Two! There were two of them, those arrows had followed too swiftly one upon the other to have come from
one bow. One brave was in the open, erect and clear in the half
light, black against the sky, his hand reaching up to his back for
a second arrow. Portugee fired and the figure crumpled and
disappeared.

The echo swept eerily over the pass. A flurry of snow beat
down upon the scene. Portugee crawled to the shelter of a
twisted tree stump, his keen eyes peering from under his wet
cap, searching for the second of Red Cloud's braves who had
trailed him up the valley. No movement, no sign. The first
Indian had vanished although Portugee was sure he had hit
him: below and to the right a clump of rocks seemed to move.
Something came gradually out against the white snow. An
arm? A bow? A shoulder? Portugee leveled the rifle round the

tree trunk, squeezed the trigger tighter, tighter and then, as he was more sure of his aim, fired. Bow and rifle, the primitive weapon of the Indian and the white man's modern gun, sent their deadly missiles towards each other simultaneously. The brave's aim was accurate, almost lethal. The arrow actually struck the rifle barrel, glanced along its silver length, gouging the metal and smacking its stone-tipped head against the frozen tree strump. Portugee's numbed hand almost let the rifle drop.

The wind tore the noise of the shot swiftly away. For a moment all was still, then he saw the Indian pitch forward from the rocks. The brave fell slowly, buried his face in the snow, his hands crumpled under him as if he was praying. His rump stuck up in the air, propped against the tree. Portugee moved cautiously. The brave's bow lay beneath him almost buried, already the snow was stained with his blood. A little farther down the slope the other Indian lay on his back—his eyes wide open in surprise. The arrow he was reaching for when the shot hit him was still clutched in his hand. The wind shook his feathers and whipped the black strands of hair over his face.

Portugee left them where they lay, and a few seconds later was urging Fortune over the top of the hill—into the teeth of the wind, on to Fort Laramie.

11
THE HUNTING PARTY

The full light of morning found Portugee some forty miles from Fort Phil Kearny and crossing the last of the massive hills that circled the fort. Low clouds and driving snow had held down Fortune's pace. Deep drifts in places had forced the pair to abandon the trail in favor of higher, rocky ground where they could travel without fear of being buried. But although it was clear of snow, the high ground had the disadvantage of being exposed to the bitter winds that swept down off the mountains in the north. Flakes of ice stung the scout's face; he hunched his shoulder forward and dug his chin in the collar of his coat in an effort to ward off the knife-edge particles. On the ridges Fortune, too, turned sideways, butting his head into the wind, his grey mane streaming out to one side and whipping over Portugee's mittens as gust after gust tore at the struggling horse and its rider.

At times the very ground beneath them seemed to be moving, transformed by snow and wind into a river of white that whirled and streamed over the curved hills like smoke. Into this, Fortune's feet struck and stamped, ringing on the ice-bound stones even above the moan of the storm.

In the occasional lulls between the gusts Portugee scanned the trail ahead and urged his horse into a canter. Through screwed-up eyes he sought anxiously for landmarks, and at last made out the low walls of a deserted staging-post some little way ahead. He was on the right track. He rode by the old building, ignoring the chance of shelter that it offered, still striving to put the miles between himself and any Indians who might be dogging his steps.

Presently, the trail began to climb again and the scout found himself riding through a narrow defile. Great rocks reared up on either hand, plastered white with snow, dark and threatening in the gaps between the boulders. "Just the place for an ambush," Portugee muttered to himself, thinking of the ruined building below that could offer shelter to a party of braves, determined to keep the route to Laramie securely closed. But he shook his head—no, Red Cloud was far behind. He felt confident that he had seen the last of the hostiles.

The wind, which was now directly behind them, increased in fury as they scrambled to the top of the hill. Once over the crest, however, they found that they were sheltered from the blast. High overhead it roared, flung up by the slope of the hill, carrying the snow with it for a while and then letting it drop in a drifting curtain of white that smothered the top of the valley and made the going slippery and treacherous.

Fortune and his rider slithered downhill at an increasing pace for nearly an hour. High rocks shut them in on all sides at first, but as they dropped down they began to pass scattered, bent pine trees and, where the floor of the valley widened, whole copses, white and laden on the top-most branches but dark beneath. Here the snow had only just begun to penetrate and the ground still promised the warmth of layer upon layer of pine needles.

By mid-morning the fall of snow had ceased and Portugee began to look for a place where he could feed the horse and snatch a moment's rest before pushing on. They had been traveling now for some six hours and the scout felt confident that he had successfully penetrated Red Cloud's ring of death. Only the natural hazards of the trail and the wild weather lay between him and his destination.

Fort Laramie was still far away. There were one hundred and ninety hard miles ahead. Crazy Woman's Creek lay some forty miles below, and then there was the wide-open plain that swept round the foot of Laramie Peak and the bleak, black hills that struck down into the Great Plains themselves to form a magnificent but forbidding background to the fort. A thousand disasters could happen before the lone rider arrived with news

of the garrison's plight at Fort Phil Kearny and the Army units
stationed at Laramie went hurrying out to the rescue. The
minutes that followed brought Portugee's epic ride nearer to
disaster than anything else that had happened so far.

The scout was halfway down the valley when he saw them.
He swung Fortune to the side of the trail, under the shelter of
the overhanging trees, while his mind raced feverishly, considering what to do. Advancing up the winding floor of the
valley, not more than a quarter of a mile away, was a group of
Indians. Through narrowed eyes he counted five braves. They
were carrying something between them slung on a long pole
that bobbed and sagged as they trudged through the snow. It
was a deer, its forefeet and hindfeet tied together and slung
over the pole. Of all the luck! To run into a hunting party here,
in the middle of a valley where the snow-capped sides made
impossible going for a horse and where retreat, because of his
tracks, could only bring discovery in a matter of minutes!
There was no chance of going into hiding until the party had
passed; he must find some way of getting far enough beyond
them before they stumbled on his trail and raised the alarm.

Pulling Fortune round, he dug his heels into his flanks and
urged him up through the trees at right angles to the trail. He
had to bend low in the saddle to avoid being hit by the snow-
laden branches. A stone or two rolled down the slope behind
them, but for the most part they climbed in silence save for the
thump of hooves on the wet ground.

Coming out at the top of the trees, he found a rough track
running alongside the copse between the tree trunks and the
loose scree that piled up towards the ridge of the hill. Crouching low, he steered Fortune along the narrow path; for nearly
three hundred yards they were able to move down the valley
parallel to the trail. When he judged that he had gone far
enough Portugee halted and slid from his seat. Holding Fortune's muzzle he led him quietly down the slope; pine needles
under a thin layer of snow muffled their movements and they
drew near the trail like two grey ghosts. Through a gap in the
foliage Portugee could just see the path below where it turned
sharply in its widing ascent of the valley.

He had not long to wait. With a light moccasined step that was barely discernible from where the two waited, hardly daring to breathe, the first of the braves crossed the open space below. Fortune stirred, trying to shake off Portugee's restraining hand. Then came the two braves carrying the deer. Portugee could see the head hanging down and the brown, bloodstained hide. Behind, with the bows and lances, were the last of the little party. All were walking slowly, as if the hunt had been a long one and they were glad that it was almost over. None of them paid particular attention to their surroundings, but they would not be able to miss Fortune's track higher up the valley unless they were walking in their sleep, thought Portugee grimly.

When they turned the bend of the trail Portugee knew that he would have to move out into the open, mount his horse and put as much distance between himself and the warriors in as short a time as possible.

He edged the horse downwards, bumping against the dark trunks of the pines, listening for the slightest sound that would indicate danger, making for the open ground at the edge of the timber. In a few seconds he was there. Holding back the branches of pine he peered out up the trail. The redskins had passed—their moccasin tracks marked the white ground up to the turn and then disappeared. He had three or four minutes at the most before they found his scent and turned to give chase. He flung the reins over Fortune's head, led the horse out from the shadows, turned for one last look down the valley—and stared into the savage eyes of one of Red Cloud's warriors!

For a fraction of a second neither moved. Surprise held them rigid. The Indian, who was tall and powerful, had been following some distance behind the hunting party and had been unseen by Portugee when he first spotted the braves in the valley. He carried an old muzzle-loading rifle in his right hand; vivid vermilion war paint streaked his cheeks—these things Portugee noticed before he hurled himself into action.

Leaping to one side he wrenched the long knife from his belt, taking the point between the thumb and mittened fingers of his other hand as it came free. In one swift movement, with

all the force he could find, he flung the knife at the Indian. Almost simultaneously the brave leveled the rifle and fired. He was
a second too late. The knife left Portugee's hand as the old gun
roared.

Fortune reared, frightened by the noise so close to his head,
his hooves lashing the air. Both men fell backwards in the snow.

The scout felt a great numbing blow in his chest as if he had
been hit with a sledge-hammer. Gasping and choking, tears
blinding him, he struggled on to his hands and knees. Wet snow
clung to his face; the white world rocked around him as he
fought for breath. From up the valley came a call from the
hunting party as the sound of the shot reached them.

Brushing away the tears, Portugee could see his opponent on
his back, one hand clutching convulsively at the ground, the
other holding the haft of the knife that protruded from his
stomach.

Dazed and sick, the scout rose to his feet, his breath coming
in spasmodic gasps, his mind still reeling.

He clutched at Fortune's bridle with one hand and made an
effort to mount. The horse backed away, and with one foot in
the stirrup Portugee was flung against his side. The shouts of
the Indians grew louder but Portugee could not find enough
breath even to quiet his frightened horse. Grimly he flung an
arm across the saddle and pulled himself up. He got his leg over
and fell desperately forward, groping for the reins with his
free hand. Fortune had turned in a half-circle and was facing
down the trail. Portugee beat ineffectually with clenched fists
to urge the animal forward, but before Fortune could move
something suddenly fastened on Portugee's foot.

He looked down. It was the wounded brave! With a superhuman effort he had crawled forward and, in a last despairing
attempt to stop the white man, had flung himself at the horse,
his clawing hands fixing on the stirrup. There he hung, his eyes
staring, his legs dragging. The haft of the knife in his body ran
with blood and red patches spattered the snow.

Portugee kicked out savagely but the brave hung on, almost
pulling him sideways from the saddle. The yells of the Indians
came closer. Again Portugee lashed out. The redskin's grasp

remained tight on the stirrup. The hunting party burst into sight, racing round the bend in the trail. Fortune began to prance sideways, dragging the brave over the snow. An arrow hummed viciously by. . . .

A feeling of panic swept over the scout and he tried to bring the horse round so that the Indian's body came beneath the stamping hooves in a frantic effort to break this grip of death. Suddenly Fortune screamed and lunged high into the air. The warrior's hold broke and he rolled in the snow. Portugee clung to the pommel as Fortune landed, and with another great leap the grey horse rushed headlong into a wild gallop down the valley. Trees and boulders whirled by. Portugee kept his seat by a miracle of balance. The yells of the Indians grew fainter as the two raced down the valley to safety.

For nearly a mile the horse galloped without a pause. As his stride lengthened and steadied, Portugee's breathing became more even; he took control of the reins, allowed Fortune his head and, once even, looked back up the empty track to make sure that they were not followed.

At last, when he felt safe from pursuit, he reined up. The valley began to level out and he walked Fortune to a group of trees where a tiny stream broke through the ice and ran in the open for a few yards.

The dull, numbing pain in his chest was still there and he could feel the wet running down his body. He pulled off his mitten to investigate and, as he did so, caught sight of a long red gash in the horse's rump. So that was what had made him jump! An arrow wound; a lucky wound, for without that startled leap the brave clinging to the stirrup might have held them back long enough for the others to reach the spot.

From Fortune's wound Portugee turned to his own. Unbuttoning his jacket, he slipped his hand under his shirt and dabbed at his chest. Slowly he withdrew his fingers and found them wet and sticky—with sweat! He heaved a sigh of relief, that turned into a fit of coughing as the pain caught at him again. Searching further he felt something hard and, pulling it out, found that he held a flattened, irregular lump of lead with shreds of torn cloth clinging to it.

But he was still puzzled and, digging down under his jacket, came across another solid object. Gold gleamed against his grimy palm. There, flattened and misshapen, was the locket Lieutenant Grummond's wife had given him. It had taken the full impact of the Indian's bullet.

12

FORTUNE'S LAPSE

Crazy Woman's Creek ran through the bottom of a gorge that lay like a dark crack across the white countryside below them. Portugee had reined in Fortune at a point where the trail turned and began a winding descent into the depths. A freak of nature, a trick of soil succumbing to the eroding forces of wind and water, the gorge ran for miles in either direction. It was as if a giant spade had scooped across the foothills, dropping the level of the ground a few hundred feet or more and scattering boulders along the bottom for good measure. It was a creek in name only. Floodwater at each rainy season for a thousand years had lacerated the bed of the gorge into a hundred channels which roared with the white mountain torrent and threatened all who attempted the passage with a swift and watery end if they relaxed their caution for a moment.

It was a tough enough crossing last summer, thought Portugee grimly. Then, the river had boiled over the rocks, sung in the yellowstone caverns and sent horses and men stumbling and gasping for their lives—until the Army had built the bridge.

Now, on the threshold of a bitter winter, snow cloaked the gorge. Icy fingers hung by the falls and the streams, strangling the flow of the waters day by frozen day until the whole roaring canyon was stilled. That stage had not quite been reached. Gazing down over the loops of the descending trail, Portugee could see the dark turbulent center of the river where it poured through a narrow gap in the snow-covered rock. Ice clung in fantastic patterns to the edges of the boulders and jagged pieces bobbed along with the current. A low murmur reached the scout even up here on the heights. Winter's grip was not yet complete on Crazy Woman's Creek, and as Portugee looked up and down the narrow canyon, seeking the crossing, he could see other patches where the waters still ran black and ominous before sliding beneath the ice that already covered the wider reaches of the river. Almost directly below him the scout suddenly found what he was seeking. The unfamiliar appearance that the snow had brought to the scene and the strange shapes of the ice had deceived him so that for a moment he could not be sure that the bridge still existed.

Built when Colonel Carrington's expedition marched north in those dusty summer days before Red Cloud had taken the warpath, the bridge consisted of the trunks of four great firs laid across the narrowest part of the gorge and secured with heavy slabs of rock at either end. Trunks of smaller trees split in half were pinned across the four main timbers at right angles and the cracks filled in with mud to give the wagons a smooth crossing. Beneath the lips of the rocks upon which the bridge was perched, the waters rolled swift and deep.

The site of the bridge had been chosen for two reasons: here the river was at its narrowest and firm rock rose at either edge; above, the sheer sides of the gorge were broken and permitted the trail to run down to the river in a series of steep bends that were dangerous enough but could be navigated by the heaviest wagons with a trained team of horses and a steady driver.

All this passed through Portugee's mind as he sat on Fortune's heaving back and looked down, remembering that summer crossing. What had kept the bridge hidden from his eyes today was the great mass of loose ice that piled against its upstream edge, disguising the sharpness of the parallel tree trunks and confusing it with other icy mounds in the valley. For fifty yards above the bridge the whole river was jammed, and as the scout moved down the trail he wondered what had caused this phenomenon.

It had stopped snowing, but the grey, low-bellied clouds trailed ceaselessly across the sky and added a somber note to the late afternoon light. Portugee pulled his jacket tighter and, as he rode lower into the gloomy canyon, a shiver of apprehension ran through him.

Sliding and stamping, Fortune came at last to the river. The scout dismounted and, leaving his horse to rest after the hair-raising descent, walked forward to inspect the bridge. A weird moaning noise came from the timbers. Stepping on to the round trunk of the nearest fir, Portugee felt the vibration that was shaking the whole structure.

Below, the river rolled strongly. Jammed up against the edge of the bridge which faced upstream were the torn and twisted branches of a dead fir. The heavy trunk went deep into the water and piled against this was a solid mass of snow and ice brought into the river by the recent blizzard. As Portugee watched, some pieces escaped and bobbed away downstream, but the main weight remained there, heaving with the movement of the water beneath and growing heavier every minute as more and more chunks lodged against the mound.

The scout stepped off the bridge. He could no longer feel the vibration that the press of the ice and the running waters sent constantly through the timbers, but he could still hear the creak and moan of the wood as it bent beneath the weight. Even as he watched there came a sharp crack and the timbers gave a slight lurch.

There was no time to lose if he was to cross while the bridge still held. Fortune's weight and his own might be enough to cause the already overstrained timbers to go, but that was something that had to be risked. There was no other crossing for miles in either direction and the ice over the wider stretches of the smooth water would not be thick enough yet to bear them.

Portugee did not hesitate. He grasped Fortune's reins and, leading the horse forward, stepped firmly onto the bridge. The mud between the logs had long since broken away, but the snow took its place and the path was smooth. Fortune's two forefeet came up on to the planks as the scout edged out above the water, keeping the horse well behind him, feeling the way and spreading their combined weight as widely as possible.

Then Fortune's hind legs stumbled onto the bridge and his ears pricked in alarm. He sensed the ground trembling beneath him and his eyes showed white with fear.

"All right, boy, all right," Portugee murmured gently. He liked the situation no more than his mount did. The vibrations seemed more violent as they trod gingerly to the center of the bridge, and the groan of the timbers, the sullen roar of the waters and the gloom that hung over the scene gave the whole episode the quality of a nightmare. A sudden lurch of the heavy planks beneath made Fortune pull back and stamp his hooves as if to seek firmer ground. Portugee sensed rather than saw the danger and jerked the reins violently forward, at the same time calling urgently: "Hup, boy, hup!" but his yell was almost drowned by a splintering crash as one of the upstream trunks gave way. Like the straw that broke the camel's back, the weight of man and animal hastened the end. The whole mass of ice, pushed continuously by the rushing water, bore down on the bridge. The remaining timbers splintered and the sagging center buckled downwards beneath the horse's frantic hooves. Water began to flood over the planks. The snow fell in great chunks from the gaps in the logs.

Portugee flung himself forward, grasping at the timbers, hauling himself up the slowly toppling surface. Fortune's hooves scrabbled on the wood as, crouching somehow like a great grey cat, the gallant horse scrambled towards the far edge.

It all happened in seconds, but time seemed suspended for the scout. He felt the bridge breaking in two; saw the great mass of ice loom up on his right. The branches of the dead tree clutched at his back as if to drag him into the river. Man and horse reached the end of the bridge almost at the same time. It now hung at a crazy angle, broken in two halves, roaring water pouring through the gap in the center and the ice thudding down, jarring the bridge horribly with each successive blow. Portugee slipped back. The cold water splashed over his legs. Digging as hard as he could with his mittened hands, he clawed his way up again, feeling the planks beneath him begin to slide.

The nightmare had become reality. For a terrible moment it

seemed as if he would hang there forever, climbing frantically up a slippery surface that slid continously downwards. Then his hands found the firm rock; his coat, caught in a projecting branch, ripped open as with a last heave he rolled onto solid rock while what was once the bridge tumbled with a noise like thunder into the torrent. Ice, broken branches, tossing planks and churning foam were carried swiftly away downstream.

Fortune stood trembling above him. The scout climbed shakily to his feet and looked back. Nothing remained of the bridge; two piles of rocks on either bank marked where the trail ended; the river rushed between.

Portugee turned his back on the scene and reached up to pat the horse, but Fortune shied violently away.

"Steady, boy, you're safe enough now," said the scout and, catching up the trailing reins, led the horse away from the river's edge. But Fortune still showed every sign of alarm and when they reached the tumbled rocks at the roadside, began to toss his head and pull sideways.

"Steady," said the scout sharply—and then he, too, caught the sudden pungent scent!

The meaning had hardly become coherent in his mind before the bear came out with a rush from the rocks. It moved like lightning towards the horse. Fortune reared, his forefeet lashing out wildly, his teeth bared as he neighed in fright. The bear rose up, too, sweeping one great paw forward and catching the horse on the chest with those long razor-like claws.

At that moment Portugee fired. The long Navy pistol smoked in his hand, conjured like magic from inside his flapping jacket. The sound echoed back from the rocky walls. Stung by the bullet, the grizzly turned to face this new attack. He was a big, brown brute, savagely hungry after the blizzard and not yet over his winter's sleep. His forefeet came down rasping on the rock. Despite its bulk, a bear moves with terrible speed when it attacks.

Portugee backed away, his feet tripping on the uneven ground. He brought his other hand up to steady the gun, heard the clash, clash of the grizzly's claws as it charged at him—and pulled the trigger . . . again . . . and again . . . and again

. . . and again . . . but the fifth shot went wide, for by then the bear was on top of him. A terrible grunting noise, an over-powering smell, an obliterating weight that crushed his head and shoulders to the ground and swept suffocating blackness over him . . .

He didn't see the grizzly roll on, carried by the impetus of its rush, blind with the five bullets in its face and neck, slipping and sliding over the icy rocks into the wild river.

He didn't see Fortune, bleeding from the savage gash on his shoulder, gallop madly up the trail into the gathering gloom.

He lay on his back, dead to the world, one hand clutching the pistol, the other flung across the wallet that was strapped round his body and which contained the dispatches from the beleaguered garrison at Fort Phil Kearny.

13

THE RING TIGHTENS

It was Jim Bridger who first put their innermost fears into words. The long day had passed without event at the fort. Smoke from Indian fires had been seen at intervals on the surrounding hills, but although a constant watch was maintained there was no other visible sign of the hostiles. The guards did their turn of duty on the stockade and were relieved. Women and children kept to the log huts. The cooking ovens burned brightly and men paused before the red glow to soak the welcome warmth into their bodies before going about their tasks.

Grey afternoon lengthened into dusk. The wind rose and brought ragged clouds of snow down from the hills. Vigilance was redoubled as the trees became lost in gloom. But although the guards peered anxiously this way and that, thrashed their arms round their bodies to keep themselves alert, their thoughts were with Portugee Phillips. How was he faring? Would he get through in time to bring help before Red Cloud gathered his warriors for the final assault?

"It's a hundred to one against him gettin' there." Jim Bridger stroked his grey beard reflectively. "And the weather ain't helpin' none."

He watched the snow whirling down.

"Yet if anybody can do it, Portugee's the man," he added.

His listeners turned away, their confidence somehow restored despite the terrible odds that they knew their messenger was facing. Where was he now, they wondered?

"He should have crossed Crazy Woman's in daylight," said the Colonel. "He should be on the plain by now, despite the snow."

The soft touch of flakes on his upturned face aroused Portugee. At first his mind refused to respond. He wanted to drift
back into the restful blackness, silence the thudding pain in his
head, but something kept urging him to move; to fight the killing cold and struggle on to . . . where?

When he went to brush the snow from his face he was surprised to find that he was clutching the pistol. He had some
difficulty in getting his fingers free for the ice had stuck them
to the metal. It was like a burn. He struggled into a sitting position, pushing the gun back into its holster. He pulled the mitten
over the stiff fingers. The Navy was empty, he must remember
that, but at the moment he could hardly hold it, much less reload! There was a strong, sickening stench of bear about him
and his jacket was patched with frozen blood.

In a rush the whole scene came back. Somewhere in the
darkness to his left the river roared. He rolled over in the snow
and slowly, painfully began to crawl away from the sound.

The Indians killed four men in the early hours of the morning. Neither the darkness, nor the snow, nor the watchful
guards stopped them. They came silently out of the woods as
a work party struggled to clear the deepening drifts from the
stockade. There was a warning shout but it came too late. The
deadly arrows flew in silence as the men struggled for shelter.
The guard's rifle shattered the night but the foe had melted
into the trees.

Three soldiers and one civilian lay huddled and still below
the stockade.

Red Cloud was tightening the ring of death.

Portugee found a cave and crawled into the farther corner
out of the wind and snow. Sure enough, there was wood
there; dry and splintered, flung up by some freak summer
flood and lodged in the crevices as the waters retreated.

Fire! He had to have warmth! With clumsy fingers he swept
the brushwood into a pile and tried to spark it into life.

After several attempts the flame caught. It leaped swiftly upwards and the smoke stung his eyes. He'd risk the redskins!

The fire would keep away the wolves, or any other savage animal abroad in the night. The scout huddled towards the flames, rubbing the circulation back into his arms. His leggings steamed in the heat. He began to think about Fortune.

"He's got a fine horse," said the Colonel. "Pure Kentucky stock, toughened up for this country. If there's one horse that can take him through, it's Fortune."

"Why did they attack like that?" asked the adjutant, "just a small party, on their own."

"Some young bucks out for glory, I reckon," said Bridger. "Red Cloud ain't quite ready for a full-out attack yet. It's my guess this bunch was just a mite impatient."

"Do you think they found Phillips? Do you think they stopped him?"

"Nope," replied the old plainsman decisively. "If they had they'd have told us. You can bank on that. They'd have paraded the horse or some of his clothes, or his scalp," he added grimly, "just to let us know there was no hope. I reckon Portugee's got past Red Cloud all right. But that ain't half of it."

Portugee stamped out the dying fire. The warmth had revived him. A search through his pockets revealed a few biscuits and a wad of tobacco. The biscuits were dry but as he chewed the tobacco the saliva came back into his mouth.

His head still ached but otherwise he seemed to have suffered no harm from the grizzly's attack. Outside the snow had stopped. He reloaded his gun; strapped his jacket down over the dispatch wallet and crawled out of the cave. When his eyes had become accustomed to the blackness he began the long climb up the trail out of the gorge.

The next time the redskins came, the guards were ready for them. It was a larger party and they approached unexpectedly from the south side of the fort. They carried a long slender tree trunk, tied with cross branches to form a crude ladder. They came with a quick noiseless rush across the clearing but the guards saw them and the warriors left four of their number staining the snow with blood before they abandoned the attempt to get into the fort.

Their intention, had they succeeded, was not quite clear. Was Red Cloud massing for a dawn attack? Was this a mere diversion?

Wearily the defenders stood to arms. The fort on the Little Piney watched for the dawn . . . and the Indian enemy . . . and prayed for their last-hope messenger.

14

ACROSS THE PLAIN

It took Portugee more than two hours to climb out of Crazy Woman's Gorge. In the pitch darkness, stumbling and sliding on the frozen road, expecting at any moment to pitch over the edge of a precipice where the trail swept round in a sudden turn, it was a frightening experience. He had no time to think about his horse; what had happened to Fortune after the bear's savage attack, where the horse had galloped to during the time when Portugee lay senseless by the river, he had no means of knowing or finding out. For the present every ounce of concentration must be devoted to the hazardous climb out of the valley. Out of the mist of uncertainty only one fact was clear. Fortune must have gone up the trail, there was no other way. And so, up after him, the scout went; not thinking of the disasters that may have overtaken the grey, not worrying about his own predicament but simply struggling onward, driven all the time by the picture at the back of his mind—that of the hard-pressed garrison at the fort on the Little Piney, depending solely on him for help.

He could feel the end of the trail coming before he could actually see, in the almost black night, any appreciable difference in the terrain. There was the sense of trees closing in on the trail and, if it was possible, a thickening of the darkness. Once, relaxing his guard a little as the fear of pitching over a cliff receded in his mind, he blundered into some branches. Snow fell in a cold cloud about his head; he stumbled to one side and went on blindly, his feet feeling for the smooth trail, his eyes aching as he strove to pierce the gloom.

Presently, as he tramped on beneath the trees, he heard a distant cry. His heart leaped as he thought of Fortune and he stood quite still, trying to identify the noise, or at least the direction in which it had come. Something stirred in the wood much nearer at hand. It could have been a fall of snow, it could have been an animal. Portugee longed for the light of dawn to help him, but after the long hours in the cave and the period on the river bank when consciousness had left him, he had only the haziest notion of the hour. He lowered his head and began to march onwards.

About this time, an hour before dawn perhaps, he saw the first sign of wolves. An increase of light told him that he had emerged from the close woods into a clearing or open country, he could not tell which. The snow was deeper and he floundered on without much sense of direction when suddenly he became aware of a movement away to his right. A dark shape showed against the snow, bunched up, drew apart, separated. More he could not see, but as he stood there peering uncertainly this way and that, startlingly clear, ringing eerily across the snow came the long-drawn-out hunting call of a timber wolf!

Portugee was apprehensive but not frightened. He'd long expected this: the great wolves that roamed the prairies at the edge of the hills would be out seeking food after the blizzard. He slipped his hand inside his jacket and drew the heavy pistol. He held it in his mittened hand and looked around. There was little need for caution. In fact, the quieter he was, the more encouraged the wolves would be to investigate. He shouted at the grey pack. It moved, huddled together and seemed to fade into the darkness. But the wolves were still there all right and they'd stay there . . . until he collapsed in the snow or was rendered helpless by some unexpected accident.

He began to move forward again, the gun swinging by his side, his eyes peering from left to right. Occasionally he would stop to look behind him, but the wolves came no closer and he moved on with increasing confidence.

He had little notion of direction as he left the woods. Perhaps he was even now in open country, the low foothills that led gently on to the plain, or perhaps this was just a clearing in the trees. He reckoned that this last thought was correct, reasoning that he hadn't gone far enough to reach the plains, somehow feeling the trees all round at a distance.

And then he had the biggest stroke of luck since leaving the fort. The snow was perhaps knee deep in the clearing; the ground, level. Plunging forward, breaking a path as he had done across the open ground outside the fort, he almost fell into another trail through the snow. He stopped abruptly. There it was, dark against the white ground, a broken, ragged line that crossed his own path at right angles. He almost ceased to breathe. He dared not hope . . . and yet there was only one thing it could be!

Gingerly he knelt down, pushing his gun into his belt, and then, with long fingers he began to feel the ground beneath him. It was churned up, lumpy with fallen snow. But suddenly, there was what he had been seeking . . . the clear, hard outline of a hoofprint!

There was only one horse it could be at that time, in that one spot, in that wild and desolate country. Fortune! The thought that perhaps by a millionth chance it was the trail of some Indian brave's steed crossed his mind but he dismissed it. His fingers explored the ground quickly. This horse was shod; he could feel the impression of the iron shoes stamped as clear as a plaster cast in the snow. It must be . . . it *had* to be Fortune.

Portugee straightened up, hope flooding into his weary body at the thought of finding his horse. He peered at the trail again. It ran off into the darkness to left and right. Which way had the horse come? Which way was it going? The scout bent swiftly down again and with both hands this time felt the trail. He moved a little to his left. Yes. There were the hard, crisp curves of a hoofprint and another and yet again. Fortune had come up on Portugee's left, crossing the path that the scout was making through the snow and had gone off into the darkness on his right.

By the very clearness of the tracks, by the feel of the hard edges and the absence of drifted snow, the scout knew that the trail could not be very old. An hour ago, perhaps less than that, Fortune had crossed the clearing. Was that, then, the cry he had heard whilst struggling through the trees? Was Fortune at bay in the woods with the wolf pack snarling at his heels?

Portugee drew his mitten over his frozen fingers and stepped into the horse's trail. At a faster pace now he plunged onwards.

After about a quarter of an hour, Fortune's deep tracks through the snow petered out but the scout seemed to be following some sort of natural trail and he went grimly forward. The going became hard again and he found himself among trees—but this time he was not alone. One either side of him the wolf pack ran. They kept well back, invisible in the blackness, but when he paused in his stride, head cocked to listen, he could hear them—the soft patter of feet through the trees that continued a fraction of a second after he had stopped, the occasional crackle of a snapped stick. Then all would be silent until he moved again, and then once more the movement began, keeping pace with him as they pushed through the branches. Once when he stopped he fancied he could hear the panting of breath close by. The hair on the back of his neck crept as an involuntary shiver of fear hit him. Then he marched on, noisy, defiant, his gun in his hand, keeping up a bold front to hold the pack at bay, his feet feeling the way along the trail.

Perhaps it was because of the noise that he was making as he pushed through the trees that he did not hear the horse until he had almost blundered on to him. A great black bulk towered up. There was a flurry of snow, a frightened snort and the crack of branches. Suddenly Portugee could smell horse and he almost cried out in joy. It was Fortune!

Trapped somehow in the trees, for the moment Portugee didn't question how or why, the big grey horse stamped and whinnied as he approached.

"Fortune, hey feller. Quiet, boy, quiet!"

Portugee stumbled forward, his arm outstretched. He felt a rope cut across his face and at that moment the wolves closed in.

They came in a savage, silent rush: dark shapes against the snow, teeth snapping. In his relief at finding Fortune, Portugee was almost caught off guard, but not quite. Jerking the Navy

forward, he turned to face the advancing pack. He had no time
to take off his mittens or to find the trigger with his stiff, frozen
fingers. The gloved palm of his right hand slammed the hammer of the pistol back in the swift fanning movement that was
to become famous among the gunfighters of the plains.

The pistol flashed vividly in the trees and by a stroke of luck
the shot took the leading timber wolf as he lunged. The scout
had fired by instinct at the nearest sound. There was a shrill
yelp of pain, a thud and threshing in the snow. Again Portugee
fired; again the gun flash lit up the scene. The shot wolf was
jumping, his head twisting from side to side in an effort to tear
at the burning pain that was spearing his body. Fortune
stamped and neighed in fear, but the wolves had had enough
for the moment and drew off.

Portugee ducked under the quivering rope and stepped towards the horse. He stroked the trembling neck and saw the
great grey head toss dimly in answer. Through a tangle of
reins and rope he felt for the saddle which was twisted across
Fortune's back. He slipped the Navy into his holster as his hand
reached the roll of feed, still there behind the blanket. Pulling
handfuls out, he piled them in the snow a little distance away.
Talking all the time to the horse, watching for the wolves, he
next pulled down some branches and broke off the dry stems.

It was the work of seconds to clear a space and spark the
dry wisps of hay into flame. He threw on small, dry twigs that
crackled instantly into life. The dark shadows leaped back and
the menace of the wolves receded.

In the light of the fire a strange scene was revealed. Fortune
was "tethered" to the trees. The rope from the saddle had
worked loose and, trailing behind in the snow, had tangled itself round the trunk of a young fir. In pulling against this the
horse had only further entangled himself. The reins, broken
and twisted, were wrapped round another branch. The saddle,
straining the girth, was at a crazy angle over his back. Portugee had got there only just in time. A few minutes more of
wild struggle and the horse would have perhaps broken free.
Portugee could scarcely believe his luck. He'd seen many a

plainsman stranded while the horse, hobbles broken, kept his
irate rider at arm's length and led him an exhausting dance over
the prairie before being recaptured.

Working swiftly he freed the rope, hobbled Fortune neatly
and securely and proceeded to straighten the saddle. Then he
pulled some more feed from the pack and threw it down in
front of the horse. While Fortune was eating he piled more fuel
on the fire and then, pulling the precious bottle of brandy from
the saddlebag, took a long, warm, choking swig and leaned
back against the trunk of a fir to take stock of the situation.
Things began to look better.

Half an hour later, watching the green glint of the wolves'
eyes as they moved in the darkness beyond the range of the fire,
he stood refreshed, and confident. He had made a meal of biscuits and brandy. He had inspected the gash on Fortune's
shoulder where the bear had mauled him; it was raw but clean
and the icy air had rapidly congealed the blood. Fortune had
eaten the best part of the hay, crunching the fragrant summer
grasses and pressed flowers with evident satisfaction in the cold
winter night. Banging his cap inside out, Portugee had filled it
with melting snow and, generously lacing the resulting water
with brandy, had given Fortune a drink. The scout had checked
his equipment. His rifle was gone. The long hunting knife he
had left in the body of the Indian warrior in the valley. He had
used some ammunition, but there was plenty left. The pain in
his chest from the impact of the bullet from the old Indian gun
still stung him as he bent over the fire, but all things considered
the pair were ready once more for action.

The last part of the journey lay before them. Dawn would
soon be here and from the edge of the woods Portugee could
find his way across the plain. If Laramie Peak, towering above
the final range of hills, showed up, so much the better, but in
any case the going would be easier now—as long as the blizzard
held off.

The scout took a last look round, pulling his jacket together
against the cold. Then he kicked out the embers of the fire and
swung into the saddle. Horse and man moved off through the
gloom, the rider ducking low to avoid the branches. When

they had gone the wolves came to the edge of the clearing and sniffed uncertainly at the smouldering fire and hissing snow. Silence and darkness crept down again over the woods.

There was no dawn, just a gradual lessening of the darkness. The grey clouds appeared; leaden, almost motionless in the still air. The thinning trees were flat black shapes behind him and the white rolling plain spread out at his feet. Protugee urged Fortune down the slope. The snow flew under the pounding hooves. The miles dropped by. The blizzard's driving wind had brushed the snow over the foothills, swept it on across the plain, allowing it to pile deep only where the ground dropped suddenly in shallow, scooped-out valleys. There Fortune would flounder, thrusting sometimes chest deep through the snow, and several times the scout sprang from the saddle to lead his mount forward through a particularly treacherous drift. The cold was intense. Icy fingers sought and found the openings in his jacket. His forehead was numbed and he had to tie a scarf up round his nose in order to keep his breath from forming into tiny icicles on his unshaven lips.

After a few hours on the plain he came to an Indian totem. Three thin branches stuck up from the snow with rawhide thongs running between. From the center of each cord a totem hung, swaying. One was a tuft of feathers with something dead and bloody and frozen dangling beneath. The other was part of the head of a buffalo. Red powder was sprinkled on the skull in the form of some mysterious sign. Portugee rode by without stopping. This was a Sioux totem—Red Cloud's warning sign that death lay in wait for any man who journeyed into the mountains. Death was certainly present at the fort, thought the scout grimly. Death had breathed on Fetterman's company, death waited outside the stockade for the defenders in the fort to weaken and succumb to attack—or until help arrived from Fort Laramie.

Determinedly Portugee spurred his horse. The totem dropped behind out of sight, the sky seemed to creep lower until he was riding between two flat planes of white and grey that merged in the dim distance to a cold grey mist.

For hours he struggled on without rest. About noon he halted, giving the horse nearly all that remained of the hay and chewing on biscuits soaked in brandy himself. He peered anxiously at the lowering sky. A few flakes of snow drifted on the wind, and in the distance he could see the plumes of little snow showers sweeping across the horizon. He remounted and, holding his course by the unerring instinct that had guided him so often across the plains, rode on into the gathering gloom of the storm.

15

THE PASSAGE OF
THE MOUNTAINS

Fortune found the pass.

All the morning Portugee had struggled across the plain. Snow showers sweeping over the mountains blinded the pair of them for minutes at a time but the falls came only occasionally, and despite the wind, they kept up a good pace. Like a great ocean frozen when the waves were at their highest, the prairie rolled towards the last mountain barrier between the gallant messenger and his destination—the fort on Laramie Creek. Fortune's hooves pounded the snow. The wild sage that grew over hill and hollow showed dark and twisted where the horse had been, and once a startled hare leaped from almost beneath the grey's hooves and went bounding away across the white wastes. The wind increased as the afternoon wore on. A tall conical hill looming up out of the grey sky on his right told Portugee that he was on the trail, and as they left the plain the ground began to dip and twist. Ice lay thick on frozen pools where the beaver had dammed the mountain streams in the summer and Fortune's hooves rang crisply on the wintry air as he galloped across.

Here, the scout recalled, he had hunted the antelope, sable and marten. There had been friendly trade with the Indians in those days, and Portugee had been shown the secret way through the mountains by a party of young Sioux braves.

He brushed his hand across his face, dusting away the snow for the thousandth time, feeling more acutely the bite of the icy particles as his mind dwelt on happier times. But things were different now—savagely different. This very pass, dis-covered with hunting companions who were now sworn ene-

mies besieging hard-pressed Fort Phil Kearny, was the quick-
est route to take him to Laramie in time to effect the rescue of
Colonel Carrington, Jim Bridger and all his friends at the fort.

With renewed vigor he spurred Fortune on.

A line of buttes loomed up a few miles distant, the snow-
covered crests giving off plumes of white as the wind whipped
around them. The ground began to change as he approached
the mountains. He rode over the first craggy hills, head down
against the wind, Fortune's mane lashing back as he cantered
staunchly on. At times the creak of saddle leather was audible,
and the steady, even breath of the horse, but for the most part
the constant moan of the wind drove all other sounds out of the
scout's head. Soon they were involved among the treacherous
ravines on the other side of the buttes. Turning and twisting,
Portugee strove to follow the old trail. Fine powdered snow
covered the bottom of the ravines hiding the slippery boulders,
lying in wait like spiteful traps for the stumbling feet of the
horse. Steadily, relentlessly, Fortune moved on, sure-footed,
even daintily, where the going was tricky, lengthening into a
mile-eating loping stride where he found the going good.

What a horse, thought Portugee. The Kentucky breeding
was proving itself "just like the Colonel said," the scout murmured. "Fortune—if we're going to get to Laramie it'll be
largely thanks to you." And despite the driving wind he leaned
forward and stretched a hand out to rub the throbbing shoulder
beneath him.

Fortune lowered his head and plunged on.

The landscape darkened. Firs began to appear, clinging to
the grim rock, their boughs bending beneath the weight of
snow, their tops swaying in the wind.

There was nothing picturesque about the Laramie Hills in
winter. Desolate as could be imagined, their black and broken
rocks permitted little vegetation to grow. Streams of swirling
snow ran and hissed like rivers in the winding ravines, death
place of many a good frontiersman caught by tempest or blizzard and hopelessly lost. Portugee began to wonder if he would
ever find his way.

By now the mass of the mountain that swept north to Laramie Peak loomed above them. They had been climbing slowly towards a seemingly impenetrable wall. At one spot the way was marked by the huge footprints of a grizzly and while they skirted a steep valley lined with trees, the howling of wolves and the barking of foxes came out of the darkness. The wind still roared down at them but its main force was spent in battering against the highest slopes, the white faces where the snow piled and waited in an avalanche ambush to engulf the traveler below. Continuously now, a fine fall cloaked them as they struggled on. Twice they came to a blank end of the trail . . . great granite walls barring the way. The wind laughed hollowly and smote them as they turned. Twice Portugee cast back in a half-circle as the entrance to the pass eluded them.

Despair began to ride with the scout. The strain of the journey, the pain in his chest, hunger, lack of sleep, all pressed down on the bowed, furred figure urging his horse blindly through the rocks.

"It must be near here. I know it . . . I *know* it."

The way grew narrow, the snow deeper. Dismounting, the scout led the horse, breaking waist high into the deep drifts. Above him, the top hidden in the falling snow, towered the mountain.

It was no good. At last he had to face it. He was lost. He turned wearily about, pulling the reins. Fortune, obstinately, refused to follow. The horse tugged on towards the rocky wall.

"It ain't no use," said the scout. "We can't get by that way." But he let the horse have its head and now the procession was reversed. Fortune led through the snow; Portugee, clutching the stirrup, stumbled alongside.

For perhaps a quarter of an hour they moved thus. Fortune seemed to be hugging the foot of the cliff. The track—if track it was—twisted and curved with the rocks. The late afternoon light was dimming when the horse at last stopped. Portugee was almost out on his feet. Breathing in great gasps he jerked the stirrup.

"Get on, get on," he mumbled.

Fortune stamped and tossed his head as if to say "Look, look up there," and then, through frost-rimmed eyes, the scout saw it.

The mountain was cracked from top to bottom. Fortune had found the pass.

Portugee had negotiated the secret trail once before, but even on second sight the defile overawed him. Sheer precipices shot up hundreds of feet on either side to become lost in a cloud of drifting snow. Along the bottom of the crack, in darkness and gloom, ran the trail, so narrow, so tortuous that the snow barely penetrated and the rocks and stones lay black and bare.

The scout drew the horse into the comparative shelter of the pass—passage would have been a better word to describe the way—and pulled him out the last feed of hay. Awakening himself with a mouthful of brandy, he set about tightening the girth and otherwise preparing for the last stage of the journey. After a short rest he patted Fortune's neck and mounted.

"Good feller," he whispered. "One more effort and we'll be there." Hope ran high as he shook the reins and the grey trotted forward over the shingle of this incredible road.

Closer and closer the rocks pressed in on them. Here, out of the wind and snow the temperature was higher. A stream foamed over the stones occasionally filling the entire bottom of the defile as it wound through the mountain until at times they were forced to move in icy water.

Looking up, Portugee could just distinguish a narrow, lighter strip far above him. It was the distant sky. All around was dark as night.

They climbed steadily for nearly an hour. In one place the rocks loomed so close that the scout could reach out and touch them on either side. Bushes clung in the crevices and stung his face. Presently, the ground leveled and they emerged into a tiny amphitheater. Here the snow lay thick, and as they crossed towards the ravine on the other side to begin the descent of the mountain, Portugee could feel the bitter north wind gathering strength. This was the face of the mountain that was taking the brunt of the storm.

Once more the narrowing walls of rock. Once more the

gloomy and twisting trail, but downhill this time and covered with snow.

Fortune slipped and recovered. The echoes rang back from the granite cliffs. Portugee took a firmer hold on the reins. In this way they went on for a long time. Suddenly it grew darker. It was as if the faint light from above had been extinguished. Portugee looked up at the sky—but it wasn't there!

He reined in, his gaze riveted upwards, looking at the danger that hung two hundred feet above his head.

Held by trees or what he could not tell, the driven snow, streaming across the mountain top, had packed down into the crack that formed the secret pass. For hour after hour as the blizzard raged over the last few days, it had accumulated. Now, like a fairy-tale bridge, it lay across the ravine, thirty or more feet thick, seemingly solid, weighing a thousand tons. Beneath this arch the trail disappeared into a pitch-black tunnel.

Portugee expelled his breath in a long incredulous whistle. For some moments he remained there looking at the ice and calculating the chances if he rode beneath. From the darkness came the sharp bark of a fox. This decided him.

"If you can get through, so can we," he muttered and rode forward.

Under the icy bridge it was eerily still. Fortune's very breathing echoed in the dark. The chill struck at the scout and he shivered. Every step was danger. Noise might bring the whole edifice crashing down upon them. Foot by foot they moved through the darkness. Again, somewhere ahead, a fox barked.

Then the light increased; the echoing of Fortune's hooves ceased and they rode from under.

The defile widened suddenly. Snow and bushes appeared . . . and the gaunt grey shapes of timber wolves.

Automatically the scout pulled up, reaching for his gun. Then he stopped as a thought struck him with all the impact of a bullet. What would a shot do in that narrow spot, with the ice packed precariously high above? He had seen rocks jerked into an avalanche by the sudden noise of a gun. He must get by, if he could, without firing.

The wolves ranged right across the pass, in a wide semi-circle. Fortune, ears pricked, muscles trembling, stood rigid, sensing the menace of the pack. The scout dug in his heels hard.

"Get on, boy," he cried, "get on!"

Fortune did not budge.

Again Portugee tried, but still the horse did not move.

A great grey wolf, nearer than the rest, ran forward a short distance and stopped, head low, snarling and snapping. Fortune backed on stiff legs.

Slowly the whole pack moved forward.

The scout pulled off his mitten and, stuffing it in his jacket, slowly drew his pistol. In the gloom at the bottom of the pass, the lone horseman and the killer pack faced each other. Hundreds of feet above the wind moaned across the top of the ravine and all the time the cold powdered snow fell like a fine rain. Behind, the great ice bridge cut off the sky.

Portugee tried once more. "C'mon, Fortune feller," and he slapped the cold grey rump behind him with the barrel of the heavy Navy. Fortune moved a step or two, and at that the nearest wolf crouched back on his haunches ready to spring. Portugee saw what was coming and reluctantly raised his gun. He fired as the wolf leaped, and, twisting over, the great grey beast crashed to the ground midway between the pack and the horse.

The shot echoed like a hundred cannons in the narrow space. The whole pack moved forward, an army of snarling lips and slavering jaws. Portugee fired again.

Crack! The noise echoed with an almost physical shock behind him.

He flung a glance over his shoulder up at the ice bridge. It was just the same, still there, shining and massive, almost directly above. Below, the darkness of the tunnel seemed even blacker and more dangerous.

Crack! Another noise shattered the air, but Portugee had not fired again. With mounting horror he continued to look up. The whole span of ice seemed to drop a few feet and then stop. At the edges, against the black rock, a shower of snow jetted downwards like a water from a fall. The cracking noise came again; dark lines began to run across the face of the ice, and quite slowly three or four blocks as big as buffalo toppled forward into the ravine.

The scout yelled at the horse. Still Fortune faced the wolves unaware of the falling terror behind. Portugee thrust his mittens into his jacket, slammed his pistol in his holster. Then, with one backward glance at the shattering ice above him he played his last card. He rose in his stirrups. Digging his hands into the horse's mane, he leaned far forward over Fortune's neck. The grey thrust up his head, unused to the weight balanced over him. This was what Portugee wanted. Bending forward as far as he could, he thrust his face down to the horse's mouth. The soft velvet flesh came up to meet him, and as the avalanche broke above, the scout bared his teeth and bit hard into Fortune's muzzle.

Fortune gave a surprised scream. The shock as he shook his head free almost threw the scout from his back. Gamely Portugee hung on: hair and blood filled his mouth as the grey leaped forward. The wolves scattered beneath his flashing hooves. Jarred and shaken, Portugee could only cling there. It was an old, savage Indian trick but it had worked. The leap that the angry horse took carried them into the wolf pack but out of danger.

With a roar that filled the air like continuous thunder the ice bridge broke up. Thousands of tons of frozen snow crashed down into the narrow pass. Blocks of ice as big as stagecoaches pitched along the bottom like marbles. The wolf pack turned and broke. For one amazing moment, horse and rider, wolves and foxes fled side by side along the floor of the ravine while just behind them, on the spot where a few moments before they had faced each other for a fight to the death, the snow piled an enormous tumbling mass. Branches of firs broke and splintered like matchsticks as the avalanche rolled on. A block of ice crashed among the running pack a few feet away from Portugee. Lying along Fortune's back, he saw the twisted, screaming bodies of the wild killers crushed beneath.

And it was now that the horse's racing ancestors came to

Fortune's aid. With ever-lengthening strides he outstripped the rolling avalanche; left behind the remaining wolves and carried the scout on to safety.

Dazed and shaken, his frozen hands tight in Fortune's mane, Portugee let the horse have his head, feeling sorry for the cruel trick he had played, but thankful nevertheless that his knowledge of the Indians' daring horsemanship had saved the day.

A mile down the trail where the creek tumbled frozen on to the plain they burst from the mountains and, following the watercourse through the undulating ground, embarked on the last lap to Laramie.

16

IN THE NICK
OF TIME

From the top of the great double gatehouse at Fort Laramie you could see across the creek and several miles down the long prairie trail. That was in the summer; when the sun blazed down and the only thing that moved on the parched plains were the drifting eddies of dust—"dust devils," the soldiers called them. They drifted up to the fort, spinning the tumbleweeds along, scattering twigs and grass high into the air.

Corporal Rawlings would have given anything to see a "dust devil" this wild winter's night. For it was well below freezing point on top of the guardhouse and the wind howled across the newly-fallen snow, piercing his greatcoat until his whole body shrank and shivered with the cold. The fact that it was Christmas Eve and that every now and then in the lulls between the prolonged gusts he could hear snatches of lively music from the great hall where a dance was in progress seemed to add to his discomfort.

"Dancing! I'd like to see a few of them up here for an hour or two," he grumbled to his fellow guard. "They'd dance all right in this wind! Guard duty," he added bitterly, jerking his head, "on Christmas Eve, too!"

"Aw, give over, Bill," his companion remonstrated. "There's many a man worse off from what I heard tonight," and he gestured with gloved hand in the direction of the Big Horn Mountains.

"What've you heard?" asked Rawlings, suspiciously. "Red Cloud?"

The soldier nodded. "Luke Parsons and that Frenchie 'Rob-by-doo' come in before dark. Said there's Indian signs all over the plains beyond the buttes."

Rawlings shifted his grip on the rifle, hunched himself up even smaller against the wind and grunted a noncommittal reply as he looked out from the fort. The rumors had been flying all day, despite the natural high spirits that Christmas brought, even on the frontier. The Indians were out, there was little doubt about that. Two of the French-Canadian scouts attached to the garrison had bought news two days ago that there was every sign of a large gathering of hostiles to the northwest. They'd named Red Cloud, along with several other chiefs, as the leading spirits of the war parties. Kiowas, Blackfeet, as well as Sioux . . . the whole of the frontier was blazing up, he reckoned. Red Cloud had sure meant business when he'd stalked out of Laramie on the day of the great council.

All through the long autumn months messages had come in from Fort Phil Kearny reporting skirmishes with the enemy—the dreaded red man who was making an all-out effort to throw the palefaces back off the great plains.

"I wouldn't like to be with Carrington's boys tonight," muttered the soldier at his elbow. "A hundred and twenty miles inside them mountains and nobody near them except a howlin' bunch of Indians." He spat reflectively over the side of the gatehouse. "Don't give much for their chances if Red Cloud takes it into his black head to go that way."

"They got a fine officer in charge and more men than the fort can rightly hold. And this weather will keep Red Cloud pinned down." Rawlings walked across to the steps and looked towards the lights within the fort. Black figures crossed and recrossed the blazing squares of yellow that ran the length of the hall that was appropriately called "Old Bedlam." Even through the whirling snow something of the air of gaiety spread out with the scraping of the fiddles and the stamp, stamp of dancing feet. Somewhere, nearer at hand, he could hear a child crying and then hush suddenly, probably comforted with the thought of Christmas morning only a few hours away.

"Corporal! Here! Something down by the creek." He

swung round and crossed swiftly to the guard's side. The
soldier pointed.

"There," he said. "Left of the ford. I seen him clear just
now."

"Seen what? said Rawlings. He'd been too many years a
corporal in the Army to be alarmed by some youngster's fears.
On a night like this it was easy to imagine anything out there
in the wildness. The soldier sensed his disbelief.

"I *heard* him. His hooves on the ice."

"Nobody's out there in this weather, lad. Where'd he come
from in snow like this—on Christmas eve, too?" Nevertheless,
he peered carefully out, raking the white ground with a shrewd
gaze.

"By thunder, you're right!"

In a moment of respite from the wind's moan they both
could hear it plainly—the even beat of hooves on the icy
ground. Just for a moment—and then it was swamped by a
burst of music and noise from the fort.

The guard slid his rifle over the wall, unclipping the canvas
breech cover as he did so. Corporal Rawlings laid a restraining
hand on his arm.

"Careful. Don't shoot unless I say."

Two pairs of anxious eyes peered down the trail. This was
still Indian country; better to have a touchy trigger finger than
be taken by surprise.

"There he is." The guard pointed, but Rawlings had already
seen the solitary horseman riding out of the darkness.

"Hold your fire, lad. That's no Indian."

"Well, who is it? One of the scouts?"

The corporal shook his head. None of the regular garrison
were out to his knowledge. He watched the rider approach,
clearly seen now, urging his horse on as if he'd miles to go,
instead of a few score yards. The corporal could make out the
bundled figure on the horse, plastered white on the front with
frozen snow, his mittened hand rising and falling regularly as
he lashed the great grey beneath him.

Portugee had ridden blindly over the last five miles, leaving
Fortune to follow the trail, rocking with almost total exhaus-

tion in the saddle, his mind riveted on one thing only—the message for the General at Laramie. When they came to Laramie Creek he glimpsed the fort ahead, its lights winking dimly through the snow but seemingly distant still.

Suddenly the grey walls loomed above him. Instinctively he reined in. Heaving horse and half-conscious rider, two hundred and fifty incredible miles behind them, had arrived at their destination!

"Hold! The guard shouted down at the grey figure beneath him. "Who are you?"

Portugee did not, indeed could not, answer. "A message for the General . . ." The words rang through his mind but his frozen lips refused to form them. He pulled Fortune round and blundered sideways up to the great double gates. With gloved fist he hammered on the planks.

"Open up," he croaked. "Open up!"

"He looks about all in to me," said the corporal, "but keep him covered. I'll go down," and he ran to the steps and disappeared below.

Fortune neighed at the gate, as if in added exasperation at the delay.

"Who are you?" cried the guard again. Was this some Indian trick to gain entry to the fort? He was taking no chances.

Calling two men from the guardhouse, Corporal Rawlings opened the inner doors and slipped through the crack. The banging on the outer gates echoed in the confined space.

"All right, we're comin', we're comin'."

With the help of the soldiers he unbarred the gate and swung it back. The grey horse and storm-masked rider swept in. Rawlings leaped for the bridle and pulled them up.

"Who are you?" he called. "C'mon, dismount and let's get a look at you."

Portugee fumbled for the dispatch wallet, then, sensing that this was not the place to deliver his message, leaned wearily down. This time he formed the words in a hoarse whisper. "Message for the General . . ." His eyes closed and the gatehouse reeled about him. With a superhuman effort he forced the blackness away.

"Message for . . ." he began again.

"All right, we'll take you to the General." The corporal left Fortune's head and came round to Portugee's side. "Just as soon as . . ." but he didn't finish for Portugee, impatient, exhausted, had had enough. He dug his heels into Fortune's flanks and the grey began to go forward. One of the guards whipped out his revolver.

"No!" yelled Rawlings. Something about the muffled trail-worn figure on the horse had convinced him. "No, he's all right. I'll stay with him." And grasping Portugee's stirrup he ran alongside the pair as they pushed through the inner doors.

Light and music came across the square and Fortune headed for them. The gallant scout was trying to say something to the gasping, stumbling figure of the soldier clinging at his side, but only the word "Cloud" came from his cracked and bearded lips.

The lighted windows of the hall danced before him. Dismounting, he left Fortune to the soldier and weaved an erratic path up the steps. There were two doors. There must be a latch somewhere. He fumbled with frozen hands but it defeated him. Then he put his whole weight against it and pushed.

The doors flew open. Color and noise and yellow light flooded out and blinded him. He took a few staggering steps into the hall, the wind sweeping a half-circle of snow before him. The crowd of dancers surged back. There were swinging colored skirts and the brightness of dress uniforms. The conversation died. Somewhere there was a scream and for a moment a solitary violin scraped on into the silence.

The muffled swaying figure dominated the room. Behind, against the night in the doorway, the corporal hesitated, his eye wide. Then the frocks disappeared and a purposeful uniformed circle closed in on the scout. A cavalry sword glinted.

Portugee fumbled at his jacket and pulled out the wallet. Blinking in the flaring light from the swinging oil lamps, he struggled with the clip. They watched in silence—this strange, incongruous figure that had burst like a nightmare into the gaiety of the Christmas ball.

"General," the figure was mumbling. "Message."

At last, the sense of urgency got through to the motionless officers. A ramrod-straight, grey-haired man stepped forward.

"I'm General Rutledge. Who are you from?"

Portugee's face turned towards him. Behind the mask of snow his lips moved and a cracked sound came out.

"Kearny," he said. "Fort Kearny."

The buff envelope came out of the wallet and he thrust it towards the General's outstretched hand.

"Good Lord!" exclaimed the General incredulously. "From Carrington?"

Willing hands now caught at the scout, helped him forward. But he thrust them off with a last gesture of defiance. Every eye in the hall was fixed on him. A great log fire roared in the chimney and already pools of water ran about his feet as the snow melted.

Again he tried to speak.

"Red Cloud . . . rescue . . ."

The four corners of the hall began to spin about him. He could see the General's face close up to him, leaning forward now, speaking urgently as he tore open the long buff envelope, but the scout could hear nothing save a growing, rushing noise in his ears.

He made one last effort.

"General . . . Crazy Woman's . . . bridge gone . . ."

And then mercifully nature took charge. The hall began to revolve round him; darkness drove out the swaying, dazzling lights, not the nightmare darkness of the trail but the obliterating peace of sleep.

He slipped through the clutching hands and like a great tree falling, like a monument toppling from its pedestal, Portugee Phillips collapsed to the floor.

Outside a horse whinnied.

At Fort Phil Kearny they had given up all hope of rescue. Four days had passed since Portugee Phillips had slipped through the side gate and disappeared into the forest—disappeared forever, it now seemed to the defenders behind the stockades.

At first Jim Bridger had been confident that the scout had gotten safely through Red Cloud's ring of death, but as the long days and nights passed without any sign of rescue even he began secretly to admit that there was little hope left.

"Indians he knowed how to deal with," said the veteran frontiersman to Colonel Carrington, the only man to whom he admitted any doubts at all over the chance of rescue. "But the weather's been bad and there's a hundred things could've happened to him on that trail. I still believe in miracles, Colonel, but we got to prepare for the worst."

Colonel Carrington made his final preparations. After the last skirmish when the Indians had tried to get into the fort with ladders under cover of darkness, he had doubled the guards. It imposed a great strain on the little garrison but there had been no more attacks.

Christmas had dragged by. A grim, featureless Christmas without any of the luxuries that usually attend the season, save in the children's quarters, where Jim Bridger himself had played Santa Claus and distributed what presents the women folk could make in an effort to hide the truth of their situation from the youngsters.

As the days slowly passed Colonel Carrington began to plan for the end that he felt was certain to come soon. There had been no snow now for twenty-four hours; the lowering clouds had lifted and the keen wind dropped. Smoke from the Indian fires crept up all around the horizon, and the old soldier and the frontiersman both knew that it was only a matter of hours before Red Cloud mustered his braves for the last assault.

The women and children had been confined to one large log building, the magazine, in the corner of the fort. Mrs. Grummond had asked the Colonel for rifles, saying that the women could play a part in defending the place if the worst came to the worst. A picked squad of soldiers mounted guard, with rations and ammunition stored behind specially barricaded doors, and had strict orders to remain where they were whatever happened elsewhere on the stockades. They were to defend the magazine to the end and then, if all was lost, to see that none of their charges fell into the cruel hands of Red Cloud's warriors.

Food was brought round to the men at their posts. Those off duty snatched what sleep they could. Colonel Carrington and his officers, tired and haggard after days without proper rest, assembled in the Colonel's office for what was likely to be their last conference.

"Gentlemen, on all sides of the fort there are signs of increased activity by the enemy." Carrington spoke curtly; came straight to the point. "The weather's cleared and Red Cloud is gathering his army together. I don't think that there's been such a large number of hostiles in these hills before. You all know that an attack is imminent. You also know that we have little chance of repulsing the Indians when they come in full force."

He looked round the circle of grim faces. Not a man spoke.

"Two soldiers have volunteered to go to the post at the top of Pilot Hill. With their aid, we will be better able to see where the main threat lies and bring our howitzers into a position where they will be most effective. Theirs is a dangerous task, for whatever happens in the fort, they will be singled out for special attention as soon as the enemy realizes what they are doing.

"As you know, I have placed the women and children in the magazine, with a special squad for their protection. I need hardly repeat the orders I have given to their officer should all else fail and the rest of the garrison be overwhelmed.

"Fire arrows shouldn't worry us with the snow still on the roofs, but there may be more tricks than that up Red Cloud's sleeve and we must be prepared for any eventuality.

"You know your duties, and in the main you know what to expect. It won't be long now. Are there any questions?"

For some short while the conference went on. Question and answer followed swiftly one upon another. At length the conversation died. The Colonel shook hands with each man. The officers saluted. "Good luck," he said, and with a set face and an ache in his throat, turned to the inner room where the two volunteers waited for their final instructions.

They lay gasping at the top of Pilot Hill. The last scramble up over the loose boulders had taken the breath out of them and they rested where they had fallen inside the old shelter.

Presently, when they had stacked their meager rations in the corner and checked their rifles they began a long, careful scrutiny of the country.

The fort lay below them; a dark, solid square in the white snow, the trees and hills encircling it on every side. Smoke climbed lazily up on the still air. Smoke rose from the hills opposite, too; Indian smoke from signal fires; silent messages threatening them with destruction.

"Look! To the west."

The pointing finger stabbed towards a distant cloud rising some miles away above the old trail. Three short puffs followed; and a few moments later the signal was repeated.

"Great jumpin' rattlesnakes! Down there, by the river!"

Both men leaned forward, their eyes widening at the spectacle below them.

The whole long slope down to the bridge across Piney Creek seemed to be moving. First the lances and the tossing war bonnets; then the brown painted bodies; the wild heads and waving manes of the ponies . . . like a colored carpet a thousand warriors surged over the ridge and swept down to the river.

One of the soldiers leaped on the wall and began to signal wildly to the fort.

Colonel Carrington saw them as he climbed onto the roof of the guardhouse. Jim Bridger flung up an arm and gestured to the southwest, then turned back to his old black telescope without a word. The Colonel looked in the direction indicated.

It seemed that Red Cloud's entire army was on the move. The Indians continued to pour over the ridge in the direction of the old trail. Even as he watched another column burst into view from the hills on the left, a few horses with their crouching, whooping riders strung out in the lead, the main body following in a crowded, tumbling stream. Other braves appeared riding up the creek, the ponies slipping and dancing on the ice. More warriors on foot came running hard behind, leaping and spinning in the air, their tomahawks whirling in the morning light. The whole valley to the south seemed to be filled with a yelling horde of savages.

The Colonel wheeled round and looked across the fort to the hills behind. Nothing stirred; even where the pine woods swept nearest to the stockade, the friendly woods that had sheltered Portugee Phillips on his escape, there was no sign of movement.

"We've all sides covered, sir." The adjutant reassured his commander. "There's no hostiles, except by the creek."

"Lookout signals there's more over the hills, sir," Captain Ten Eyck ventured, "but they're all heading south, sir."

"What's the old devil up to?" muttered Jim Bridger, lowering his telescope. "This is the last way you'd expect them to come at us."

Still Carrington said nothing.

From the square below came the rattle of chain and the rumble of wheels as the gun-teams pulled the howitzers into position. Sweating, groaning men heaved at the ropes, slipping and cursing in the snow as they manhandled the heavy guns. With a crash the boards fell inwards from the embrasures in the stockade. The howitzers were run forward until their muzzles pointed through the gaps. The men put chocks behind the wheels to stop them running backward when they fired.

"Howitzers ready, sir," Major Powell called up from the foot of the ladder. The activity in the fort seemed to stop, waiting on the Colonel's command.

In the sudden, unexpected silence the distant, shrilling screams of a thousand war cries echoed up to the fort.

"Colonel, look, they're turning!" Captain Ten Eyck gave a hoarse shout of excitement.

It was true! The converging columns of galloping savages had swung away from the fort. A jumbled, milling throng spun for a moment where the old trail wound through the trees and then streamed off to the south. The braves running by the creek began to climb the high ground in the same direction. More smoke signals rose in the distant sky.

"What in tarnation's happening?" growled Sergeant Haggerty. "Are they fighting among themselves?"

"Major Powell, give them a salvo." Carrington's voice rang out across the fort.

The muzzles of the guns arched slowly upwards and as they did so, a weak sun broke through the clouds, glinting on the brass bands of the barrels.

"Number one gun ready, sir."

"Number two gun ready, sir."

Major Powell looked up at the Colonel. Carrington nodded. "Fire!"

The howitzers roared out in unison. Blue smoke rolled from the stockade as the guns jumped and then crashed back into place. The gunners worked swiftly to reload. Every eye on the guardhouse roof was riveted on the creek. The first shell fell short, exploding in the bed of the stream and sending a column of ice and water bursting upward. The second landed squarely on the old trail.

But still the Indians ignored the fort they had so long besieged!

And then, as the silence crept back, the lonely garrison heard firing—one sharp distinct volley rolled down from the hills. A loose rattle of musketry followed, and then another volley; precisely controlled, definite, it came like triumphant music to the ears of the soldiers.

"By thunder," shouted Bridger, "that's Army shootin'." The noise from the distant hills increased; the roar of savage war cries and the rattle of rifle shots gradually became submerged into one continuous sound of battle, punctuated again and again by the crashing volleys. The Indians could be seen thronging the whole of the ridge beyond Piney Creek. Gun smoke began to drift up on the bright air.

"Major Powell, I want five salvos into the trees on either side of the trail. But make sure you put them either side and don't fire beyond the ridge." Even Colonel Carrington's voice carried a note of subdued excitement. All along the stockades now it ran, and men on the other side of the fort turned to see what was happening down by the bridge.

"Back to your posts!" roared Sergeant Haggerty. "Watch
the woods on all sides." The blast of the howitzers cut short
his censure. Again and again they roared out, sending their
high explosive hurtling towards the milling Indians. All purposeful movement on the ridge had ceased. Smoke drifted over
part of the scene; some groups of braves could be seen firing
down the trail; there seemed to be an uncertain, hesitating
tremor among the ranks of the wild horsemen.

Into this disordered army crashed the shells from the fort,
and even through the noise came the wild screams of injured
and frightened horses. Shell after shell whined down and exploded. It was the turning point. Faced with something beyond
the hill that the watchers on the fort could not see, shattered
from behind by the deadly fire of the howitzers that many still
regarded as white man's magic, Red Cloud's warriors turned to
flee. Back over the ridge they streamed, a disorderly mob,
beyond the control of their stern chief, their strength momentarily broken.

"Captain Ten Eyck." There was almost a smile on Carrington's lips as he gave the order. "This is a privilege you and
your men have earned. Take your squad out in extended order
and stop any hostiles that cross the creek."

"Yessir!" Captain Ten Eyck leaped down the ladder, bawl-
ing for the sergeant and his men.

There was no restraining the wave of excitement that swept
over the fort now. In response to Ten Eyck's order a company
hurriedly formed up before the gates. Willing hands lifted the
bars, swung the heavy doors inwards. On the double, with the
Captain at their head, the little band passed on to the snowy
plain. Spreading out in extended order they began to advance
towards the creek, a thin, straggled line against the sunlit snow.

Colonel Carrington watched them go. Pitifully weak as it
was, the line evinced pride in every advancing step. It was a
gesture—a symbol of the courage and defiance that had kept
Fort Phil Kearny from falling into Indian hands over the long
months of siege.

The fleeing Indians reached the river. Now they turned,
back the way they had come, some struggling over the river on

horseback and on foot, fleeing towards the fort they had so lately threatened. Ten Eyck's men halted, dropped to their knees and with leveled rifles began to fire at the hostiles.

At that very moment, down the old trail from Laramie, through the trees, scattering the last of the redskins, a blaze of color in the flag at their head, the blue uniforms and silver equipment clear in the wintry air, the rescuers burst into view. The battle that until now had been hidden from the watchers on the roof, became at last apparent.

In the fort a bugle pealed out. A ragged cheer went up, growing in volume. Women and children ran from the magazine hugging each other, laughing and shouting with joy. On came the cavalry, crashing across the creek, a long winding cavalcade that spread out to thunder across the flat, white plain in the last glorious charge.

The fragile line of troops from the fort were standing now, waving their hats and cheering.

Still the cavalry came on, through the dancing line of soldiers.

On the guardhouse roof Jim Bridger was jumping with unrestrained excitement. "So he made it, he made it, what did I tell you!"

They could see the faces of the troopers now, relaxing after the charge, breaking into smiles as they saw the extent of their welcome.

The flag ducked in salute as the first of the column reached the gates and swept in.

For the moment, the siege of Fort Phil Kearny was ended!

BOOK TWO

RED CLOUD'S REVENGE

1

THE NEW COLONEL

It was early in spring when Portugee Phillips again crossed Piney Creek. The epic ride had taken its toll. For nearly forty-eight hours after his arrival at Laramie on that never-to-be forgotten Christmas Eve, the scout had lain unconscious in the hospital while the relief column struggled northwards by a circuitous route. In the days that followed, rest and good food had restored his strength—but the savage frost-bite had taken longer to heal and weeks elapsed before he was able to move about.

Now, sitting in the saddle looking back, Portugee could see signs of the battle all along the trail above the creek; broken and splintered trunks of trees told where the shells had completed the rout of Red Cloud's warriors. He reined round and looked ahead at the fort, secure and busy in the bright sunlight. Then his gaze swept up Pilot Hill, picked out the squat shape of the shelter on top, and moved on to the surrounding tree-covered country.

Were the Indians still there, watching every move, he wondered. Red Cloud's strength had been broken; the grip of death in which the cunning old warrior had held Fort Phil Kearny all winter had been smashed. But for how long, Portugee asked himself. Red Cloud was a determined and courageous chief. Surely he wouldn't leave the fort to thrive here, two hundred miles inside his hunting grounds, with every prospect of it being used as a base for another expedition farther along the Bozeman Trail!

Portugee jerked the reins and Fortune trotted on.

There was work to be done. He had orders to report to the

fort and place himself at the disposal of its Commandant. And Portugee knew, although it was a closely guarded secret outside, that those orders could send him nearly a hundred miles on, to the new outpost in the Big Horn Mountains that was going to prove another blow to Red Cloud's pride.

At the gate the guard shifted the grip on his rifle and glanced lazily up at the dark, lithe figure mounted on a superb grey horse. Visitors were common now that the winter had gone and the trails were open again and comparatively smooth going.

This chap had waited for the easy weather, he supposed; not like the nightmare ride *he'd* had, with the relief force, just after Christmas.

He sauntered out of the shade and squinted upwards as the horseman halted and raised a hand in salute.

The guard looked him over slowly; then lowered the rifle and stepped back and nodded.

"O.K., mister," he said. Then by way of explanation he added, "Can't be too careful; this is Indian country, you know."

The horseman grinned and made to ride on.

"Say, mister," called the guard again, "who are you?"

"Phillips," replied the scout. "Friends call me Portugee."

And he spurred through the gates into the fort.

Portugee swung off the saddle and dropped Fortune's reins over the hitching rail outside the Headquarters block. Before him lay the square of the parade ground, white in the bright spring sunshine. Beyond and to the left was the long, low line of the stables, built against the stockade wall, with the platform of the banquette running along the top. As he watched a sentry passed slowly along the planks and disappeared into the squat tower above the entrance to the fort.

Immediately in front of Portugee, on the far side of the square, there was a stretch of bare wall; the thick timbers of the stockade, with their roughly pointed tops, thrust upwards to the sky. The planks of the banquette ran horizontally across the space, a few feet below the top of the stockade, supported by long poles set at an angle and jammed into the earth at the base of the wall.

With all this, however, Portugee was familiar from the plans and building that had taken place last year. What caught his eye was the bustle of activity elsewhere.

Fortune shook his head and blew through his wide nostrils; Portugee reached out and patted the soft nose.

Army tents lined one side of the parade ground and behind them, dozens of soldiers, stripped to the waist, were busy with the construction of a long new barrack block against the eastern wall of the fort. Logs swung with a loud thump into place, hammers rang rhythmically and the steady rasp of a saw brought his eyes round to a gang of loggers who were cutting a pyramid of tree trunks into stout planks.

The sun poured through the holes in the stockade walls. When the barracks were finished the men would sleep literally at their action stations; the gaps serving both as windows and loopholes in the event of attack.

Farther round, almost at right angles to where Portugee stood, were the living quarters of the officers and their wives. Children ran out, playing some wild game around the big mess hall while the scout was looking.

He kept his eyes on them for a moment and then turned to gaze at the opposite side of the fort. There, beyond the long row of stables where horses were being groomed, was the hospital now completed, and farther round, another large building had sprung up with a crudely lettered sign:

STORE
Joseph H. Kidder

In rough chalk capitals someone had scrawled the word SALOON on the edge of the sign. Between the sutler's store and the hospital were jammed the eight big wagons that had left Laramie several days before Portugee had started on his journey. The canvas hoods had been rolled back and a crowd of men were unloading the wagons. A small group of women were talking excitedly to a portly figure in a white apron, anxious to find out what goods had arrived.

Behind, in the far northwest corner of the fort, where the heavy timber wall swung irregularly round, was a low building, partly screened with a mound of earth. A solitary wagon was unloading ammunition into the magazine, and Portugee's mind raced back to the desperate months of siege when Colonel Carrington had chosen the magazine as the last refuge should Red Cloud's warriors sweep over the snow-banked stockade.

"Things have changed a bit, eh, John?" said a voice at Portugee's shoulder and, swinging round, the scout was greeted by the cheerful, weather-beaten face of Sergeant Haggerty.

"Tom? How are you?" The two pumped each other's hands; grinning at one another, too pleased for the ordinary words of greeting. They walked along to the sergeant's little office at the end of the Headquarters building. Despite the spring day, charcoal was glowing in the stove and the coffee pot stood on top.

Portugee lifted off his hat, unbuckled his belt and slid the Navy Colt onto the side of the table. He settled down thankfully into a chair as the sergeant turned, putting two cups on the table and reaching for the coffee pot.

"China!" exclaimed the scout, expecting the usual tin mugs of the frontier.

"Reminds one of home," said Haggerty. "You're the first to use them. Bull train come through yesterday. Gilmore and Porter contracted to run one a month up from Laramie." He poured the coffee, thick and black, and set a tin of sugar on the table. "Joe Kidder brought some china up for womenfolk. Let me have the cups, though he charged high for them."

"Always did," said the scout, sipping the scalding coffee.

The sergeant set his cup down. "More things have changed, John."

"Meanin'?"

"The Colonel," Haggerty inclined his head in the direction of the office. "Colonel Wessells."

"I hear he's a good man."

"He's a good Army man, John."

Silence.

". . . but he don't know Indians."

There was no need for comment between the two veterans.

"First time west?" asked Portugee.

Haggerty nodded.

"Commanded a brigade in Virginia. Got a fine war record, everybody says."

"But he don't know Indians!"

"He reckons Colonel Carrington failed." Sergeant Haggerty pushed the coffee slowly round with a spoon. "Reckons the tribes oughter be split up. Deal them one blow; well planned, no respite. Great snakes," the sergeant's voice rose, "we can't get enough wagons up here to supply the garrison as it is without stores for a sustained campaign."

He drank his coffee in long gulps. "I grant you it's quiet now—but you wait."

The two sat in silence while Portugee digested the sergeant's unspoken opinion of the new Colonel.

"Tell me about Carrington."

Portugee refilled the cups.

"He was recalled to Fort Sedgewick," explained Haggerty. "Relieved of command of the fort. Colonel Wessells was appointed in the same order."

"But why?" cried Portugee. "Just because one hothead got himself killed . . ."

"There were eighty men, John."

"But Fetterman was responsible . . ."

"He was under Colonel Carrington's command," explained the sergeant. "Once the newspapers got the story back East, Washington had to have someone's head. The Colonel just happened to be the one."

Portugee was silent for a while then he asked, "When did they leave?"

"End of January. They took two wagons and an escort. And Jim Bridger went with them, thank God."

"Mrs. Carrington . . . and the children? I heard . . ."

"She reckoned where her husband went, she went too. We

bedded them down with double canvas on the wagons, blankets and food to spare. But it was a cruel order, John."

"Were they attacked?" Portugee asked.

"Nope. Indians watched them when they crossed Crazy Woman's Creek, five mile below the old bridge, but that was all. I heard two of the teamsters were frostbit . . ."

"One lost a leg and one an arm."

". . . and one died at Reno. They met the other party on the trail beyond. Colonel Wessells sure acted fine there. He sent six of his own troopers back with them and come on short-handed himself."

The coffee was lukewarm. The cold had seemed to creep into the spring air of the room. Portugee got up and moved to look out of the window.

"It was a rough winter, John." Sergeant Haggerty rose to join him and they gazed through the window at the long ridge rising up to Pilot Hill. A cluster of white posts showed in the tall grass on the lower slopes.

"We buried nigh on thirty men." Haggerty's voice was low. "And one woman and her babe. Leastways, we buried them when the ground thawed."

"And this was after the relief, Tom?" Portugee turned back to the room.

"Before and after, John. Mostly after. You see there were more mouths to feed after Colonel Wessells arrived. And supplies just didn't get through. Red Cloud didn't take a beatin' when the Second Cavalry got to us, John. Sure they fought—but it was what the Army call a 'strategic withdrawal.' And after that they harried everythin' that went in or out. The men were scurvy, livin' on hardtack and jerked beef and half of that rotten. . . ."

Portugee listened, his brown face immobile, his mind back in the bitter winter with the thermometer forty below. His hand touched the Navy holster. Haggerty went on:

"The water froze; every kettle had to be filled with chipped ice and melted for men and horses. Ever had to bury a horse, John?"

Portugee shook his head.

"You couldn't eat them," said the sergeant. "Died of disease mostly, anyways. There was no washin', leastways not for the men. Fleas, lice . . ." He slapped the table. "Kept a bit of coffee and rice for the children. . . ."

He drifted into silence, reliving the isolated months of hardship in his mind. Suddenly he clapped a hand on the coffee pot and swept it back on the stove. He stood up and vigorously shook the grid. The charcoal glowed red.

"No use goin' on like that," he said. "Things got better when the weather broke. Then the bull trains started to come up in April . . . it's been a different life since. I'll say one thing," he jerked his head in the direction of the office. "The Colonel's a good organizer."

He went to the door and gazed out at the busy soldiers. "Long may it continue. We couldn't stand another winter under them conditions."

He began to clear the table but Portugee's voice stopped him and he stood with the china cups in one hand, the other resting on the scrubbed planks.

"Tom. It ain't goin' to last and you know it." Portugee pulled the Navy towards him and toyed with the holster as he spoke. "Red Cloud's not done for by a long ways yet. I've lived on the frontier long enough to know the signs—this valley is infested with young bloods. Sure, I came through safely— on the trail of a wagon train and a parcel of troopers. But we were watched, from Crazy Woman's on."

The sergeant put the cups in a tin bowl beside the stove and lifted a can of water. "I ain't surprised," he said, pouring the water over the new cups and rinsing out the coffee grounds. He stood the cups on a board shelf above the stove and turned to face Portugee.

"They watch everything. Just watch. They followed the wood train along the road by the Big Piney yesterday. Sat up on the ridges on their ponies, just lookin'. Some of the boys loosed off a few rounds; they just turned and rode farther off, then stopped to look again. I don't like it, John. What's he up to?"

"He's learnin' the routine." Portugee leaned forward and

spoke earnestly. "The Army does everything regular. Reveille, parade, work calls. The wood train goes out certain times. Messengers go and come from Reno on a schedule. They got to do it that way, they're so big."

He gestured towards the blue hills outside. "Red Cloud is watchin'. For weeks maybe. Then when he knows the routine of the fort, he'll strike. Move one party across the Big Piney —he'll strike the Laramie Trail. Put guards on the Laramie Trail—he'll hit the Virginia City road."

Portugee leaned back. Sergeant Haggerty looked at him in silence. The scout went on quietly: "Tom, the Bozeman Trail is finished—closed. Carrington knew it; even while he was sending men a hundred miles up the trail to survey Fort C. Smith. Red Cloud's got all this country in his hand, from the Yellowstone to the Platte, from the Big Horn Mountains to the Black Hills. Colonel Wessells will find it out soon enough. Maybe even the Government."

He rose abruptly to his feet and strapped on the Navy. "I'd best report in, anyways. Is he expecting me?"

Haggerty nodded. "Message came up with the bull train. I'll go tell him you're here."

But as he reached the door the sergeant turned and thumped the timbers with his fist.

"Sufferin' bearcats! I knowed I'd somethin' to tell you," he cried. "Frenchie's here."

"Jean?" exclaimed Portugee, a smile breaking across his dark face. "Jean Robidoux?"

"None other," said the sergeant. "Came up with the first train in April. Workin' as a rider for Gilmore an' Porter. Due back from Reno with dispatches at sundown." His grey eyes twinkled as he saw the obvious pleasure that news of his old friend had brought to Portugee.

Jean Robidoux, son of the famous Robidoux who founded his trading post a hundred miles south of Laramie at Scotts Bluff in the forties when the Oregon Trail was being opened up, had long been a close friend of the scout's.

"How is he, the old French coyote?" asked Portugee.

"Oh, fine, fine," said the sergeant, straightening his jacket and stepping through the door. "He'll sure be pleased to see you." And the two walked along the porch to turn into the Colonel's office.

But the Frenchman of whom they spoke so gaily was far from "fine." Had he known it Portugee would have been filled with horror at his friend's plight.

For Jean Robidoux, French *coureur de bois*, lately out of Fort Reno with mail for Colonel Wessells, was at that moment fighting for his life in a blind gulley on a spur of the Big Horn Mountains.

2

CAPTURED!

The tomahawk whirled through the air, thudding into the tree and pinning the buckskin sleeve of the Frenchman's jacket tight to the rough bark. For a moment there was silence in the gulley broken only by the harsh rasping of breath as he gathered his strength after the desperate climb. He reached over and tugged the bright, painted weapon from the tree. His arm was barely grazed. The wet, sweaty buckskin flapped against his face as he pushed his hair back and wiped the sweat from his eyes. At least he was armed again.

He looked down the gulley. The haze caused by his scramble over the loose sandy stone was still rising silently. He could see no sign of life, not even a lizard in the hot sun. Then, in the shadow on the left, an arm slid over the smooth surface of a rock. The side of a brown face showed for a moment. The arm moved in a quick signal, and from the opposite side of the gulley a trickle of pebbles spilled down the slope.

Simultaneously the Indians hurled themselves forward. In one grimly concentrated rush, silent save for the rattle of stones as moccasined feet leaped upwards, they closed in. The scout straightened his legs, raised the captured tomahawk. The first Indian reached him and put out a grasping hand. He struck down savagely and the blade bit home. No sound escaped the brave's lips; he came on, clutching at the tomahawk as it swept upward to aim another blow. Then they were on him. A shoulder struck him violently in the chest; again he brought the tomahawk down—but it was almost over. Fierce hands clawed at his waist and his legs. A violent jab hurled his head backwards. He kicked out but they caught his feet. Brown bodies and blood-stained buckskin rolled in the bottom of the gulley. The tomahawk clattered across the stones and a cloud of dust rose around the milling figures.

With a superhuman effort the scout rose upward, four or five braves clinging to him, but a sixth flung an arm round his throat from behind and again the heaving tangle sprawled on the pebbles.

Soon it was finished. He lay there, trussed hand and foot with biting rawhide thongs. The warriors stood round him, their chests heaving in the sun. Blood dripped from a bronze arm onto the rock. His swimming senses cleared gradually and he looked up at them, eyes screwed up against the bright blue sky.

They were Red Cloud's warriors all right, he thought. Well, why didn't they get it over with? Kill him here in the gulley and leave his scalped body for the buzzards?

But that was not the plan. At a word from one brave, they picked him up. Carrying him down to the floor of the canyon, they threw him in the shade of some bushes, then split up, some going on down the sloping track, the others squatting a few yards away listening to their leader who was speaking in short guttural sentences, with the occasional movement of an arm as he talked.

The scout pulled quietly at his bonds, but they were securely tied, and after a moment or two of ineffectual effort he gave up and lay still, his eyes closed, the aches of the blows he had suffered growing more and more painful. A gash in his left arm throbbed but it had stopped bleeding. He wondered what had become of the horse that had stumbled and thrown him almost as soon as the Indians gave chase. For a time it had seemed that he might almost get away, but then the blind gulley had fooled him. On the high slopes they had caught him defenseless, his gun lost in the fall from his horse, his knife taken in the first clawing tangle as the braves closed in.

They wanted him alive, then. He shook off his weariness and tried to sit up. The braves were coming back up the floor of the canyon leading a bunch of horses—and among them his own tall pony.

There were few words spoken. They hauled him up and got him on the saddle, tying his feet under the belly of the horse so that he could not fall off, leaving his hands lashed behind him. Then they set off. He had to twist and dodge to avoid the branches slapping in his face, and grip grimly with his knees to stay in his saddle as the horse climbed and slipped on the hard trail.

Two of his captors rode in front, with a short rope leading back to his pony's bridle; the rest followed closely. At the end of the gully they turned into the canyon and the going became easier on the level ground. Now the tight lashings on the Frenchman's feet began to have their effect. Unable to ease his position by standing in the stirrups, it was not long before the limited circulation in his legs began to send shooting pains of cramp into his body.

Riding thus for nearly two hours they came out of the canyon onto the undulating slopes of the plain. The wind rippled through the long grass, running ahead of them as they turned westward and struck out into the prairie. Much later they came to the gradual decline that led, the Frenchman thought, to the Little Goose River.

A few dark patches upon the plain were the first sign of their destination. "Buffalo," thought Robidoux, but as they approached and the yelping of the dogs could be heard he knew that they were horses.

The Indian boys guarding the herds gazed curiously at the little party as they rode by. One lad leaped up and ran alongside with shrill questioning, pointing to the helpless scout. Robidoux's captors gave grunted monosyllabic answers but the boy seemed satisfied and ran off towards his companions. The group could be seen talking excitedly together. Presently, one boy mounted on a pony shot out from the group and raced across the plain ahead of the warriors to disappear over a ridge not far ahead.

Cramped and aching after the long ride, the Frenchman tugged at his bonds and tried to ease himself into a more comfortable position. The warriors took no notice but urged their mounts to a sharper pace. As they topped the ridge all the scout's discomfort was forgotten at the sight which met his eyes.

Little Goose River lay below, stretching from the far horizon in the east to disappear in gentle loops and curves in the misty west, where the distant peaks of the mountains hung in the sky. The river ran through a wide flat valley which lay some hundreds of feet below the plain. Sweet meadows, grass and bushes spread from the water's edge to the bluffs on which the warriors had halted. Groves of trees stood tall along both banks. But the scout's gaze was riveted directly below. Clustered on the green meadows, yet carefully sheltered by the trees, stood the tall lodges of the Sioux. Already a dark crowd of the savage inhabitants was gathering on the edge of the village, warned of the party's approach by guards high on the bluffs and their curiosity further aroused by the tale of the pony boy.

But that was not all; in either direction as far as the eye could see, rose the conical lodges of the Indians, each topped by a cluster of long poles, fading in their hundreds into the distance. Smoke rose lazily into the sun; thousands of savages moved like ants over the floor of the valley. To a rider on the plain behind Robidoux, only a few herds of ponies and rising smoke gave any sign of habitation. From the guarded ridge Red Cloud's secret army burst into view. Never in all his years on the plains had the scout seen such an encampment!

The leader of the warriors spoke briefly and they began the descent of the bluffs. Slipping and swearing many a French oath, the scout nevertheless managed to keep his seat until they were on the floor of the valley and moving briskly towards the village. A great buzz of sound hung over the crowd gathered to meet them and a group of braves stepped forward to speak.

But with a curt greeting the party passed by, driving the Frenchman's horse before them through the swelling crowd. A yelping pack of dogs now ran at their heels. On all sides excited voices rose as news of the captured white man spread.

Shrill cries came from the boys running and jostling to see the captive. Although they had all heard of the white man, few had actually seen one. They crowded in to touch his legs, to prod the horse on, to scream and spit at Robidoux as he rode stoically onwards as erect as his bonds would allow, trying to keep his seat with dignity amidst the milling throng. The squaws scraping at the buffalo meat, hanging in red strips from the lines stretched between the lodges, turned to stare; some left their work and with bloodstained hands and dress joined the noisy crowd.

The mob wheeled into the main track of the village. They began to pass more lodges. The painted signs glowed in the sun. From the corner of his eye the scout saw the Sioux heraldry, and then beyond, the emblems of the Cheyenne . . . and Arapaho . . . and presently the Oglalas.

Oblivious to the spittle and sticks, Robidoux's mind raced ahead across the vast camp. Little Goose River ran for ten miles or more down the valley; if all the wide meadows were as packed with Indian encampments there must be more than ten thousand warriors in Red Cloud's army. And all this was less than a day's hard riding from Fort Phil Kearny! The massacre of Fetterman's regiment had raised Red Cloud's prestige to undreamed-of heights. And he had reaped huge dividends from the deed in the shape of hundreds of warriors from tribes all over the plains. They were flocking to the leader who could wage war with such success against the hated white man.

Robidoux's horse stumbled, goaded by the mob of boys hanging to its harness. One of the scout's captors pushed forward and beat the boys off with the butt of his lance. The crowd broke, jeering and laughing. Then they were wheeling into a wide open space where three lodges stood together and off to the right, in isolation, a fourth. Robidoux could see from the circle of poles which surrounded it and from the "medicine bag" hanging outside, that it was a medicine lodge. A grotesque array of objects hung from the poles varying from bundles of herbs and plants to the horns and ornamented skins of animals and a fantastic number of human scalps. More of these terrible trophies were thrust into the bag suspended from a lodge pole.

A ring of warriors in full war paint mounted guard on the lodges. The crowd stopped short, spreading round and behind the tepees until the whole circle was surrounded by a mass of Indians. The scout's horse was thrust forward so that he rode alone to the center of the space. Gradually, quiet fell upon the scene. The breeze stirred the dangling scalps on their bloody poles. From behind the now silent crowd came the whining of dogs as they padded round at the heels of their equally wild and unkempt masters.

Robidoux looked beyond the savage, staring faces to the lodge poles pointing to the skies, ridge upon ridge of tepees appearing into the blue distance. A sound beneath his mount's head brought his attention back to the crowd and, looking down, he found himself gazing into the blazing eyes and proud face of the mightiest general the Sioux had ever known . . . Red Cloud.

The Indian wore a blanket of bright colors, with scarlet predominating and here and there vivid green. The bold nose, the small bright eyes and the wide powerful mouth set tight like a trap, gave an immediate impression of high intelligence and power. Eagle feathers, notched to show many deeds of valor, hung from the black hair that fell in two braids over his shoulders. Beneath the blanket he was naked except for a beaded loincloth and a leather belt that held a long curved knife at his hip. The absence of ceremonial dress or ornaments seemed to add to the quality of the man. He spoke, with his eyes boring into the Frenchman's face.

Robidoux shook his head, then as an afterthought raised his shoulders and jerked at his bonds.

The chief spoke again and a warrior slid from his horse, coming forward to jerk a knife at the captive's bonds. The scout almost fell from his horse which the brave dragged back to the edge of the circle. The blood rushed agonizingly through Robidoux's cramped limbs. He recovered his balance and, rubbing his arms, stood alone before Red Cloud.

Again the Chief spoke but the scout could not understand the dialect. The warrior who had cut his bonds spoke at length, and a murmur of approval ran through the crowd as the story of the chase and capture was told to the Chief. When it was finished Red Cloud dismissed the brave, let drop his blanket and advanced within striking distance of the scout.

Robidoux stood his ground. If this was the kill he'd show these Stone Age savages that a Frenchman knew how to die.

But the Chief did not touch his knife. Instead, to Robidoux's surprise, he set about talking to his white prisoner.

Sign language was universal to the nomads of the plains. Many tribes and many dialects made it difficult for even warriors of the same nation to speak together. A common language of gesture had developed to a high degree over the centuries so that now, even Sioux from the remote Missouri in the north could "hand talk" with the Commanches of Texas.

Red Cloud lifted one hand and thrust it towards the scout, all fingers extended. He bunched the fingers and shot them out again, eight, nine, ten times, sweeping his other hand from left to right as he did so. Then he pointed to his mouth and flung an arm in the direction of the encampment."

"The Chief speaks for ten thousand lodges."

Robidoux, adept at reading signs of this nature, translated slowly aloud and nodded.

Red Cloud rubbed two fingers together . . .

"Cheyenne."

. . . pointed with forked fingers . . .

"Sioux."

. . . spun one thumb on the other . . .

"Arapaho."

The scout listed the tribes as the chief signaled each one, and then watched while Red Cloud closed both hands as if grasping a bunch of sticks, hooked his thumbs together and flapped the fingers, then crooked his hand into a cup and made a drinking motion . . .

"All the tribes have come to Little Goose River."

The dark palms came together and then both arms shot forward.

"To unite."

Red Cloud's hand shot vigorously up, drawing a stiff forefinger across his throat and pointing to the scout. There was no mistaking the gesture.

"To make war on the white man."

Red Cloud nodded as the Frenchman spoke aloud and Robidoux looked at him closely, wondering whether he understood the English words or not.

And so the talk went on. The white soldiers were clearly enumerated; the council at Laramie; the treaty promises broken; the building of the forts from Reno in the south to the new Fort C. Smith in the Big Horns; the fight of the tribes against every step of the white man into their country . . . and finally the Fetterman massacre.

As he looked at the dangling scalps and the medicine man in the opening of the medicine lodge, Robidoux suddenly realized why he had been brought before Red Cloud. His capture was no mere chance. He had been waylaid for a definite purpose. The Indians knew Colonel Carrington had gone and that a new officer commanded the fort. And they wanted to make sure that he knew how bitterly opposed the tribes were to the road through their lands. He, Jean Robidoux, was to bear the message of defiance flung back to the "new little white chief," as Red Cloud called Colonel Wessells.

Suddenly Red Cloud flung up his arm and called the crowd. The circle of Indians advanced closer. Drawing his knife, the Chief extended the point until it touched the scout's tattered buckskin shirt. When he spoke again, to Robidoux's intense surprise, it was in the pidgin English that many of the plains tribes had learned from the trappers and mountain men who had explored the West long before the Army came. He emphasized each word with a little jab of the knife.

"Go," spat out the Chief. "You go . . . new little white chief. Tell . . . him . . . WAR."

A great shout went up from the circle of braves as they caught and understood this one savage word.

Red Cloud slid the knife back into his belt, pointed again at the scout and raised two fingers beside his head—the coyote sign.

"White man thief."

Again a great shout went up.

The Chief pointed to the ground with a rigid forefinger, and then the signs blurred so swiftly that the scout had difficulty in following.

"He come to steal Indian lands," he made out, and "Fort, soldiers, road, all go." A wide sweep of Red Cloud's arm as if he were brushing ants from a table.

"Tell new white chief . . . GO," once more the spitting English words came from the Indian's lips, "or else . . ." with his finger Red Cloud traced a quick scalping circle round his head and flung his other arm in the direction of the medicine lodge where the scalps of Fetterman's soldiers hung in the sun. The cheering broke loose unchecked now. The medicine man began to strike a drum and the long ululation of imitation war whoops came from the women on the edge of the crowd.

Robidoux's captors dragged him back to his horse and flung him up in the saddle, lashing his feet together under his horse's belly. Red Cloud stood with arms folded, the scarlet blanket like a pool of blood on the ground behind him.

The scout made one last appeal. He pointed to the warriors and then to his own throat. What would the Indians do to him once outside the camp, outside the stern control of the Chief?

Red Cloud understood. At his spoken command the medicine man ran from his lodge and tore down one of the totems. He handed it to Red Cloud, producing as he did so a red chalk stick from somewhere in his tattered robes. He spat upon his palm and moistened the tip of the stick.

Red Cloud took the totem. It was a thin willow branch which had been drawn into a loop at the end. Strung over the loop and stretched tight by a network of threads was a cured white scalp, the fair hair from which waved in the wind. With the moist chalk Red Cloud made his mark in the center of the skin. Then he threw the totem to Robidoux.

It was the Chief's sign; a safe pass through the guards of the great encampment.

They turned the scout's horse. This time his hands were free. Grasping the mane in one hand and holding the totem high in the other, he rode forward. On all sides were the jeering, dancing Indians. Encouraged by the excitement the dogs joined in, yelping and leaping at the frightened horse. In this way they escorted him to the bluffs, whipped him up the slope and sent him careering across the dusty plain, the totem jerking in the wind above his head, the yells of the triumphant Indians fading behind.

3

"THE GUN THAT FIRES ITSELF"

"Rider approachin' from west."

Portugee Phillips was talking to the carpenter and watching the smoke climb up from the oven chimneys as the bakers stoked up their fires to begin the day's work. The cry from the sentry on the gatehouse rang out on the still morning air, and Portugee rose from his seat on the upturned wagon.

Excusing himself quickly to the carpenter, he sprinted towards the gatehouse. Perhaps this was his friend, now long overdue on the ride back from Fort Reno. He climbed the ladder and joined the sentry on the platform behind the stockade. The soldier pointed down the trail below them, but Portugee's keen eye had already picked out the hunched figure that rode slowly towards the fort, a grey silhouette against the pale morning mist that still clung to the floor of the valley. Something about both rider and horse told Portugee that all was not well. And there was a lance that stuck up in the air above the weary pair and jogged to and fro.

Portugee swung off the platform and dropped down to the entrance to the fort. A guard was already pulling back one of the heavy gates.

The scout ran out. The horseman was much nearer now, and Portugee could see a familiar buckskin shirt—and then suddenly, the bonds tying the twisted feet to the horse's side. He raced to meet him, calling to the guards as he did so. The horse stopped and slowly lowered its head as Portugee approached. Flecks of foam spattered its heaving chest, and blood congealed on the rawhide thongs that bound the rider's feet.

"Jean!"

The name burst from Portugee's lips as he recognized his friend. Robidoux managed to smile weakly as he bowed his head to his mount's mane.

"'Ullo, mon vieux," he croaked. "Like old times, huh?" Portugee's knife was out cutting quickly but carefully at the thongs.

"Hold on, partner," he said softly. "Just hold on till we get you inside."

With one hand on his friend, who now sprawled forward over the horse, and the other holding the reins, he walked the pair towards the gateway. A soldier ran to steady the tired figure from the other side and, with the sentry above staring down, the gallant Frenchman and his weary horse were brought in to safety.

Outside the hospital they lifted Robidoux down and with an arm slung round each shoulder Portugee and the soldier helped him towards the steps. Suddenly the weary face became aggressively alive.

"Mon Dieu, non!" exploded Robidoux. "Old Kidder's store . . . not . . . not hospital."

"But, Frenchie," exclaimed the soldier, "you're bleeding, your legs are hurt."

The stubborn figure thrust him away and remained upright, nevertheless hanging grimly on to Portugee's shoulder.

"No doctors for me," he cried. "Old Kidder's firewater will cure this . . . this canaille." And he pointed to his legs. "Allons!"

The two friends walked unsteadily to the next building, the sutler's store, anxiously followed by more soldiers. Inside, they sat Robidoux on a barrel, his legs stretched out before him and his back propped against some bales of cloth. Crates and merchandise were piled everywhere in the dark interior of the huge building, where everything from a saddle blanket to a candle could be bought—if the sutler had it in stock and if he was of a mind to sell it to you.

Portugee called for glasses and French brandy.

"Brandy!" expostulated the sutler, a large man with a white

apron over his stomach and a heavy gold watch chain looped
above it into his waistcoat pockets. "Where do you think I'd
be gettin' French brandy from in this wilderness?"

"Aw, Joe," said one of the soldiers. "Gilmore and Porter's
mule train come in this week. If you didn't have some crates
among the stocks I'll volunteer to ride to Laramie myself and
get some."

"It's medicine for a brave man, Mr. Kidder," explained Portugee, jerking his head in the direction of his friend.

The sutler, grumbling to himself, disappeared behind shelves
laden with boxes of sugar, round-headed nails, jars of pickles
and a pile of thick grey socks. He came back with a fistful of
glasses and a tall bottle which he set down on the table before
Robidoux.

"Here you are, you old coyote. I guess you deserve it."

Portugee filled a glass and handed it to Robidoux, who tossed
it down his throat in one gulp. The spirit seemed to revive him,
for he reached for the bottle and then pulled up his tattered
trousers, exposing the raw flesh where the rubbing thongs had
cut him on the long ride from Little Goose River. Bending
forward, he carefully poured a little of the spirit over each
leg in turn; then he leaned back and relaxed.

Portugee continued to look at his friend. The rough cauter-
izing of a wound with brandy was something the French scout
had taught him in the early days of their adventures on the
plains. Out there in the wilderness it had been a necessity; here
in the fort, with a doctor nearby, it was an act of bravado—a
gesture to old times and old adventures before sleep and oint-
ments took over.

"Parbleu, I'm tired," the Frenchman murmured, without
raising his head, "but I've a message for the Colonel." He
struggled to rise. "Must report."

"The Colonel's sent me over to patch you up before you see
him," said a voice from the doorway. "I reckon you could do
with some bandages on those legs. And some food. Got my
own cook at the hospital," concluded Dr. Horton. "Come on,
lad, it'll tickle even your fussy palate."

He stopped, eyed the brandy bottle and, picking up a glass,

poured till it was brim full. He held it towards the scout with
a steady hand.

"Your health, m'sieur," he said. "Welcome back to Fort Phil
Kearny."

Some hours later, Jean Robidoux, fed, warmed, bandaged,
but very weary, walked with Portugee Phillips up the steps to
Colonel Wessell's office, talking earnestly. The morning sun
was high, and all around the fort rang with activity. Robidoux
paused on the steps and looked back at the stockade. He said
nothing but Portugee knew that the Frenchman was thinking
of Red Cloud and his army, miles away but somehow menacing
the peaceful scene.

They had talked while the scout was washed and treated
and feasted in the doctor's quarters. Portugee had marveled
at the fantastic Indian gathering on Little Goose River; shaken
his head thoughtfully as he listened to Red Cloud's grim message and, when his friend had finished, exclaimed:

"They're really going to make a fight of it, ain't they! But
I doubt whether the Colonel will be impressed. In some ways
he's like another Fetterman."

"But not so hot in the head, eh?" said Ribidoux. "Come on.
We'll see."

Sergeant Haggerty was waiting for them and led them into
the Colonel's room. Ten Eyck nodded silently to them as they
entered; Major Powell, whom Portugee knew from the Fetterman affair, was also in the room. Colonel Wessells was standing
by the window, one hand behind his back, the other holding
the long, gruesome totem that a trooper had pulled from the
saddle scabbard when they had groomed the Frenchman's horse.

He turned as they entered and tossed it into the corner of
the room.

"Welcome back, Mr. Robidoux," he said. "I asked Dr. Horton to see if you . . ."

"Thank you, Colonel," broke in the Frenchman. "I'm all
right now. Nothing that a couple of days' sleep won't cure!
But I must make my report first."

The Colonel motioned his visitors to chairs and sat down at

his desk, listening with elbows propped on the table and finger-
tips touching as the French scout launched into his story. His
face became stern as he heard Robidoux's description of his
capture; remained grim as the scout described the extent of the
Indian encampment, and grew positively dark at Red Cloud's
message.

There was a long silence after the Frenchman had finished
and leaned wearily back into his chair, his task over. The Colonel looked out of the window, at the sunlit hills, as if trying to
count the lodges on Little Goose River. Finally, he spoke.

"An encampment of ten thousand lodges," he said reflectively. "How many warriors would you estimate that to be,
Mr. Phillips?"

"Well," said Portugee, "allowin' for Red Cloud's natural
inclination to jump up his numbers, I've listened to Robidoux
describe the camp and I reckon Red Cloud can mount eight,
nine thousand full-blooded braves. I know it sounds a lot,
Colonel, but you got to count on the fact that he can take his
pick from four, five different tribes."

"He'll never hold them together," said Colonel Wessells,
decisively. "Sioux, Cheyenne, why they're natural enemies."

"Colonel, ain't you forgettin' Sand Creek, when the Army
raided Black Kettle's village . . ."

"That was a hostile encampment. The tribe had to be
punished."

"No, sir," broke in Robidoux. "They were not at war then;
but killin' their women and papoose soon brought them out on
the warpath. Cheyenne and Sioux, they've been united against
the whites ever since."

"I still say Red Cloud cannot organize these tribes into one
fighting force."

"Colonel," countered Portugee, "they're already organized.
A year ago these same tribes sacked Julesburg together. They
killed everyone on that wagon train at Platte Bridge."

"And Lieutenant Collin's party who tried to effect a rescue,"
broke in Ten Eyck.

There was silence in the room as the two scouts faced the
Army man. Major Powell said nothing. Sergeant Haggerty

looked from Phillips' dark, tanned face to the frosty profile of
his Colonel. "They're all the same," he thought to himself.
"Come out here new and think they can succeed where a dozen
wiser men had to give up." He gazed out of the window at the
high hills rising above the stockade and thought of Colonel
Carrington's sudden recall. Sergeant Haggerty was a loyal man
but he could not help feeling his new Colonel was wrong.

Portugee tried again. "Colonel, more than three expeditions
have tried to whip these tribes. Captain Moonlight lost all his
horses and darn near his life against the Brule village at South
Pass. And General Connor, only last year marched into the
Black Hills with three columns of soldiers. Right here, up
Powder River he comes, and what happens?" He looked at
Robidoux for confirmation and the Frenchman nodded. Portugee went on: "The columns failed to rendezvous. They lost
their horses and mules in a storm. Then fast-ridin' Arapahoe
jumped them and they had to destroy their heavy equipment
and get back to Laramie as best they could."

"In disgrace from the Army Command," broke in Robidoux,
"although, mon Dieu, they were brave men."

Portugee spoke again.

"When the railroad comes farther west, when forts can be
supplied regularly and roads kept open, it may be a different
story. But till then . . ." The scout shrugged his shoulders.

"Till then, what, Mr. Phillips?" said the Colonel harshly.
"What exactly are you advocating?"

"Let the Indians have their land," said Portugee quietly.

"*Their* land?"

"Government treaty gave them all the land north of the
Platte," replied the scout quickly, adding grimly, "Though I
don't suppose it'll stand for long if there's gold in the hills."

"Mr. Phillips," said the Colonel, "treaties are the concern of
the Indian Department in Washington. I have to obey orders
and my job is to build—and hold—enough forts to keep the
Bozeman road open and safe from Fort Laramie to Virginia
City. And I intend to do it even if I have to kill every Indian
this side of the Big Horn Mountains."

Phillips drew a deep breath.

"With all respect, Colonel," he said, "you ain't fighting a battle by the Army Manual. I've traveled and fought in these hills all my life. I know the Sioux, and I know the country. And that's what these redskins live off. Their ponies feed on prairie grass, their people *live* off the buffalo. They got all they want in the country along Little Goose River. They're not dependent on grain comin' up in wagons for their horses nor on flour and vittles humped up by mule train for their men. Sure, they may go lean through the winter, but this ain't winter, Colonel, it's spring and there's long fat months ahead for the Indian."

Captain Ten Eyck entered the battle. "They're watching every bull train that comes up from Laramie. They're up in the hills above the pinery when the men go out to cut timber. Pretty soon they'll get tired of just watching. If Red Cloud sets up another siege, we face another winter. We've more mouths to feed, more women and children who came through when the road was opened up after the snow. . . ."

"Captain," interrupted Colonel Wessells, "you're perfectly entitled to your opinion, but I'll remind you that I'm in command of this fort and I'm every bit as determined to break Red Cloud as Mr. Phillips, here, seems to be determined to give in to him."

Portugee flushed. "Colonel, I'm paid to give my advice to the Army," he said. "If I didn't say what I thought I'd be cheating my employers."

"I accept that, Mr. Phillips," replied the Colonel. "I also respect your views. But it doesn't mean I agree with them. This gathering of tribes is going to be smashed and I'm going to do it right here in this valley. Soon."

Portugee looked at the tired Robidoux, glanced at Sergeant Haggerty and the other officers lined up behind the Colonel, and made one last appeal.

"Colonel, these people don't want to be herded onto reservations to live on the white man's pity. They want to live where they were born; where there's no enclosures and everything draws a free breath. They're fightin' now for their last stronghold—and Red Cloud knows it. They're fightin' as you or I, Colonel, would fight for our homeland. And it's my guess they won't give up an inch of the plains to the Army, Washington or anyone else."

As Portugee was speaking Colonel Wessells slowly pushed the papers on his desk away from him and waited with outstretched arms until the scout had finished. Then, angry and impatient, he spoke.

"Mr. Phillips, I've listened to you at length because you're a man with long experience on the plains. Also you have already performed a great service for the Army in carrying dispatches to Laramie. But I've heard all this before."

His voice rose with increasing impatience as he went on:

"These hostiles aren't invulnerable. I grant you we may have underestimated Red Cloud's capacity as a leader up to now . . . but, I repeat, *he can be whipped.*"

He thumped the desk top as he spoke and rose to his feet. The men in the room watched him as he strode to the door.

"Corporal," he bawled, leaving the door open and turning back to face the silent scouts.

"He can be whipped," the Colonel repeated, "and by men who have held this fort through the winter. We're not waiting for any reinforcements from Fort Reno."

Robidoux rubbed his aching legs and shook his head doubtfully. But it was Portugee who put their thoughts into words.

"Colonel Fetterman had the same idea . . ." he began, but Colonel Wessells interrupted before the scout could go on.

"But I've got something Fetterman didn't have," he cried.

He swung round and caught sight of Sergeant Haggerty. "Sergeant, take the corporal over to the armory and fetch one of those crates that came off the bull train yesterday. Bring one crate from each load," he added, as the sergeant saluted and motioned to the corporal standing in the doorway to follow.

"I want them here inside five minutes," he shouted after the retreating figures, and slammed the door shut with his boot.

There was complete silence in the room as the Colonel walked to his desk and sat down. He looked defiantly at the scouts, who gazed back at him. Portugee drew a deep breath. Robidoux, with the picture of the lodges stretching mile after mile along the Little Goose River still fresh in his memory, again shook his head gently. He reached wearily up to his breast pocket and pulled out a small oilskin package. Methodically he filled his pipe while they watched. He was still packing down the black tobacco when noisy footsteps were heard on the boards outside.

"Right, straight in there, on the floor by the Colonel's desk." Sergeant Haggerty's voice could be heard above the clatter, and then the door burst open and the corporal with two troopers staggered into the room carrying two heavy packing crates between them. With a crash they dropped them to the floor. Colonel Wessells sprang up.

"All right," he barked. "Now where . . ." and then broke off as Sergeant Haggerty silently slipped two steel bars with forked claw levers at the ends from behind his back. He tossed one to a trooper and motioned him to open the crate. He then dropped on one knee and began to prize open the lid of the longer box with the other himself. The board top splintered and came up with a crack, the long silver nails glinting in the light. Sawdust poured in streams on to the floor.

Colonel Wessells strode forward and tore a board from the box. The smaller box came open with a second crack and the trooper pulled the brown oiled paper away to reveal a row of square cardboard boxes.

By now the Colonel had brushed Sergeant Haggerty aside and was scooping sawdust out in great handfuls. The entire company in the room pressed round the boxes, as if expecting one of Red Cloud's warriors to spring up fully armed and uttering his war whoop.

Instead, the Colonel dragged a long heavy object from the box and deftly catching hold of the end of rag, spun the thing in the air.

Blue metal shone dully in the light. As he caught it in his other hand and stripped the remaining rags from the butt, Portugee saw a short, heavy rifle. Just visible among the sawdust and rags in the box were the outlines of five more.

"Now, gentlemen," said the Colonel, breathing hard, "we shall see." He took a cardboard box from the trooper, threw it on to the desk, broke open the top and began cramming the contents into his right-hand side pocket.

"Repeating rifles," breathed Robidoux. "Henrys. Like those Fisher and Wheatly had when they went out with Fetterman."

"No," said Portugee, "these ain't Henrys; these're breech-loaders. But they're new. Springfields, by the look of them."

The Colonel strode across the room, kicking the rags and sawdust aside. He went out of the door, across the porch and jumped down the steps. He carried the rifle in both hands before him. He didn't look to see who followed, but the whole crowd jostled out of the office, spilled on to the porch, watching him stride out of the shadow on to the dusty sunlit parade ground. A trooper lounging in a doorway jumped upright as he saw the advancing figure. Colonel Wessells came to a stand-still and waved one arm in a wide, sweeping gesture.

"Clear the square," he bawled. And again, "Clear the square."

Little groups of soldiers all around the parade ground came to the alert as the Colonel's words reached them. Two figures walked by the high wall of the fort, stopped and looked toward the orderly room. They were in the very center of the portion of the great timber palisade exposed between the buildings opposite.

"*Get out of the way!*" roared the Colonel. "*I want that wall cleared.*" The figures hesitated, then ran off to the side.

"Parbleu, what does he do?" exclaimed Robidoux, his unlit pipe still clutched in his hand.

Before Portugee could answer the Colonel had taken a step forward with his left foot. He crouched slightly, then threw the rifle up to his shoulder. A second's pause and then a shot rang out across the parade ground.

A puff of dirt and dust showered up where the bullet hit the wall. The guard on the lookout tower above the gate jerked round and looked down at the scene. Heads appeared at doors and windows all round the square.

The Colonel brought the rifle down; there was a quick movement of his right hand, and then once again he threw the gun up to his shoulder and fired. A further shower of splinters flew from the fort wall.

The time between the shots was perhaps four seconds. "Sufferin' bearcats," said an astonished voice at Portugee's elbow.

Another shot rang across the square. Again the rifle came down. Again the same quick motion of the Colonel's right hand, only this time a little swifter. Again he flung the gun up and fired and the dark shadow on the ground mimicked his movements.

Running figures appeared between the buildings of the fort. A growing buzz of voices could be heard. There were cries from excited children and anxious mothers. The bakers came out of the bakery, bared arms white with flour. The hurrying figures were brought to a standstill by the crowd already gathering along the sides of the square. Gradually the shouting and noise subsided. On Pilot Hill the lookouts could be seen gazing down at the fort. And still the shots went on and on and on. But now there was only a fleeting second or two between each report.

The Colonel's figure was wreathed in blue smoke. Each shot spat down between the silent ranks of watchers and dug its way into the timbers of the wall.

"He's a danged good shot, I'll say that," muttered Sergeant Haggerty, watching the splinters fly from one small patch of wall.

"And he knows how to handle that rifle," rejoined Portugee, as he watched the Colonel's hand jerk open the breech, saw the spent cartridge fall out and the hand slap in a fresh one taken from his side pocket. The pile of spent cartridges on the ground at the Colonel's right foot grew steadily.

"Le bon Dieu help the Indian that has to face such a gun," said Robidoux, adding, "It fires itself!"

At last the firing stopped. The last echo rang back distantly from the hills. The Colonel lowered the rifle. The crowd remained staring at the wall of the fort as though any minute it would burst into flame. Dust rose lazily in the air.

Colonel Wessells wheeled and marched back to the steps.

His eyes gleamed up at the watchers in the shadows. He held the rifle up; smoke still issued from the hot barrel.

"This is it," he almost snarled. "This is Red Cloud's ticket to the Happy Hunting Grounds."

He flung the gun with a crash on the boards at Portugee's feet and strode up the steps into his office.

The men on the porch crowded round looking at the rifle as it lay on the boards.

"Springfield-Allen."

Someone read out the name engraved along the breech.

"The Sioux will wonder what's hit them when they come up against a repeating gun like that," said another excited voice. "They're used to taking the first volley, but they always bank on rushing into close quarters while we reload."

"Maybe the Colonel's right after all," said Robidoux, looking quietly at Portugee Phillips.

His pipe was still in his hands, unlighted.

4
DEATH ON THE TRAIL

The summer now burst upon the valley in all its splendor. The sun, hot even in the early hours of the day, blazed down on the fort by the Little Piney. The timbers on the new buildings warped. Dust hung in a plume behind every rider. The long grass yellowed, the water in the streams shrank to a shallow trickle and men, working stripped to the waist, were as bronze as the Indians who haunted the hills.

As June passed, both the Colonel and Portugee were proved right in their predictions.

The new Springfield-Allen rifle was all that Colonel Wessells had claimed; it was fast and efficient and every soldier felt a surge of confidence as he handled the new weapon. Portugee's grim forebodings that "Red Cloud was not done for by a long ways yet" turned out to be only too well justified. In the first days of July the Indians struck swiftly and savagely in a series of daring attacks.

Training with the new rifles began the very day after the Colonel's dramatic demonstration of fire-power on the parade ground.

Some breechloading rifles and indeed "repeaters" had been in use during the Civil War which had just ended. But in both the Union and Confederate armies the muzzle-loading rifle was the infantryman's main weapon. True, these muzzle-loaders were far removed from the long Kentucky rifles used by the pioneers, with their powder horn, greased patches and ball; nevertheless, eleven separate motions were still needed to load the army rifle and three shots a minute was considered fast firing.

The Springfield-Allen rifle was miraculous in comparison.

The breech was thrown open in one movement, which also ejected the spent shell. A cartridge containing *both* powder and bullet was slapped in, the breech closed and the rifle was then ready to fire. The number of shots one man could pump out in one minute became the subject of great rivalry between the soldiers. Eight, nine, even ten bullets a minute whined towards the targets set up in the meadows outside the fort.

Day after day the squads marched out to the long mounds of earth thrown up to make a range. The crackle of musketry echoed between the Sullivant Hills on the one side and Pilot Hill on the other.

"Danged waste of ammunition," growled a burly teamster in the cool shadow of Kidder's storehouse. "They wouldn't make so free with it if they had to hump it over every danged mile of the trail from Laramie."

"A lot of these lads are learnin' to handle a new weapon," rejoined Sergeant Haggerty, who was snatching a moment of well-earned rest from the Colonel's rigid training program. "Every shot you hear now means a mite more accuracy when they're facing Red Cloud's bloods."

"And that can't be much longer," put in Portugee, coming through the doorway in time to catch the gist of the conversation.

"Maybe so. Maybe so," said the teamster, getting to his feet and moving past Portugee. He stood in silence a minute, head cocked, listening beyond the general noise of the fort. "Anyways," he added, "here's more ammunition for your boys to blaze away with." And saluting the sergeant, jauntily he moved off across the square towards the gate of the fort.

Portugee and the sergeant walked outside. Faintly came the "crack-crack" of whips across the valley. Climbing the stairs at the side of the guardroom, they looked out from the platform over the stockade to the south. Sergeant Haggerty cocked an eye up at Pilot Hill. From the cabin on top of the conical peak the lookout was flag-wagging a message. A sentry dropped down from the banquette by the gatehouse and doubled across the square, disappearing into the orderly room.

"Here they come," grunted Portugee, leaning on the rail.

"Pity old Jim Bridger ain't here with his telescope. Might see
if Jean's with them."

Down through the foothills beyond the meadows on the far
side of the Little Piney, where the trail from Reno wound
towards the fort, were the white, swaying canvas tops of the
huge Conestoga wagons.

"Seven . . . eight . . . no, ten, by thunder!" exclaimed
Portugee. The white road smoked behind them. The riders, to
avoid the suffocating dust, moved out abreast of the wagons
as they crossed the meadows.

The bullwhacker's whips cracked more fiercely as the oxen
reached the Piney crossing and bent to drink thirstily at the
stream. The bull train straggled to a halt, the wagons in the
bed of the stream, eight oxen in each team heaving and
spluttering at the water, quenching their thirst after the long,
hard haul over the mountain road from Crazy Woman's Creek.

Several riders came on towards the fort, but the bulk of
troops escorting the train remained grouped near the wagons.
Even so near their destination they still seemed apprehensive.

"Something's up, John," growled Sergeant Haggerty. "Look
at that wagon by itself. It ain't stoppin' to water with the rest.
Comin' straight on."

It was true. The crack of the long heavy bullwhips and the
bellowing of the animals as they were urged across the stream
came clearly to the ears of the watchers in the fort.

"C'mon," said Portugee. "Let's meet them."

By the time the two had reached the entrance the gates
were wide open and the first riders from the bull train came
cantering up.

"There's Frenchie," said Sergeant Haggerty.

Jean Robidoux rode at the head of the group and as they
clattered in beneath the gatehouse, raising a cloud of dust, he
saw Portugee and the sergeant and swung sharply round, reining in to bring his heaving horse to a standstill before them.
He slid from the saddle. White dust puffed from his clothes.
His kerchief had been tied round his nose and mouth to keep
the dust of the trail from his lungs, and a white patch of sweat
and grit caked the top half of his face. He saluted the waiting

pair but cut immediately through the preliminaries of greeting. "We were attacked," he said briefly. "Fifty young bloods jumped us at Crazy Woman's." He gestured at the single oncoming wagon. "There's four wounded men in there . . . and two dead." And as Sergeant Haggerty turned to the nearest soldier and ordered him to the hospital to alert Dr. Horton, the French scout swung up into the saddle again.

"See you soon, mon vieux," he called, pulling his horse round. "Tell you about it then." And he rode across the square to report to the Colonel.

Portugee and the sergeant turned to join the crowd that was gathering at the gate as the first of the wagons came rumbling in.

The next day Red Cloud struck again.

As well as contracting to bring a bull train up each month from Laramie, the firm of Gilmore and Porter had taken on the task of building a sawmill in the fort. To supply the timber that was used daily for fuel and to build up stocks for the coming winter, loggers worked in the pinery beyond the Sullivant Hills. Each morning a wood train, provided with an escort of troopers, drove through the hills to the pinery to bring back the logs felled the previous day.

It was well after noon on the day following the arrival of the bull train when the returning wagons from the pinery, under the command of Major Powell, ran into trouble.

The six loaded wagons, with the loggers and teamsters riding on top, had nearly reached the end of the trail through the Sullivants when Major Powell spotted several figures peering over the crest of a hill to the right.

Leveling his fieldglasses he saw a dozen mounted braves. With a wave of his arm Powell summoned his sergeant.

"Hostiles," he cried. "Get the wagons into two columns. Bring all the spare horses between. Dismount at my signal and prepare to fight on foot."

The sergeant wheeled away. Powell galloped to the leading wagon and headed it off the trail. Slowly the second wagon drew level, the loggers looking anxious and already handling their weapons. Gradually the other wagons fell into place, until they were moving in pairs, with only a short distance between each. Into the gap in the center the herders began to lead the spare horses, some twenty draft animals that were used to supplement the teams when the heavy wagons were hauled over the steeper inclines of the trail.

"They'll have a job to stampede that lot," thought Powell, with satisfaction, as the maneuver was completed.

Heavily loaded, the wagons proceeded at a brisk walking pace along the trail.

"Dismount," signaled the captain, and the troopers, now in a regular circle enclosing the wood train, swung off their horses and pulled rifles from their scabbards.

By now the number of Indians on the hills had gradually increased until about a hundred braves could be seen moving leisurely down the slopes in advance of the slowly moving train. They approached within easy range and yet not a shot was fired, Major Powell having given strict instructions to his men to reserve their fire for close quarters. Suddenly, with a wild, ringing war cry the Indians wheeled and charged. On they came, screaming and whooping in an effort to stampede the horses.

Still the wagon train held steady, every man looking anxiously from the major at the head of the column to the enemy thundering down upon them. Coolly, Powell rose in his stirrups, swung off his horse and, leveling his pistol, fired.

Instantly the troopers dropped on one knee and, taking deliberate aim, poured a volley from their rifles into the ranks of the Indians. Several reeled in their saddles; ponies fell, bringing others down on top of them, and suddenly the charge broke into two yelling streams which flashed down either side of the wagon train.

Reloading, the troopers fired into their flanks as they tore by and ragged fire broke out from the loggers on top of the wagons.

The Indians rode on out of range, bunching again as they passed beyond the wood train, and reining round to renew the attack.

The bugle rang out with the call to mount, and at the pre-arranged signal the whips cracked and the teams broke into a run. The troopers closed in against the two lines of lumbering wagons. On the last two, a group of teamsters put aside their rifles and began climbing along the piles of jolting logs towards the back.

Major Powell rode close, looking anxiously over his shoulder at the Indians circling behind them. Another charge was imminent.

The whole pace of the teams had now increased to a canter. The wagons were swaying dangerously as they approached the crest of the trail. Another mile and they would be in sight of the meadows leading down to the Little Piney. The teamsters were standing in their seats lashing the horses.

The Indians, lying low over the necks of their ponies and urging them on at full speed, once more bore down on the flying train. The circle of troopers had broken at the back, forced against the wagons by the narrowing trail and leaving a gap which seemed to entice the howling braves on. Closer and closer they came. A few wild shots flew over the wagons but their whole effort seemed bent on reaching close quarters, to stampede the loose horses between the wagons and to sep-arate and massacre the escort and drivers in the confusion that followed.

Still Powell held his fire. The loggers clinging to the bounc-ing wagons seemed like sailors on a stormy sea. Almost within tomahawk range came the exultant redskins, already rising in their saddles to leap on the rattling tailboards.

"Now," yelled Powell, and fired his revolver into the air twice in rapid succession. The loggers on the two rear wagons heaved. The tailboards fell with a crash, and as the men scrambled back the piles of round logs tumbled out on to the trail. Straight under the flying hooves of the Indian ponies they rolled, while at the same time the troopers wheeled on the hill-side to halt and pour a deadly volley into the struggling mass of Indians. Brilliant as the Sioux horsemanship was, dozens of ponies fell. The charge broke completely over the stratagem of jettisoned logs.

A cheer went up from the wagon train, now rumbling over the incline and increasing speed as it swept down the hill.

The Indians drew off, the chiefs circling, their war bonnets flying out in the dust as they attempted to rally the braves.

Again the bugle sounded and the escort formed up on the trail. For a moment the two parties faced each other and then the rearing, prancing ponies of the Indians split up, racing off over the ridge of the hills, their reckless riders intent on resuming the attack on the timber train as it rolled out on to the meadows almost within sight of the fort.

"Forward!" The tiny column of cavalry galloped down the trail. The Indians streamed along the ridge on either side after the disappearing wagon train.

Whether it was a new bunch of braves on fresh, fleet ponies or whether some of the attacking Indians had been held in reserve for this separate effort, Powell and his men never knew. Whatever the reason, suddenly, with a loud whoop of triumph, half a dozen fast-riding warriors swept down the hillside ahead of the troopers and on to the rear wagon. Smoke belched out from the guns of the loggers of the leading teams but the weaving Indians seemed to bear a charmed life.

A logger stood up in the rear wagon leveling his rifle as best he could over the jolting boards to draw a bead on the leading braves.

A lariat shot out from the warriors. The noose fell round the logger's shoulders, pinning his hands to his sides, the rifle falling in the dust. For a second he stood there, pulling vainly at the taut rope and then he pitched over the side.

Two ponies appeared from nowhere, their riders hanging with legs crooked over the necks of their mounts. Outstretched hands then swept up the rolling logger, the ponies closed for an instant—and then with the insensible man hanging over the horse before him, one brave wheeled away and galloped back towards the crest of the hill.

In vain Powell urged his troop after the captured man. Yelling Indians swept between the troopers and their quarry: a brief, fierce flurry of shots; a wounded trooper; confusion as the redskins scattered in all directions; the captive hidden; the fight over.

In silence, Major Powell assembled his men. In silence they rode down the trail. The timber train was rolling slowly towards the distant fort, the horses steaming in the sun, the attack successfully repulsed.

But one white man had been left in savage hands—alive.

They found him the next morning on the edge of the hills beyond the Big Piney. His legs were tied to stakes, wide apart; his arms spreadeagled between two bent saplings. Strips of flesh had been torn from his naked body and the poor, raw head still slowly dripped blood. A small fire smouldered nearby.

Colonel Wessells surveyed the meeting coldly. A lantern smoked at his elbow and a soldier came to the table to adjust the wick. The council of war, begun late in the afternoon, had continued well into the night. Five days had elapsed since the attack on the wood train, five days in which Red Cloud struck at every man and party who ventured out into the surrounding hills.

"Nine separate attacks in the past week," said the Colonel slowly and deliberately. "Two men killed, fourteen wounded and one taken by the hostiles."

He looked at the grim faces around his desk. Powell tense and tired; Ten Eyck grim and angry; Portugee and Robidoux silent; Sergeant Haggerty and Dr. Horton, back in the shadows watching.

"Well, we've done with waiting. This time we take the fight to the enemy. With God's help we'll bring Red Cloud to battle on our own terms—once his power is smashed, this army of savages will melt like snow in summer."

Colonel Wessells smoothed the map before him, and pointed to the black pencil marks below the pinery. Once more he began to go over the plan they had discussed during the long hours of the evening; summarizing the details, making sure each man knew his part. They gathered closer round the table, the murmur of question and answer rose and fell. The lights dimmed elsewhere in the fort. Only the lanterns in the Colonel's office and the guardhouse remained to rival the stars in the clear night sky.

The Colonel's plan was simple. It took a leaf out of Red Cloud's book in that it set a small force out on the hills to sit as bait. And just as Fetterman had been lured over Lodge Trail Ridge into an ambush that had cost the life of over eighty men, so Colonel Wessells planned to tempt the Chief of the Sioux down into the valley—to face a hidden force of picked infantry, fully trained and armed with the new Springfield-Allen rifles.

5
A TRAP IS SPRUNG

In the early morning at the end of July fourteen wagons rolled out of Fort Phil Kearny, turning west along the wood road through the Sullivant Hills.

At the head of the column, Portugee Phillips urged Fortune into a canter and, with a corporal trooper in close attendance, rode forward to the first ridge of hills. Here he pulled off the trail and, reining Fortune round, sat watching the wood train moving towards them.

To any curious eyes—and Portugee knew the Sioux too well to believe that the wagons were leaving the fort unobserved—it seemed like any other wood train that departed daily at this time on its way to the pinery. Perhaps there were more wagons, but they creaked along in the same casual fashion, the loggers riding on the empty boards, the teamsters hunched on their seats flicking their long whips over the walking teams. A white dog ran, tongue lolling, beside one of the wagons. Five or six spare horses trailed behind each tailboard, and in the rear an escort of twelve troopers trotted behind their sergeant, the blue uniforms bright in the clear air, the occasional glitter of light winking upwards like a mirror as the sun shone on some polished accoutrement.

Just like the routine departure of the wood train for the hills . . . or was it?

"What do you think, Corporal Riley?" Portugee turned to the man beside him. "Is there anythin' out of place?"

The corporal shook his head slowly. "No, Mr. Phillips, I don't think so. Few more wagons than usual. Few more men, naturally." He grinned. "But they sure don't look like the Twenty-Seventh."

Portugee smiled too. For although Gilmore and Porter's teamsters drove the wagons, and although the logging teams were dressed in their usual rough clothes, the battered hats, colored shirts and belted jackets covered a specially selected squad of the Twenty-Seventh Infantry—crack marksmen all. And the rough board timbers on which they lounged were in reality a false floor covering the long crates of Springfield-Allen rifles and seven thousand rounds of ammunition.

"If Red Cloud only know'd what was slipping through his fingers," mused Portugee. He walked Fortune down off the crest of the hill and with Corporal Riley close behind, took his place at the head of the column as the wagons came level.

Some two hours later they came out of the far end of the Sullivants into the wide valley that ran roughly north and south from Lodge Trail Ridge to the wooded slopes of the pinery. The Big Piney ran down from the hills in the south and meandered across the meadows before swinging east and passing behind the Sullivants towards the fort where it was joined by its tributary, the Little Piney.

On the level valley floor, a green meadow perhaps a mile across and about six miles as the eagle flies from the fort, Portugee turned the wagons and brought the column to a halt. The dog, who had ridden the last few miles on one of the wagons, jumped out and ran yelping round the teams.

For a long while the scout sat in silence, occasionally patting Fortune's neck as the horse bent down to crop the lush meadow grass. To the northeast the ground rose in a gentle ridge, then dropped again until it reached the hills that formed the eastern wall of the valley. Across the Piney in the opposite direction were the pine-clad hills where the loggers worked. It seemed an ideal spot for their purpose, and when Sergeant McQuinty rode over and asked, "Is this it, then?" Portugee nodded and slipped to the ground.

Quickly, quietly, at a signal from the sergeant, the troopers and disguised infantrymen went about their allotted tasks. Few commands were given; every man knew what was expected of him. The dog explored the camp site, scratched a few fleas and sat down to watch.

First the fourteen wagons were drawn into a tight oval; then the teams were unhitched and with a mounted guard circling them watchfully, put out to graze on the meadow. Next the wagons were unloaded, great care being taken to stack the ammunition boxes and rifle crates as unobtrusively as possible in the center of the camp. Finally the men gathered round Portugee as he prepared to put into action the plan so carefully conceived days before at the council of war in Colonel Wessell's office. Confidently he directed the first operation.

Thick timber blocks were hammered into place beneath the axles of one of the heavy wagons, lifting the great wheels a few inches off the ground. The axle-pins were pulled and the wheels themselves were removed. Bringing the nearest team of horses into the circle, Portugee had them hitched to the balanced wagon.

"Steady," he called, "steady," as they strained against the ropes. "Watch 'em when she falls."

With a crash the wagon came down off the balks of timber. Dust rose in a cloud. The horses jumped, startled, and then again took the strain as Portugee urged them forward. Gradually the great wagon-box came up, the bare axle biting into the earth, the timbers creaking.

While the straining horses held it there at an angle, Portugee placed some of the scattered timbers under the raised ends of each axle and signaled for the team to be backed.

With a thump the wagon-box came down, the timbers held and it lay there at a gentle angle, the planks of the floor facing inwards, the outer wall a foot or two high in the air—a perfect breastwork for a rifleman.

A growl of approval went up from the soldiers. Corporal Riley hammered with his fist on the stout inch-thick planks.

"Indian arrows won't pierce it and Indian musket balls will bounce off. Lads, we've got us a fort."

One after another twelve of the heavy wagons were stripped of their wheels and dragged into place. Portugee planned the long oval with spaces between each wagon-box just wide enough for a man to walk through but not large enough for a horse. Across each end of the oval, to the north and south, were left openings across which the two remaining wagons could be driven. These were placed just outside the corral, and left on their wheels, ready to roll across the gaps at the first sign of danger.

As the afternoon wore on and the work on the wagon-box corral proceeded, Portugee had the uneasy feeling that every move was being watched although no visible sign of the enemy could be detected on the wooded slopes.

By late afternoon, the cooking fires were blazing and tents had been pitched within the corral. The men rested and ate, talking warily about the Indians, playing with the white dog, chaffing each other as soldiers do under any circumstance and enjoying their temporary freedom from uniform.

"All right, all right," growled Sergeant McQuinty at last. "There's a guard to be mounted. Some of you had better be gettin' some sleep."

The horses were driven into the corral and tethered; the wagons rolled across the gaps to shut them in. The fires died, the evening light crept out of the valley, hung on the distant peaks of the hills, vanished, leaving the camp in darkness.

Portugee leaned against the wagon-box in which he had decided to sleep, his saddle beneath his head, a blanket over him, listening to the wild sounds of the night.

Owl or Indian? Who could tell?

Once in the night he was roused by the frenzied barking of the dog. He threw off the blanket and walked over to the wagon where a shaded lantern burned dimly, and Sergeant McQuinty cursed the dog under his breath.

"The beggar won't keep quiet!" he explained to Portugee. "Keeps goin' off down there towards the water and raisin' hell every trip."

The dog came up and out of the darkness as he spoke. His hackles were up, he sniffed out into the meadows and growled.

"All right, boy." Portugee patted the big white head. "I'll take a look round," he said to Sergeant McQuinty and, easing the Navy on his hip, went off soft-footed on a tour of inspection.

All was quiet. Whatever had disturbed the dog had gone. Out in the meadows an owl hooted. On the distant hills its mate answered eerily.

Owl or Indian? Who could tell?

The grey light of the first day of August crept slowly over the quiet valley. Already men were up in the wagon-box corral, stirring the fires to life, driving out the horses to graze by the river. Breakfast was eaten standing among the tilted wagons and then, with a quiet word to Sergeant McQuinty, Portugee and a party of the loggers saddled up and set out for the pinery.

The sun was already brushing the top of the great pines when they reached the slopes of the hills and set to work. This was all part of the plan to allay suspicion in the hearts of the Indians watching the valley. For Portugee was convinced that every move, from the arrival of the wagon train to the building of the corral, had been observed. A telltale movement on a distant hilltop; the brief flash of light that could have come from a signal mirror; the uneasy prowling of the white dog during the night . . . it all added up to a constant watch on the camp by Red Cloud's warriors.

The day crept by without incident. Portugee and his squad alternately watched and worked and the number of fallen pine trunks grew steadily. Shortly after noon, the guard posted at the edge of the woods to keep contact with the distant corral, came up through the trees to report the arrival of the daily wood train and a large escort of troops. Soon the rattle of approaching wagons could be heard. Under the direction of Mr. Porter himself, the loggers brought their teams along the rough track to the piled trees. Wood-cutting stopped and all hands turned to tackle and lever to load the timber.

Returning to the corral, Portugee was surprised to find Sergeant Haggerty among the new arrivals.

"Aw, I couldn't let them keep me out of this," said the old soldier gruffly in reply to the scout's greeting. "Besides, I knowed somebody should be lookin' after you, if Red Cloud showed up." And he slapped an arm round his friend's buck-skinned shoulders.

Two of the big Conestoga wagons stood outside the corral and soldiers were busy unloading more stores. Major Powell and a young lieutenant were talking to Sergeant McQuinty. On the western side of the corral, where the ground sloped very slightly towards the Big Piney, a row of tents was already up.

"I sure hope there ain't too much activity around the corral to scare Red Cloud off," remarked a soldier, passing close to the friends. Sergeant Haggerty looked at Portugee and raised his grey eyebrows. The scout shook his head.

"There's 'sign' everywhere," he said. "Red Cloud don't scare that easy."

A sharp bugle call cut across the bustle of the camp. Sergeant McQuinty saluted and left Major Powell. He took the reins of his horse from a waiting soldier and mounted. The commands rang out; the loggers on Porter's wood train called their farewells. Twelve mounted troopers and the sergeant took up their position at the rear of the wagons and the wood train rolled on the road to Fort Phil Kearny.

All in the corral watched it go, the blue uniforms bobbing in the dust behind the rocking log loads, the hunched figures of the teamsters with their long whips raised in a last salute as the teams wheeled eastwards out of the valley. The white dog ran down the trail after them, changed his mind, stood barking at the vanishing horses for some minutes and then came panting back to the corral.

"Good boy," said Major Powell, watching the dog run into the circle. "We'll probably need every bit of help we can get before this is over."

That night they tethered the horses in the corral and doubled the guards. Major Powell, Lieutenant Jenness and Sergeant Haggerty took charge of each shift in turn. Portugee slept through the night beside the wagon with Fortune. The men of the Twenty-Seventh Infantry, in uniform or loggers' shirts, lay in their tents and slept or listened according to their fancy.

On the hills the owls still hooted.

August the second dawned hot and fiery, the red sun coming up with a rush and painting the face of the hills in the west while the valley floor was still dark. The same routine was followed, only this time as Portugee led his party of thirteen loggers up into the trees he had the satisfaction of knowing that Sergeant Haggerty and a company of over thirty picked riflemen waited hidden in the corral, under the capable command of Major Powell—ready for the whole Indian army if they chose to come.

They were joking about the young soldier's big borrowed shirt when it happened. The soldier-woodmen had paused for a rest. The early morning sun slanted down through the trees and one man had spread a blanket between four slender poles to give a patch of shade in which he could sit with rifle across his knees and keep watch.

From his position he could see the other half of the party about two hundred yards away on the far side of a decline that ran down through the trees to the open meadow below. Portugee Phillips, half hidden, motionless, mounted guard a little higher up the slope. The horses were tethered between the two parties, watched by Corporal Riley with a rifle under his arm.

"I reckon the logger that loaned you that shirt is havin' a tight time in your uniform," said one of the soldiers, leaning on his ax and grinning at the offending red check as its wearer leaned back against the trunk of a pine. The other men were guffawing at the joke and their laughter drowned the "whirr" and "smack" of the first arrow.

Nor did they see the red blood stain the vivid shirt. The logger was transfixed, his eyes wide in surprise, his mouth still open with dying laughter. The arrow was through his shoulder pinning him to the tree.

Almost in the same instant Portugee fired from the opposite slope. Up the hill, an Indian sprang to his feet, reached forwards as if he were diving into water and, with the bow still clutched in his outstretched hand, fell face down on the pine needles. In this position he slithered across the slope, leaving a long furrow behind him.

One awful second of stunned hesitation held every man
where he stood.

"Hostiles!" bawled Corporal Riley unnecessarily. "Watch
out!" Acting on a prearranged plan, both parties grabbed their
guns and ran for the horses. The guard beneath the blanket
awning leaped forward and reaching up to the shocked soldier
in the check shirt gave a violent wrench that pulled the arrow
clean out. White-faced and reeling, the logger clutched his
shoulder. Blood ran between his fingers as the pair staggered
down the slope. Above them Portugee fired again, trying to
cover the retreat.

The Sioux slipped like red ghosts through the trees. Again
came the "whirr" of arrows. This time the horses were the
target. Corporal Riley, hanging grimly on to all the reins he
could gather, was dragged down the gulley as the frightened,
wounded beasts reared and plunged in confusion.

The first man had almost reached them when the tethers
broke. Kicking and twisting, ten horses scattered into the
woods. Riley hung desperately to the reins of the remaining
three, although a blow of one threshing hoof knocked him
nearly insensible. The soldiers bunched in the bottom of the
decline, kneeling with rifles leveled, seeking the elusive foe;
Portugee came slithering down the slope as the guard and
wounded man tumbled together into the group.

Corporal Riley was now sitting dazedly on the ground, his
arm twisted up in the reins, his forehead split open from the
kick. Portugee took quick command as arrows sang towards
them.

"You two—on that horse," he yelled. "Get down to the
meadows. Run. We'll hold them here as long as we can."

Two soldiers climbed up on to one horse and with a man
hanging alongside on either stirrup they set off down the
gulley A group followed, dodging from tree to tree. The
guard had pushed the wounded Check-shirt to Corporal Riley's
side and was calmly leveling his rifle up the hill. He fired,
cursed briefly and fired again. The flitting red shadows seemed
on all sides. It was only a matter of minutes before they were
overrun.

Portugee dropped his rifle and loosed Fortune's reins from Riley's arm. He pulled the horse over to Check-shirt and, calling to him to stand, swung the man's uninjured arm round his own shoulder and heaved him upright. Somehow he got the logger half over the saddle and was struggling to push one leg up when a hand appeared from the other side, clutched the logger's pants and dragged him farther on to the horse. It was Riley, dazed and blinded by blood, but trying to help.

"Hang on," said Portugee. "He'll take you, just hang on." And he wacked Fortune's rump and sent him careering down the hillside after the others. That left three men and one horse.

Riley collapsed again to the ground. The guard was still shooting carefully whenever he saw a movement in the trees, but all around the painted bodies began to jump forward and shrill war hoops resounded through the woods.

Portugee pulled out his Navy, and helped Riley to his feet. The guard flung his rifle down, ammunition gone, and picked up a long woodsman's axe.

"Get goin'," he cried to Portugee. "I'll hold them—long as I can."

"Not likely," yelled the scout. He swung the Navy up and fired twice at the warriors gathering on the immediate slopes above. "Help me get the corporal up."

Between them they pushed Riley into the saddle.

"I'm all right now," he gasped. "Get! Get!"

"Right," yelled Portugee. "C'mon."

The horse neighed shrilly as he spun it round to face the meadows. Riley, recovering, reached out and grabbed the reins, jerking like mad and urging the beast forwards as with one shrilling war cry the Indians surged down the slope.

And then they were careering down the gulley, Portugee and the soldier on either side of the horse, their hands wrapped round the stirrup straps, their feet hardly touching the ground in gigantic strides. Arrows whistled by, smacking into the trees as the three weaved an erratic path to the meadows. The long, bloodcurdling cries of the braves followed them closely as they burst out of the trees.

Far ahead in a scattered line were the others, running for the

distant camp. Fortune and the wounded man were with them
now, the whole desperate cavalcade strung out like the field at
the end of a race—only this was a race for their very lives.
Dust hung over the trail and the heat beat up in waves from
the grass after the cool shade of the woods.

Out of the corner of his eye Portugee saw many Indians
breaking cover along the whole stretch of woodland. Painted,
near naked figures, hideously colored in yellows and blues and
greens. The sun flashed on the tomahawks.

The scout hung on grimly to the stirrup straps and pounded
along beside the corporal's horse. On the other side the guard
ran determinedly, his shirttails flapping behind him, the ax still
grasped in his free hand, glinting as it swung up and down.
How can he carry it? wondered Portugee, and then became
conscious of the heavy Navy swinging in his own right hand.

Corporal Riley had recovered enough to lash the horse and
yell encouragement. The flying hooves churned the grass, and
every lurch forward seemed to drag Portugee's arm out of its
socket. He clung to the strap and tried to keep up, his mind
shouting to the swearing rider above him to slow down, his
breath coming in great rasping gasps, but he was too winded to
give words to his thoughts. The sky began to blind him; lights
flashed before his eyes and blood colored his vision. They'd
never do it.

Behind them the Indians came on, some thirty of them
running at an incredible pace and gaining slowly.

Suddenly Portugee was flung through the air. A great blow
shot him away from the horse's flank, the prairie spun and
he was rolling over and over in the dirt. Clutching his pistol
in a torn and bleeding hand, he came to his knees.

The horse was on its back, its legs lashing. The saddle was
on the ground beneath it, the girth snapped. Ten yards in
front, Corporal Riley crawled in circles on his hands and
knees. A weird, sustained howling came from the pursuing
Indians, swooping now like hawks to the kill.

Portugee scrambled to his feet and ran to the corporal,
jerking him upright.

"Run," he yelled in Riley's ear. "Run."

Riley hesitated. "My horse," he croaked thickly. "Got to have my horse."

"No time," cried Portugee, his straining face close to the wounded and bewildered man. "C'mon."

The corporal shook himself and stumbled towards the horse, which was now staggering to its feet, flanks heaving. Two arrow shafts stuck out of its rump.

The scout hesitated. The guard with the ax had run on. Riley, oblivious to his danger, was walking back toward the horse, his hands outstretched. The Indians whooped again, their prey was almost within scalping distance.

Portugee brought the Navy up with both hands to keep it steady but the pistol waved in a crazy arc; he couldn't hold it still, try as he might. The Indians came on, yelling in triumph, brown bodies glistening in the sun. The nearest brave ran with long effortless strides, his arm raised behind his head with the tomahawk poised to throw.

Portugee's finger tightened on the trigger, but suddenly the Indian's face disappeared. For an infinitesimal second the brave hung poised in the air, a great red hole where the right eye had flashed a moment before. As the body crumpled, Portugee heard the echo of a shot far behind.

With a great effort he swung the Navy and dropped the second Indian in his tracks. Far away a fusillade of rifle fire broke out. The panting Indians hesitated. Another fell to his knees, sprawling forward over his scalping knife.

Portugee called hoarsely to the corporal, and once more they broke into a stumbling run. As they came towards the shallow river Portugee could see the kneeling figures of the infantrymen firing coolly, rifles raised in the classic Army Manual pose. The shots from the Springfield-Allens whistled past the fugitives into the scattering Indians. Through the cool water they splashed and up the bank beyond. Then they were all running together, the riderless horse cantering before them.

A last arrow slithered at their feet but its sting was gone. It bounced on the trail.

So they came to the high boards of the wagon-box corral.

The guard first with his ax, then the horse, and far behind, Corporal Riley and Portugee, surrounded by the riflemen who had run out to their rescue. Through the gaps they slithered, sprawling on the grass, rolling over, gasping for breath.

Dimly Portugee heard the ringing notes of a bugle sounding the alarm.

6

THE
WAGON-BOX FIGHT

"Great heavens, Major. Look at the Indians."

Portugee sat up as he heard the words and found that he was still grasping the naked Navy in his right hand. He was breathing heavily from the run, and other exhausted figures sprawled round him. He reloaded the pistol, sitting where he was on the grass, and then got to his feet. A strong arm grasped his as he did so and helped him up.

"You all right, John?" Sergeant Haggerty bent towards him, deep concern on his bronze face. "Your hand's bleedin'. Are you hurt?"

Portugee shook his head. "I'm all right! How are the others? The corporal was . . ."

"Riley's all right." Haggerty nodded towards the big Conestoga wagon that stood just inside the corral, its canvas covers partly drawn back. "Gettin' his head bandaged. The others are O.K. too. I've tethered Fortune by the wagon there."

Portugee looked around the corral. Fortune and a small group of horses were roped tight against the other Conestoga inside the north end of the corral. The two timber wagons were already in place across the entrances to the wagon-box. All around the circle, men were standing in small groups looking out across the meadows. Some were in uniform, some were still wearing the tattered loggers' "disguise." A further party of soldiers were staggering back and forth across the corral under the direction of Major Powell, carrying the heavy ammunition boxes from the central dump and distributing them in the upturned wagon beds.

"Look at them come. Just look at them."

The astonished voice of the soldier standing near the captain caused Portugee and Sergeant Haggerty to turn their attention to the scene beyond the circle of wagons.

From every direction the Indians were approaching. Over the hills from the north and west, along the ridges to the east, everywhere they made their wild and barbarous appearance, chanting their war songs and filling the whole valley with sound. Riding in and out of the war parties, beating drums and shouting words of encouragement to the young braves, were the medicine men and older warriors.

"Red Cloud's sure made plans to swallow the whole dang corral," growled Haggerty. "You think we can fight him off, John?"

Portugee swung round. "We can have a durned good try, Tom—but first I must get me one of these new rifles." And he strode across the corral to the pile of crates in the center.

"You all right now, Mr. Phillips?" asked Major Powell as Portugee selected one of the Springfield-Allens and started to cram fistfuls of cartridges into his pockets. The scout nodded and Powell pointed to the south entrance. "Perhaps you'd have a word with Lieutenant Jenness, then. And tell him not to delay too long out there."

Portugee looked out of the corral. The lieutenant was standing with a small group of soldiers by the cooking fires about twenty yards outside the wagons. He was sweeping the hills with fieldglasses and talking to the sergeant at his side. As Portugee made his way through a gap between the wagons he noticed that most of the horses were herded together near the end of the row of tents on the west side of the corral. Although they were hobbled and watched by several soldiers they were moving uneasily, their heads tossing and ears twitching at the growing din around them. "We'll probably lose the lot when it starts," thought the scout as he walked out towards Lieutenant Jenness, his rifle under his arm.

"We reckon that's Red Cloud up there," said Sergeant Hoover, as Portugee came up.

"Take a look, Mr. Phillips," added Lieutenant Jenness, holding out the fieldglasses to the scout.

The group of Indians on the peak in the east leaped large into view as Portugee adjusted the glasses. There were perhaps half a dozen of them, mounted on war ponies, their heads bedecked with gorgeous war bonnets, their lances bearing crimson pennants that waved in the breeze. Portugee moved the glasses slowly to the right. Behind the chiefs, other groups of Indians were scattered in an extended line down the ridge into the woods.

He brought the glasses back to the mounted chiefs. They were on a fine vantage point, just beyond range of the soldiers' guns, looking straight down into the corral and commanding a view of the whole valley beyond.

"Red Cloud, all right," grunted the scout. "The others . . . I ain't sure but . . . Crazy Horse, maybe. And Man-Afraid, there at the end."

"Man-Afraid?" Lieutenant Jenness frowned, perplexed.

" 'Man-Afraid-of-his-Horses' is his full Indian name," explained Portugee, "Chief of the Oglalas."

"Well, we'll make him 'Man-Afraid-of-the-Soldiers' before the day is out," said the lieutenant. At that moment a great shout went up from the corral, and, turning, they saw that the whole imposing army of Indians on the north side of the valley had reached the Big Piney and were urging their horses across.

In one great line they forded the shallow stream, the water spuming upwards before them like white smoke as a thousand flashing hoofs churned the riverbed.

"Men, take your places in the wagon-boxes." Major Powell's voice cut across the hubbub. Lieutenant Jenness turned towards the corral and a few seconds later they were inside. The men crouching by the wagons rolled the heavy wheels across the gap. The fight, which had started in the pinewoods in the early morning, was about to blaze into a full-scale battle.

Portugee took a place in a wagon-bed on the west side of the corral. Two men were already in the box, an anxious young

soldier peering out over the top boards at the advancing warriors and an old man, whose logging clothes could not disguise
the bearing of an experienced soldier. Methodically he was
removing the laces from his boots. Portugee clambered over
the lower wall of the wagon and squatted down on the ammunition crate inside.

"Frank Robertson." The old soldier introduced himself.
"This here is young Sam Gibson. Never seen so many Indians
before in his life." He went on with his task.

Portugee nodded to the youngster and watched Robertson
as he joined the laces together and made a large loop in one
end. This he carefully tied over his right foot and then made a
smaller loop in the other end. Portugee noted that several old
hands in the other wagon-beds were doing the same thing. If
the Indians broke the barricade and all was lost he knew that
these men were determined not to be captured. They would
stand up, slip the smaller loop over the trigger of the rifle
and then, putting the muzzle under the chin, would take
their own lives. The fate of the logger lariated from the wood
train a few days before was a clear indication of what to
expect if Red Cloud won the day.

Portugee looked slowly around the circle. Everywhere the
men were crouched in their positions. Lieutenant Jenness was
in a box next to the southern entrance of the corral with
Sergeant Hoover and several other soldiers. Beyond them, the
cooking fires still smoked, and Portugee could see the blackened coffee kettles that the cooks had left beside the fires in the
hurried retreat into the corral. Farther round the circle he
could pick out other familiar figures; the wounded logger with
his shoulder now bandaged, leaning back against the boards, a
rifle in his hand; the guard who had run with them through
the woods, the ax which he had carried now stuck into the
top of the wagon-box; Corporal Riley, his head bandaged,
standing upright watching the Indians on the eastern peak;
Sergeant Haggerty, who silently raised a thumb in greeting as
he saw Portugee looking. And in the center, Major Powell,
standing on the remainder of the ammunition boxes, gazing

across to the Big Piney. An orderly and a bugler were with him.

There was a complete, uncanny silence within the corral as the fifty-seven men waited and listened to the thousands gathering on every side.

"Hey, look at this." Young Sam Gibson turned round and pulled at the scout's shoulder. Portugee and Robertson rose and the three gazed out at the enemy.

The mass of Indians had halted on the bank of the Big Piney and their line of battle stretched in a curve almost as far as the eye could see. All were arrayed in the full finery of war. Each face was painted in brilliant colors, yellow, blue, green, vermilion—no two alike, each seeming more horrible than its neighbor. The proud warbonnets tossed in the wind, the buffalo war-shields were brandished on high. Vivid pennants waved from the lances; bows were strung; quivers full of barbed arrows; scalping knives, tomahawks, old muzzle-loading rifles flashed in the sun . . . and here and there a brave more impudent than the rest rode rorward to flourish a captured modern rifle, a shocking souvenir of the Fetterman massacre.

Chiefs could be seen riding up and down along the line, exhorting their warriors to deeds of heroism, shouting Indian chants and occasionally wheeling their horses to hurl pidgin-English taunts at the waiting soldiers and challenging them to come out and fight like men. Dust rose in a cloud above the straining army.

But this spectacle, as impressive as it seemed, was not the thing that had caught young Gibson's eye. Following his outstretched arm, Portugee saw a small group of Indians on foot running along behind the line of tents outside the corral. They carried bells, shaggy buffalo hides and whips.

"They're after the horses," he said to the young soldier. "They'll try and stampede the stock."

At that moment a party of mounted warriors detached itself from the end of the Indian line and thundered towards the corral. They came individually at regular intervals, circling nearer and nearer the wagon-box as rapidly as their fleet-footed ponies could carry them. And at each turn the rider would suddenly disappear, throwing himself upon the side of his pony, one foot in the rawhide loop on the pony's chest, the other leg crooked over the top of the neck, half hidden by the tossing mane. With both hands free the brave would bring rifle or arrow up beneath the racing steed's neck.

The pony seemed to fly, unguided by bridle rein or spur. In this position, hidden from the soldiers, each warrior would fire, load and fire again as often as he was able.

The first arrows streamed over the wagons and dug slanting into the ground behind the defenders. The first musket balls thudded into the boards.

Gibson ducked hurriedly.

Under the cover of these daring horsemen, voluntarily running the gauntlet of possible fire from the corral, the shrieking braves with the bells neared the struggling herd.

Major Powell signaled to Lieutenant Jenness, who immediately stood up and waved to the guards. The three soldiers began a crouching run back towards the wagons while the men in the lieutenant's wagon-box opened a steady covering of fire.

"Why don't we bring the horses inside?" demanded Gibson above the din.

Old Frank Robertson gave him a pitying glance. "Major decided to let them have the horses," he said. "We got a dozen in here already. What you think is goin' to happen when musket balls and fire arrows start rainin' down?"

Portugee glanced at Fortune and the other horses packed tight against the Conestoga. They seemed quiet enough for the moment.

The bedlam of bells and dancing Indians finally panicked the hobbled herd. They scattered in all directions; running among the retreating guards and galloping wildly across the open plains when their hobbles snapped.

Lieutenant Jenness's party continued to shoot steadily. A brave suddenly clutched the buffalo robe he was waving and rolled forward. The bunch of tiny bells bounced over the ground, to be caught by a flying hoof and tossed high above the dust-filled air.

"There go last damned horses," came a weird English cry from one of the Indians.

A guard fell, struck by an Indian bullet. Almost as he crumpled to the gound one of the circling horsemen, a powerfully built brave on a superb war pony, dashed at full speed between the wagons and the tents towards him. The warrior grasped the pony's mane with one hand and leaning down seized the soldier with the other and lifted him across the pony in front of him. Without slackening speed he swung round behind the tents and, racing out at the other end, cast the body to the ground, reared the pony on its hind legs and waved a bleeding scalp derisively at the corral.

Young Sam Gibson slid his rifle over the wagon boards and in a fit of horrified rage, pulled the trigger.

"Hold your fire," roared Major Powell, and Portugee pulled the boy down.

"Wait, lad, our turn will come," he said quietly.

The Indian horsemen now turned to the running braves and, without stopping, each man leaped up behind a mounted warrior and was carried out of range. The two guards reached the wagon-boxes and slipped inside. Lieutenant Jenness ordered his men to cease fire.

Again silence settled over the wagon-boxes. Old Frank Robertson nudged Portugee and jerked his head to the hills in the east. Major Powell was watching through his glasses. Suddenly he put them down and turned to his men.

"Here they come," he said. "When I give the word, shoot to kill."

Up on the hill, a blanket waved once, twice, above the heads of the mounted chiefs.

A great, spine-chilling, prolonged screaming rose from the assembled Indians, and as Portugee and his companions flung themselves to the top of their wagon-bed the whole front line of Sioux cavalry exploded towards them.

Across the length of the valley advanced a tidal wave of hurtling horseflesh and frenzied warriers. The thunder of hoofs rose in a continuous drumming that drowned even the war whoops, and it seemed as if nothing could stop the charge sweeping over the corral and engulfing all within it.

The very earth vibrated. The arrows sticking in the top of the wagon-box quivered as the sound rolled onwards. The rifles over the boards lifted, steadied, and the defenders took aim between the feathered shafts.

Nearer and nearer came the Sioux cavalry; a dark line of bobbing horses, the wild colors of the painted warriors poised above them. Behind, like a curtain, rolled a dun-colored cloud of dust. Suddenly the advancing wave winked and flashed with light as the braves fired their muskets in a ragged volley. An arch of arrows rose in a black, graceful curve against the sky and sang down towards the wagon-boxes.

Sam Gibson swallowed hard and crouched a little lower.

"Steady, lad," said old Robertson quietly, out of the corner of his mouth. Portugee was watching Major Powell's upraised hand.

A hundred and fifty yards. A hundred yards. Seventy-five . . .

The fingers tightened on the triggers. The arrows fell "smack-smack-smack" into the wagons.

The Indian faces loomed up. Gibson could see the straining open mouths that curiously made no sound against the fantastic thunder of hoofs.

Powell's hand dropped.

"Now!" yelled Portugee.

A long sheet of flame rippled down the entire side of the corral. The crash of shots and rolling blue smoke followed.

The center of the Indian line reeled before the deadly volley. Horses and warriors came plunging down but others were waiting behind and into the gaps made by the rifle fire leaped the second wave of war ponies, each warrior lashing his mount to an even faster pace in an effort to be the first to reach the barricade and "count coup."

Now, according to every experience of warfare against the white foe, was their moment of triumph. Their sheer weight of numbers filled the empty places in the line. The whole

charge came confidently on towards what they thought were
the defenseless soldiers struggling to reload their empty
rifles.

Only this time it didn't happen. With barely a second's
pause another sheet of flame came from the corral. And this
time the blow was worse, for the very nearness of the Indians
prevented even the wildest shot from failing to find its mark.

Down tumbled the wonderful ponies. Backwards staggered
the dazed warriors, and into the growing heap of heaving
bodies the relentless bullets from the new rifles tore without
respite.

The long line of Sioux cavalry broke and poured in two
streams around either end of the corral, seeking a gap in the
defenses and relief from the awful stream of fire. But from
every side the tiny fort spat flame. More riders dropped as
daring young bloods forced their ponies straight at the wagon-
boxes in vain efforts to reach the defenders.

At last, the puzzled Indians withdrew to the south. The
Springfield-Allens, one by one, grew silent and a dark cloud
of dust drifted slowly across the quiet corral.

Out from the wagons bounded a small white shape, barking
furiously at the retreating enemy. It was the white dog who
had remained discreetly hidden throughout the action but
who now deemed it prudent to join the attack. The tension
broke. Sam Gibson sat back on the wagon-bed, the sweat pouring from his face. Frank Robertson reached in his jacket
pocket and pulled out a plug of tobacco.

"Well, the Colonel was right," said Portugee. "They never
knowed what hit them."

The old soldier said nothing. He was watching the low
ridge to the north of the corral.

"I reckon there's a whole parcel of the varmints over
there," he grunted and, opening the breech of his rifle, lifted
it up and blew gently down the barrel, never taking his eyes
from the distant ground.

Sergeant Hoover ran across the corral and spoke urgently
to Major Powell. The major sent his orderly for Sergeant
Haggerty, and while Portugee's old friend adjusted the cap-

tain's fieldglasses and set watch on the distant Indians, Powell walked to the wagon beside the south entrance.

"The lieutenant's been shot."

"Lieutenant Jenness is dead."

The word passed rapidly round the circle. Portugee saw Powell pull a blanket over the huddled shape beside the wagon-bed and, after a moment's pause, come striding towards him.

"Mr. Phillips. I want a man from each wagon to go out there to strike those tents. They give too much cover to the hostiles."

Portugee rose to his feet and looked at the line of tents in question.

"I'll need five men," said the scout quietly. "We'll cut them down."

"Can we cover them, Major?" asked Frank Robertson. He jerked his rifle in the direction of the ridge. "There's a parcel of braves crawled up over there and I aim to keep them pinned down where they can't do no harm."

Major Powell nodded. "You act as you think fit, Robertson. But don't waste ammunition."

Robertson looked at him steadily and said nothing. Portugee gathered four men from the nearby wagons, looked at Gibson and said, "Come on, lad." The six slipped out between the wheels and with bared knives ran towards the line of tents.

Almost immediately Frank Robertson's rifle cracked behind them and a puff of dust went up from the crest of the ridge. Sam Gibson flung himself face down on the ground at the sound of the shot, then seeing who was firing, got up and ran shamefacedly after the others.

They reached the first tent, split up and swiftly slashed the guy ropes. The canvas crumpled slowly. Gibson kicked the poles away and the billowing sheets collapsed to the ground. They made for the second tent. Back in the corral, Robertson watched the ridge like a hawk, and more soldiers by the north Conestoga wagon climbed out to give them added covering fire if necessary.

The second tent came down, and then the third. The little

party moved slowly down the line, hacking and kicking at the tough canvas. There were only two tents left standing when a cry of warning came from the corral.

"Look out! Hostiles!"

From the bed of the Piney, down which they had come half hidden by the drifting dust cloud, a small band of Indians rode up on to the meadows and urged their ponies towards the tent line.

At the same moment, methodically, Frank Robertson began shooting at the low ridge to the north where a crowd of redskins, wriggling through the grass, had gained a position from which they could fire directly into the corral.

Portugee paused, his knife at a guy rope, coolly calculating the distance between the tents and the oncoming braves. The soldiers with him redoubled their efforts and, even as the scout turned back to cut the rope, the dirty green canvas collapsed at his feet.

"Right," yelled Gibson, now beside himself with excitement and satisfaction. "The last one," and he ran forward to the remaining tent.

"Back, the rest of you." Portugee saw no sense in risking more lives than were necessary. "We'll see to this." And he tore after young Sam. The remaining soldiers scattered back towards the corral.

The last tent proved a brute—or else with only two of them to do the job it took twice as long to sever the guy ropes. Whatever it was it seemed to the scout that he had sadly miscalculated. Gibson was still at the far end pushing the tent pole, and one whole line of ropes remained holding the tent wall taut when the redskins came within range.

Two bullets tore through the canvas, but whether from the rifles in the fort or the Indian muskets Portugee couldn't tell. Frank Robertson had turned his attention from the ridge and was firing now at the war ponies bearing down on them. One pony crumpled to the ground, flinging the rider over its head, and Portugee heard the sickening snap of bone as the Indian struck the ground.

He dropped the knife and jerked the Navy loose, yelling

at Sam Gibson to run for the wagons. In one practiced movement he lifted, cocked, aimed and fired. A second Indian swayed forward, clutching the pony's mane before him. The others were almost on them when a third shot from Frank Robertson hurled another brave from the saddle.

The frightened pony wheeled, cannoned into the one next to it, and both ran straight into the swaying tent. A rope snapped, twisted round Portugee's leg and dragged him to the ground. The whooping brave, still clinging to the one pony, tried desperately to extricate himself from the tangle of canvas. The scout was dragged, clawing the ground with one hand, his pistol waving wildly in the other, as he sought to bring down the warrior.

Sam Gibson suddenly appeared brandishing his long knife. He took the strain on the rope twisted round the scout's leg and with one blow cut him free. Portugee rolled over.

The Indian on the pony jerked out of the crumpled canvas and wheeled his neighing mount round on its two hind legs. The second wounded brave staggered behind him. In a flash the warrior had seized his companion and hauled him up on to the pony. At breakneck speed they raced away from the line of fallen tents. A third rider wheeled in the distance amidst a fusillade of shots from the fort and spurred after them.

Sam Gibson charged from the tent line and in an excess of zeal hurled his knife with a yell at the vanishing riders.

"Come on, lad. You've done enough," cried Portugee, and in answer to shouted commands and waving arms from the wagon-boxes the two sprinted for shelter.

"Durn young fool," growled Robertson, pulling Gibson over the barricade. "You want to collect scalps or somethin'?"

"Thank you, Mr. Phillips," said Major Powell as the scout tumbled behind the wagon-box. And to the young soldier, "You did nobly, lad."

Gibson grinned and picked up his rifle. At that moment Sergeant Haggerty cried from his vantage point on the ammunition boxes, "Major, here they come again!"

And once more the defenders stood to arms in the hot sun.

The second attack on the wagon-box was prefaced by a sudden burst of fire from the Indian snipers to the north. Crawling up the bed of the Piney from the hills beyond, some scores of braves now lay below the long low ridge. The occasional dark head, the notched eagle feathers flashing in the sun, the forked sticks in which the braves rested their muskets were all that could be seen of the force that had so patiently assembled some seventy-five yards from the corral.

Frank Robertson had kept them pinned down behind the brow of the hill with his steady, accurate shooting, but now several braves had rolled small boulders up through the grass and, sheltering behind them, began to drop shots directly into the corral. Although, as with most Indians, they were poor marksmen, the whining musket balls forced everyone to keep behind the shelter of the wagon-beds, and men going for more ammunition had to crawl across the clearing to avoid being hit.

As the Sioux cavalry to the south began walking their horses in circles and chanting war songs, a sudden column of smoke rose from behind the hill.

"Here it comes," grunted Frank Robertson, who had hardly taken his eyes from the ridge. The words had no sooner left his lips than a dozen black trails of smoke shot into the air and came blazing towards the soldiers.

The fire arrows fell at random, some in the wagon boards, to be knocked out by the nearest soldiers, some in the churned-up center of the corral. Soon the crackle of burning grass could be heard everywhere and acrid smoke spiraled upwards dimming the bright sunlight.

"One man from every wagon," roared Sergeant Haggerty, trampling out the flames round the ammunition boxes. "Th' rest keep shootin'."

Cursing soldiers stumbled among the flames, stamping at the smoldering grass, beating down the flames with hats and jackets. Portugee heard the neigh of frightened horses. He looked anxiously towards Fortune but kept his place in the wagon-bed. the white dog had jumped up on the covered wagon and was barking at the thickening smoke. The scout could barely see the defenders on the other side of the circle.

Bullets whistled in the thick air, plunging through the canvas of the Conestoga wagons, churning into the stores. A sack of flour, punctured by a ball, poured its white contents in a steady stream over the tailboard; a punctured water barrel emptied unnoticed over the feet of the nervous horses.

Through the confusion rang the urgent bugle call of the "charge," Major Powell's methods of warning everyone that the Sioux cavalry were once more bearing down on the fort.

"All right, all right," said Robertson, easing himself up against the stout planks as the bugler repeated the call. "Only it ain't us that's goin' anywhere."

The Indians roared in once more, only this time they did not advance en masse but, with greater caution, resorted to the habitual "circling" attack favored by the tribes of the plains. First the chiefs led off, followed at regular intervals by the warriors until the entire force of more than a thousand riders was circling the wagons as rapidly as the fleet-footed war ponies could run. In this order, keeping up a savage chorus of yells and war whoops, the braves gradually contracted their circle, coming nearer and nearer the smoking wagon-box until close enough to let fly with bullet and arrow at the soldiers.

The tops of the wagon-beds ripped and splintered under the constant shots and gouging arrows. Forced below the boards, the soldiers thrust their rifles through every available loophole . . . and still they waited.

Made bold by the continued silence, the warriors closed in, rising in their saddles as they imagined the defenders all dead and victory in their grasp.

"Fire!"

Once again the deadly rifles roared out without cease. Once again the shattered ranks of the pitifully brave Sioux hurled themselves at the barricade.

And once again they were repulsed with bloody loss.

Up on the eastern peak, as the smoke from the dying fires cleared, the chiefs could be seen in agitated council. Mirrors flashed their messages across the Big Piney. The cavalry withdrew to the edge of the valley and the Indians began to debate a new plan to overwhelm the gallant fort.

"Sergeant Haggerty's wounded."

Portugee heard the shout as he wiped the barrel of his hot rifle. He put down the gun and, with a brief word to his companions, set off in a rapid crawl across the clearing. The occasional musket ball from the snipers on the ridge screamed across the fort and the scout had to push aside the blackened arrows still sticking up in the earth in fantastic numbers like bent corn.

The sergeant was sitting on the ground by the covered wagon, his left arm limp and sleeve bloodstained. He grinned weakly at Portugee.

"Get back to your post, John," he whispered. "I'm all right."

Corporal Riley was cutting away the sleeve with a knife. "Got hit first off," he said. "Wouldn't lie down. He was firing with one arm—I don't know how he managed to load."

"We'll get you comfortable, Tom," said Portugee. "When that bandage is on, I'll help you to . . . "

"When that bandage is on," roared Haggerty with a sudden burst of energy. "I'm goin' back to that wagon-bed and I'm goin' to use this." He waved a Colt in his sound hand. "You get back to your position." His voice dropped and he grinned again although there was a tired look in his old eyes. "And thanks, John," he added quietly.

The lull now gave the defenders time to take stock of their perilous situation. The battle had commenced in the early hours of the morning with the skirmish in the pinery. It was now well past noon and the absence of any messenger between the wagon-box corral and the fort, as well as the smoke visible from Pilot Hill, would have told Colonel Wessells that they were under attack. A relief force might be on its way even now. But could they bank on this? And what was Red Cloud planning in his hurried council-of-war?

Major Powell made a round of the corral. Lieutenant Jenness and the soldier scalped as the horses were stampeded were dead. Another private had been killed in the second attack. Sergeant Haggerty was wounded and five more men besides. Out on the plain the Sioux dead lay in scores; the loss suffered by the gallant defenders was miraculously low.

But the long hours of tension, the smoldering grass and the burning sun now brought an altogether different hardship—thirst! The water barrel had almost run dry before the leak was discovered. A few men had canteens of water with them in the wagon-boxes but these were soon drained as the fighting proceeded. Now, with the temperature on the open plain reaching its peak, some of the wounded began to cry for water and brush clumsily at the flies that buzzed around their unwashed wounds.

Portugee spoke to Sam Gibson, the picture of Sergeant Haggerty's drawn and tired old face fresh in his mind.

"Are you game for another trip outside, Sam?" he asked as the young soldier knotted his kerchief round his forehead to stop the sweat running into his eyes. The boy looked at him, puzzled, but nodded.

"If we take a rope apiece and slip out the back of the big wagon, I reckon we can crawl over to the cookin' fires and reach them kettles," the scout explained. "Cookie tells me they're filled for coffee. Then we could drag them back by the ropes."

Sam Gibson stood up, ready. Portugee started to say something to Frank Robertson but the old soldier picked up his gun and cut the scout short.

"If you two are fool enough to go out again I'd better do all I can to keep them varmints quiet." And he eyed the ridge shrewdly and began to adjust the sights of his rifle.

Permission given—with a caution—by Major Powell, the two volunteers slipped out from the north end of the wagon-box, moving through the long grass on their bellies and each dragging a rope behind them. Inside the corral two soldiers paid out the ropes slowly, watched anxiously by Corporal Riley.

Stealthily the pair moved forward. From the low ridge to the north a thin spiral of smoke climbed upwards, ceased and was followed by two thick puffs in quick succession. The hidden braves were signaling to the Indians on the eastern peak. "Probably too busy sending messages to see these two," prayed Riley as the soldier and the scout sneaked through the grass.

Ten yards before the cooking fires they met an obstruction. Sam Gibson, pushing aside a tuft of tall prairie grass, came face to face with a painted warrior!

The eyes glared at the young soldier. The mouth was wide open to draw a breath for a whoop. A fly crawled across the yellow stripes of war paint!

Sam buried his face in the grass and swallowed hard. He let the tufts spring back into place and crawled round the body. Portugee, on his left, grasped his arm and pointed. Just ahead, against the sky, were the black handles of the kettles.

They wriggled past the ashes of the cooking fires and fastened the ends of the rope to each kettle. Then they gave two tugs on the ropes and in answer the lines tautened as the soldiers in the corral took up the slack. Slowly each kettle jerked through the grass; the scout and Gibson wriggled rapidly behind, guiding the bumping vessels.

Suddenly the high-pitched whine of a bullet and the crack of a shot behind them told the two that they were discovered. Flattening closer to the dusty earth, they sneaked forward as quickly as they dared.

Another shot came, the bullet plowing into the grass beside Portugee. Frank Robertson began to shoot back, and two other soldiers opened up a steady fire at the ridge.

The kettle in front of Portugee "twanged," jumped as a musket ball plowed into the top. Water splashed over the scout's face. Reaching up he grabbed the handle with one hand, tore off a tuft of grass with the other and stuffed it into the hole. To do so he had to rise up on one elbow. The corral loomed closer. Gibson's feet were scrabbling the ground a few yards in front and under the wheels of the end wagon Portugee could see the group of soldiers hauling on the ropes.

Bullets kicked up the dust around the scout, stinging his face and causing him to duck involuntarily.

"Get down, down!" yelled Corporal Riley. Portugee

crawled on. The kettles rocked as the soldiers hauled more
swiftly on the ropes. In one last scramble Sam Gibson got to
his knees and bolted through the gap. Portugee rolled sideways and with one swift movement heaved himself under the
wagon. As they rested panting just inside the corral, Corporal
Riley dragged the kettles into shelter. The white dog sniffed
round them, licking at the wet sides. The firing stopped.

Riley held out a tin mug to the panting pair.

"Here," he said. "You two sure deserve first taste."

Sam Gibson took a mouthful, screwed up his face and splut-
tered. "Gee," he cried. "Have we gone all the way for that?"

Portugee swallowed. The water was warm, gritty. The
cooks had poured it over the coffee grouts, ready for the next
boiling.

Corporal Riley lifted one of the kettles and moved round
the wagon towards the wounded men. "Coffee grouts or not,"
he called over his shoulder, "these boys can sure use it."

While Sam Gibson made his way round the circle of weary
soldiers, the scout went to speak to Sergeant Haggerty. The
veteran's arm was in a sling but . . . "Comfortable as you
can expect," he said. Portugee spent a few minutes with his
friend, then set off in a crouching run across the corral. He
plumped down on the hot boards. Frank Robertson lay back,
seemingly asleep, his kerchief over his head, his rifle across his
lap. Sam Gibson leaned against the end of the wagon-box,
looking out towards the Big Piney, his head cocked slightly on
one side. He appeared to be listening intently.

Across the corral, Sergeant Hoover called Major Powell's
attention to the Indians on the eastern peak.

"Something's up," cried the soldier, watching a stir of activity on the southeast side of the valley.

A large force of mounted Indians rode slowly out from the
foot of the hills where Red Cloud and his chiefs had appeared
once more on their vantage point. The signal mirrors began to
flash again in the sun.

Major Powell walked out to the center of the corral, a tall,
upright figure, stalking defiantly among the arrow shafts.

When he reached the ammunition boxes his voice rang out briskly to the tired soldiers.

"Take your places, men."

Sergeant Hoover circled the wagon-beds. "They're up to something different this time," he told the occupants of each box. "So you've got to increase your rate of fire. One man to load while the other two shoot. Get it?" He moved slowly round the circle, making sure each man knew the drill.

Frank Robertson snored. He had the old soldier's ability to snatch sleep at any odd moment. Without turning, Gibson reached out with his foot and prodded. Robertson woke up with a snort, pulled the kerchief from his face.

"What the . . . " he exploded.

"Listen," said the boy, so urgently that both the scout and the old soldier looked at him attentively. He turned from the wagon boards. "It's over there," he said, jerking a thumb towards the ridge near the Piney. "But what it is, heaven only knows."

A low, prolonged humming sound came to their ears, growing louder even as they listened. The men across the far side of the corral could hear it now and were looking over their shoulders apprehensively. Major Powell was motionless, his glasses trained on the slope. Far down the valley the party of mounted Indians had reached the trail from the Piney and were drawn up in a long extended line, motionless.

Waiting, it seemed, for something to happen.

The moaning from behind the ridge rose and fell. It had an unearthly quality about it as if all the dead were gathered there to protest at the continuation of the savage battle. Portugee felt the back of his neck prickling and the hair beginning to rise. White-faced, Sam Gibson reached out a shaking hand for his rifle.

Calmly Frank Robertson said: "Ain't nothin' to be afeared of, boy. I heard the Papago at it in the south. They call it an 'eagle song'; a song they sing when they reckon they're nearin' the happy huntin' grounds."

Portugee looked at him and nodded.

"I heard tell of it," he said, "but I ain't never heard it. Why are they doing it now?"

"Get some courage up, I reckon," drawled the indomitable old soldier. "Going to try harder this time."

The chanting from the hidden warriors now rose to a crescendo. There was a cry from the north end of the corral, "Here they come," and the entire line of defenders stood spellbound by the sight that unfolded slowly before them.

It was something Portugee never forgot.

Slowly, so slowly that it held all the defenders hypnotized, unable, it seemed, to lift a finger, the naked bodies of hundreds upon hundreds of Indians wound into sight. They were chanting in terrible unison. They were all on foot and the dust rose in spurts to the crash and stamp of their feet in time to the chant. Only their weapons gave evidence of their warlike intent. Spears, clubs, tomahawks, lances swayed rhythmically above the packed, painted bodies.

In one huge wedge, like a great "V" pointed at the corral, they came on, led by the imposing figure of a chief in a beautiful war bonnet.

"No!" whispered Sam Gibson. "They can't be going to charge. Not on foot! Not against these guns!"

It was Red Cloud's last throw, an attempt to take the corral by sheer weight of flesh, in defiance of the "guns-that-fired-themselves," the terrible shooting they could not understand.

The leading warrior raised his shield and spear as if invoking the Great Spirit in the sky to help him. Then with one ear-splitting scream seven hundred braves hurled themselves at the wagon-box.

A sheet of flame went out from the corral. The warrior leading the charge fell, pierced by a dozen bullets. Undaunted, the wedge of braves came on. So closely were they packed that the dead in the front line were carried forward for several yards by the press of bodies before they fell.

The soldiers fired, and fired and fired again. The rifles burned as they changed from loader to marksman and back to loader. Portugee's head reeled at the ghastly rain of death before him. Right up to the barricades the warriors came. The powerful rifles sent their bullets through not one, but two, or three, bodies at a time.

For one desperate moment the battle hung in the balance. In several places the warriors actually reached the wagons and clawed at the bristling arrows in the boards. The loaders rose with their rifles, prepared to sell their lives dearly if the Indians broke into the corral.

Portugee was using the trusty Navy now, no time even to snatch up more shells for the rifle. Frank Robertson reversed his gun and stood up on the wagon-box, swinging it like a scythe. Hope seemed gone.

And then suddenly the Indians broke and fled.

They could stand no more of the withering fire that poured without cease from the corral. Backwards over the bodies of their comrades they stumbled, deafened by the repeated crash of the Springfield-Allen guns. In a scattered mob they ran for the shelter of the river banks and suddenly the battle was over.

A silence fell on the valley. The defenders stood shaken by their narrow escape. The little fort shimmered and smoked in the sun.

The mounted Indians in the south, who had watched the final charge without attempting to help their brothers, began to ride forward. Silently Sam Gibson pointed and raised his rifle. Frank Robertson gently pushed the boy's arm down.

"No, son," he said. "There's dead enough already."

The Indians were performing the last honor for their dead. No body would be left on the field of battle. They rode a-mong the fallen, watching for a wounded warrior to lift his arm, and then sweeping him up and away without dismounting. Others crawled up from the banks of the Piney and, fixing a loop round the body of a dead brave, began to drag it where it could be carried in mourning to the burial grounds.

The soldiers watched in grim silence. The groups of Indians on the ridge began to disappear down the hill until one lone chief sat there looking down. Then he, too, wheeled his horse and rode away.

Suddenly Portugee heard voices calling his name on the far

side of the corral. A chill clutched his heart, and as he ran a-
mong the broken arrows and scattered equipment he heard
the first "boom" of the cannon from far down the valley. A
thin skirmishing line of blue uniforms was advancing along the
wood trail and the tops of the wagons of the relieving force
from Fort Phil Kearny was just turning the foot of the Sullivants.

When the scout reached the wagon-box, a group of men
silently parted to let him through.

The figure lay back on the boards, the white sling around
the left arm, the fingers of the right hand spread gently on the
ground where a few inches away the Colt lay silent. A faint
smile still lingered on his face but there was blood on the
white hair.

Sergeant Haggerty had fought his last fight for the Twenty-
Seventh.

4th August, 1867

To asst. adjutant-general,
    dept. of the platte,
    fort sedgwick

Sir,
The Colonel commanding Fort Phil Kearny announces to
this command the defeat by units of the Twenty-Seventh In-
fantry of a large force of Sioux Indians under the celebrated
chief Red Cloud, reinforced by the Arapahos and the Chey-
enne, on the 2nd instant, by the Big Piney River south of the
Sullivant Hills, Indian Territory, resulting in the loss to the
savages of over two hundred and eighty warriors known to
have been killed (including the nephew of Red Cloud in the
final assault by the Indians on foot) and the capture of rifles,
saddles, bows, arrows, buffalo robes and other quantities of
equipment left by the hostiles on the field.

The loss to the Twenty-Seventh Infantry was one officer killed, Lieutenant Jenness, and seven enlisted men killed, four in the pine woods during skirmishes preceding the main attack and three in the corral from which the prolonged attacks were repulsed. Three men were wounded (badly) and two slightly.

The energy and rapidity shown during the period preparatory to the action and the bravery displayed resulting in such signal success, reflects the highest credit on both officers and men of the regiment, in particular Major Powell, who commanded throughout the engagement, Lieutenant Jenness and Sergeant Thomas Haggerty, who fell while gallantly leading their men, and also by the civilian scout, Mr. John Phillips.

An estimated total of three thousand Indians participated in the action, and the defeat prompts me confidently to suggest that the present threat to Fort Phil Kearny has been averted and that work aimed at the completion of Fort C. Smith can now proceed, with the eventual re-opening of the Bozeman Trail to follow, providing the necessary reinforcements to staff and maintain these posts are allocated to my command.

Respectfully, I await your instructions.

Signed ....

FORT PHIL KEARNY, HEADQUARTERS POST,
BY THE PINEY FORK OF POWDER RIVER,
INDIAN TERRITORY

7

THE SIOUX
STRIKE BACK

Colonel Wessells paused before reaching for the pen to sign the report. The orderly at the table waited, but as the silence continued he scraped the nib clean, dipped it afresh in the ink and after a few trial scratches on paper turned the report back towards him again and waited for his commanding officer to resume. Perhaps he wished to amplify his request for reinforcements, or add more details of the defeat of the Indians; the orderly coughed politely and held the pen poised.

But Colonel Wessells was lost in thought. A frown creased his forehead as he gazed out of the window. On the slope behind the fort the fresh white crosses of graves stood out from the yellowing grass. The Colonel's hands were clasped behind his back and the fists clenched and unclenched at the sight of the new mounds in the growing cemetery. He turned back into the room and paced thoughtfully across the floor to stop and gaze up at the map on the wall behind his desk. The dark line of Little Goose River, bordered by many red crosses marking the extent of the Indian encampment, leaped to his eye.

What was taking place there now, two days after the battle around the wagon-boxes? *Could* he confidently report that Red Cloud's power was broken; that the great gathering of the tribes was "melting like snow in the summer," as he had once predicted?

It was true that the new rifles had proved effective almost beyond his wildest dreams. It was also true that the hostiles had completely vanished from the valley since their defeat . . . and yet . . . and yet . . . the words of the civilian scouts, the opinion of frontier-hardened officers like Ten Eyck and old soldiers like Sergeant Haggerty returned to trouble his mind. He wished at that moment that he could be in the wide sheltered valley of the Little Goose River, could see for himself Red Cloud's prestige on the wane as the lodge poles came down and the tribes scattered. He *wanted* to believe it, but somehow, for the first time in his army life, he was not quite sure. A tiny flame of doubt burned in his mind. Perhaps the bitter defeat had only hardened the savage's resolution to drive the hated white soldiers back across Crazy Woman's Creek. . . .

The Colonel took refuge in the word "suggest" in the last paragraph of his report. This was his opinion and he had expressed it guardedly. Let General Sherman work it out. He'd go north to establish the third fort along the Bozeman Trail —or hold Fort Phil Kearny for another winter, whatever order came.

He took the pen from his orderly, signed the report swiftly and waved the man away to arrange its immediate dispatch. Then he turned and stood staring at the map again, at Little Goose River.

Had Colonel Wessells been in the valley at that moment it is doubtful whether he would have even considered signing the document. The lodges were still there, stretching away into the distance as far as the eye could see. The villages were deserted but only because every warrior had gone to the great war council, to listen to Red Cloud and the other chiefs as the great Sioux general argued with every ounce of guile and power he could muster to hold the army together.

The return to the vast encampment had been a sorrowful event for the army that had set out the previous day, confident of victory. Carrying their dead and wounded, the procession trailed for more than a mile over the prairie. Runners, mounted on fleet ponies, had taken news of the fighting back to the villages and, as was the custom, all the occupants, young and old, had sallied forth to meet the returning warriors. The scene was boisterous and horrible. Instead of the shouts and songs of victory which greet successful war parties, screams and wails were heard. The war paint and bright colors of victory had given way to a deep black with which all the mourners and friends of the fallen warriors had smeared themselves. And as each family recognized the body of some relative they immediately began hacking their faces, arms and bodies with knives, even cutting off their little finger at the first joint if the dead man was a close relative. Piercing and horrible lamentations rose on all sides as the procession of weary braves wound through the camps.

Aloof, alone, his face, too, daubed with black in token respect of the men killed under his command, Red Cloud rode to the circle of tepees where he had haughtily faced the French scout, Jean Robidoux, weeks before. The medicine men moaned and beat their drums as he dismounted. Stooping, he disappeared into his lodge.

A short time later, before the despair of the squaws had time to spread through the whole encampment, the drums began to throb to Red Cloud's orders. The women and boys grouped beneath the saplings on which, some twenty feet above the ground, platforms for the bodies of the dead braves had been raised in customary Indian "burial," turned to listen to the summons.

Despair changed to curiosity and curiosity to anger as the message spread. The drums summoned a council-of-war, a meeting at which all could speak of the way to revenge their fallen brothers.

Red Cloud opened the council as dawn broke in angry, red light over the valley next morning.

The meeting was long and bitter, and the sun was well beyond its zenith when Red Cloud made his final impassioned speech.

Standing before them, the sun glinting on the eagle feathers of his war bonnet, he looked steadily along the rows of grim faces—at Man Afraid, proud leader of the Oglalas, jealous of Red Cloud's prestige and power—at Crazy Horse, most brilliant captain of the Sioux cavalry—at Black Kettle of the Cheyenne, hereditary enemy of the Sioux but united with them

ever since the terrible massacre by the white soldiers at Sand
Creek—and at many more chiefs and sub-chiefs who had
come to join him after the great council at Laramie. When he
spoke his voice was deep with emotion.

"My people. We have talked the sun through the sky until
we are weary of talking. Some are for giving up the battle;
others for avenging our dead brothers.

"I cannot express the grief that is in my heart. But this sad-
ness does not make *me* weak. Because many lay dead from the
soldiers' bullets *I* will not hide in the hills and watch the white
man eat up the land."

He raised his arm in a gesture that embraced the earth
from horizon to horizon.

"The Great Spirit gave all this to his children; the mountains, the rivers, the prairies. There was room enough for many
tribes and all were happy in their freedom.

"When the white man came we let him come in peace, for
he said that he did not want the prairies but merely to cross to
the mountains in the sunset. We made treaties dividing the
land. But that was not enough."

Red Cloud's voice rose.

"Soon he grew envious and when the yellow metal was
found in the hills he forgot the treaties and came with soldiers
to take everything."

A murmur of agreement ran round the circle of chiefs and
spread through the watching braves. Red Cloud leaned forward, his piercing eyes traveling slowly from one painted
face to another.

"My brothers, I tell you this. The white man's government
does not want just to make a road through our land. He wants
to herd us into little corners and shut us up behind fences, like
guilty ones, watched by men with guns. I was born free. I do
not want to live within walls. I will not give up the sun and the
wind."

His fine voice rang out like a clarion and a shout of assent
went up from the young men. Red Cloud went swiftly on.

"If we give in now we will *never* be left again in peace.
The Government will build more forts, more roads, bring

more 'thunder guns,' eat more of the land until only the desert places are left to the Indian."

"No. No. No!" Many chiefs were on their feet now, shouting their agreement. The Sioux general knew that he had won over all but the few jealous leaders.

"Now," he cried, striking his heart with his fist, "now, when the bitter taste of defeat is still in our throats, we must smash the fort on the Little Piney."

"But what about the magic guns?" cried Man Afraid. "What about the bullets that fall like rain?"

Red Cloud turned on him with a contemptuous look. "The white man has learned how to make terrible weapons, much better for war than these bows and arrows." He kicked the quiver at his feet and raised his proud head again to the crowd. "But if we cannot stand breast to breast and fight like men, then we will strike where they are weak.

"We will strike like wolves!

"When they send food in their wagons—we will take it.

"When they send guns—we will take them.

"When they send messengers—we will kill them."

The war whoops shrilled out.

"We will bar every trail that leads to the fort and starve these jackals into surrender.

"No more treaties! No more battles!

"We will hound them at every turn until they slink like dogs from our land."

The crowd pressed forward, eager to touch their great chief and assure him of their loyalty. Only a few hung back.

Man Afraid left with the Oglalas the same day for the wilderness. The Arapahos struck their lodges and followed . . . but the rest of the great army held firm, strengthened by Red Cloud's words, determined more than ever to shut the white road through the hills.

War parties set out the next day. At Crazy Woman's Crossing they surprised a soldier riding along the trail carelessly, in the belief that the hostiles had taken too much of a beating at the wagon-box to venture on the warpath again.

He paid dearly for his carelessness.

"Hostiles approachin' from the east!"

Jean Robidoux dropped the iron comb he was holding and ran to the stable door. A sentry on the banquette was stabbing a finger out across the stockade wall and calling to the guardhouse.

Figures appeared running to the ladders. The Frenchman joined them and climbed up to the platform to be met by Portugee, who had beaten him by a few yards.

"What is it, mon vieux?" he asked. Portugee pointed to the east without answering.

A small band of Indians on tossing war ponies was racing towards the fort, about half a dozen braves, bunched round a pack horse. They rode in silence, the manes of the ponies flying in the wind, the eagle feathers bobbing above the black heads. Dust rose behind in a long, climbing plume.

As they came within rifle range they wheeled off to left and right, swinging round until they were headed back towards the hills, but each brave twisted in the saddle to watch the lone packhorse gallop on.

Portugee suddenly gripped his friend's arm as the beast came nearer.

A bundle lay across its back and a fan of feathered sticks swayed to the steady rhythm of hoofbeats. The horse came on, slowing as the stockade walls loomed up, until it finally stopped beneath the watching soldiers.

In silence the men looked down at the naked white body and the red head rising and falling with the heaving flanks. A hundred arrows pierced the flesh, arched and tied across the horse's back. Dark streaks mingled with the animal sweat.

When they cut him down and gently removed the gag they found Colonel Wessell's report crumpled into a ball and streaked with war paint, stuffed into the mouth.

The Sioux themselves had answered the Colonel's question. When he wrote again he made no prophecy. The second messenger left with an escort. And from Fort Laramie, along the telegraph wire to the east, flashed the call for instructions—and reinforcements.

8

THE RIDE
INTO PERIL

The order came a week later.

The wires between Fort Sedgewick and the east had hummed with activity for days. General Cook, in his head-quarters by the wide Platte River, had pressed for immediate action. General Sherman had gone to talk with the Indian Department in Washington.

Finally, the great voice of Government that had grandly dispatched the Bozeman Trail Expedition under Colonel Car-rington from Nebraska in May, 1866, now quietly called a halt—and a parley with Red Cloud.

The answer reached Fort Phil Kearny by a solitary, dar-ing messenger, traveling at night to avoid ambush. For Red Cloud had wasted no time in throwing a new ring of death around the fort. He no longer came into the valley, but posted his war parties at a distance; holding the crossing at Crazy Woman's Creek, infesting the Virginia City Road be-hind Lodge Trail Ridge and roaming the lower reaches of the Piney beyond Pilot Hill.

In the north he sent a band to the site of Fort C. Smith, ransacking and burning everything they could find on the way.

A wagon train attempting to reach Fort Phil Kearny with stores and ammunition from Reno Station was turned back by war parties that harassed it without cease every mile of the way. Cursing and chasing the elusive warriors, the escort made futile sallies into the hills. The Indians melted away before them, only to reappear again as soon as vigilance was relaxed and take ugly toll of mules and men with wicked barbed arrows shot from overhanging rocks and pines. Eventually the train turned back for Reno without even reaching Crazy Woman's Crossing.

The dispatch rider was more fortunate. In the dark moonless night he gave the roving bands the slip, and on the third day of his journey approached the fort as dawn was breaking over Pilot Hill.

The instructions he carried were brief.

But Colonel Wessells could not read beyond that one word for a long time. He stared at the creased dispatch in disbelief while the tired messenger stood to attention before the desk.

Again the Colonel read the opening words of the order and stopped. With one hand he waved the messenger away, his eyes still on the dispatch.

"EVACUATION."

No. It could not be true. Not after all this work, all this effort. Not after all this heroism and death.

But it was true.

Colonel Wessells took the dispatch into the orderly room where the officers and the scouts waited impatiently, and handed the paper to Ten Eyck.

"Read it," he said bitterly. "Aloud. I can't." And he turned away.

Captain Ten Eyck took the dispatch and began reading in a curiously quiet voice. He stumbled over some words but there was little doubt as to their meaning.

TO: OFFICER COMMANDING FORT PHIL KEARNY,
BY THE PINEY FORK OF POWDER RIVER,
INDIAN TERRITORY

I am instructed by the Indian Department of the Government of the United States, in Washington, to order the immediate evacuation of Fort Phil Kearny.

You will proceed with the evacuation of this post and of any posts north in the vicinity of the site of Fort C. Smith, without delay.

All equipment you are unable to transport will be destroyed.

Your prime concern will be the safety of the women and children with the garrison.

I am also ordered to request that you report on the possibility of informing the paramount Chief of the Sioux of a council meeting to be held at Fort Laramie at a date in the near future. Advise receipt of this dispatch.

> ASST. ADJUTANT-GENERAL,
> DEPT. OF THE PLATTE,
> FORT SEDGEWICK

Ten Eyck finished and lowered the paper to his side. There was complete silence as they all looked at the Colonel. From outside, the noises of the morning crept into the room, the tramp of feet as the guard assembled, the cries from the cook-house and the jarring clang of the triangle as the duty cook summoned the early risers to breakfast.

Colonel Wessells turned to face the waiting group. For a second his reserve broke. "Why?" he burst out. "Why, when by thunder we had them licked?"

Robidoux grunted. "Seems like the Government seen some sense at last," he remarked. He pronounced the word "Government" in the French fashion making it seem like something alien and remote. Colonel Wessells regarded him with steely eyes.

Portugee spoke up. "What Washington has at last realized is that it ain't some raiding party of young bloods that they're up against—it's a full-scale Indian war. And licking Red Cloud in one battle don't end it."

He looked round the room. Ten Eyck was nodding in almost imperceptible agreement.

"Red Cloud's taken a hidin'," the scout went on, "but it ain't in his nature to give in easy. He's fighting for the life of his whole nation, don't forget. Sure, some of the tribes will leave him—but he's still got the bravest army of fighters these plains have ever seen. The Sioux will back him down to the last warrior. We know it, Colonel. You know it, though you won't admit it. And General Sherman knows it too!"

"But Sherman!" broke in Colonel Wessells. "Sherman's a

fighting general if ever there was one. Why——" He drew
a deep breath and his voice tailed off.

"Bridger's in Washington," said Portugee quietly.

"Who?" Colonel Wessells turned sharply.

"Jim Bridger," repeated Portugee. "Leastways, I heard
he was in Washington. Could be he talked to Sherman."

"You mean Bridger's behind this order?" Colonel Wessells
warmed to the attack, his disappointment with the order ex-
pressing itself in anger as he sought to place the blame for the
evacuation.

"Not directly; of course not." The scout's voice rose a
fraction. "Bridger was a good friend of Colonel Carrington.
Could be he went to see Sherman to put in a good word for the
Colonel. Sherman knows Jim's a man to speak his mind. Could
be he wanted to get to the truth of the Fetterman affair and
sent for Bridger."

Wessells digested this news in silence. It was true that
General Sherman was unorthodox in his methods; his sympathy for the outspoken independence of the frontier scouts
was well known. He could have obtained a very different picture of the situation in the Powder River country from Jim
Bridger than he could read in official reports.

"Jim had little time for this expedition from the start,"
Portugee went on. "He knows the Indians and he knows Red
Cloud, and he might just have told the Army what they're
really up against."

Powell and Ten Eyck looked at the scout in silence. Long
experience of warfare on the plains told them that Portugee
and his fellow scouts were probably right, that the Bozeman
Trail could not be opened and that the Government was acting in the only way possible. But they remained loyally silent.

It was a bitter pill for Colonel Wessells to swallow. Every
inch of him burned to get into action; to sweep out against the
hostiles and drive them out beyond the mountains. Yet he was
no fool.

What if Red Cloud refused to fight? What if the warriors
faded into the hills before every thrust, leaving the cavalry to
exhaust itself in march and counter-march while they slowly

throttled the fort by ambush and unexpected assault where it was least protected? How long could they hold out against such guerrilla tactics without supplies, without reinforcements and with winter approaching?

For long minutes he stood there, with his shoulders hunched and his head bowed. The others waited in silence and in sympathy as they sensed the struggle that was going on in his mind. At last he gave in.

"Right," he said decisively, once again the efficient Army officer. "We have our orders. The only thing that remains is to see that they are carried out with dignity and without endangering the lives of those who have defended the post for so long."

He looked along the tense faces before him.

"The evacuation of the troops is not difficult," he said, and then added slowly, "But the evacuation of the women and children, the belongings that they will wish to take with them —that is a very different matter. Red Cloud is waiting for us on every trail. A slow-moving wagon train will become a tempting target from the moment it crosses the Piney."

The tension in the room relaxed as they concentrated on this new problem. The die had been cast by hands other than their own. Now, all that remained to be done was the efficient organization of the wagon trains to safety.

At a word from the Colonel, the officers drew chairs around the orderly room table. Robidoux pulled his pipe from his pocket and spoke while he pushed the black tobacco down.

"It need not be a slow-moving train, Colonel. If we traveled light, taking a minimum of equipment . . ."

"You're forgetting the wounded, Robidoux," said Captain Powell. "We've upwards of twenty men sick. They're not all stretcher cases, but even one loaded ambulance wagon will slow the whole train."

"With the women and children, we'll be one of the biggest caravans that's ever tackled the Bozeman Trail," added Ten Eyck. "And we'll need every man we can muster to fight it through."

"*Must* we fight it through?"

They all turned to look at Portugee. His chin rested in the cupped palm of one hand, his dark eyes looked straight at the Colonel. After a moment's silence he went on: "I reckon this parley with Red Cloud must come before we leave. That way we can bargain for the safe evacuation of everyone in the fort."

"But how are we going to get him to talk?" Colonel Wessells leaned forward across the table, his hands clasped before him over the crumpled dispatch from Washington. "They don't recognize a flag of truce. Any man or company going out from here will have a fight on their hands as soon as they've crossed the Sullivants, we've proved that. And anyway —who'd trust a hostile's word under the circumstances?"

Portugee said nothing but his look implied that he respected Red Cloud for more than his prowess as a leader in battle.

He pushed back his chair and went into the Colonel's office. They heard him searching for something in the corner; presently he returned with a long, dusty, decorated stick in his hand. Jean Robidoux gave a cry of recognition as he saw it; it was Red Cloud's totem scalp.

"I'll take this," said Portugee quietly. "I'll parley with Red Cloud."

"Et moi—I'll come with you!" cried the Frenchman, leaping to his feet.

Everything was in readiness for the trip before daylight came. In the flickering light of lanterns, the blacksmith had checked both horses, tightening a shoe here and there with an additional nail.

Fortune blew loudly through his nostrils as Portugee led him out by the stable doors. The sky was grey in the east. Robidoux, already in the saddle, puffed on the black pipe and looked round at the dim outline of the hills.

Portugee pushed the Navy firmly down in its holster and swung up on Fortune's back. For the last time he checked swiftly over his equipment, patted Fortune on the neck and

gently dug his heels into the soft flanks. Slowly the pair walked
their horses towards the gate.

A group of dark figures huddled beside the stockade. Under
the gate itself, Corporal Riley and Colonel Wessells were waiting. The Colonel spoke briefly to the scouts, shook hands with
each in turn, stepped back, saluted them formally and then
turned on his heel to climb the ladder on to the parapet. The
other figures pressed forward to wish the scouts good luck.
To his surprise, Portugee saw that some of them were women
with their children.

The gates swung open. The trail gleamed white in the growing light. With a sudden clatter of hooves the pair moved
bravely out.

"God grant them a safe return," murmured one woman,
the boy at her side clutching an old rifle almost twice as tall
as himself. "That Mr. Phillips, he'll save us if anyone can."

They watched the riders growing smaller on the plain,
the wicked totem jogging in the morning breeze above the
Frenchman's horse. When the sun came up in a golden rush
they were mere specks climbing the distant ridge.

The Colonel remained watching the blue hills long after the
scouts had disappeared.

Before they sighted the buttes that marked the approach to
Little Goose River, the Indians had found them. The first
raiding party of braves had rushed up over the open prairie,
already giving tongue to their ringing war cries before they
saw the totem.

Robidoux was riding with his rifle balanced across the
pommel of the saddle. He eased it up as the Sioux approached.
He had faith in the totem, it is true, but a finger curled round
the shining trigger of the Springfield-Allen somehow gave
the painted scalp an added potency.

The Indians drew off and debated together while the scouts
continued to ride forward. Presently one brave dashed off
over undulating ground to reappear after a short time with a
second band of Indians. The painted warriors circled the
scouts, talking and pointing to the totem.

The two parties then took up station on either side, riding in single file at a distance of some twenty yards from the pair, their war ponies keeping to the same steady pace.

"We have an escort of honor, mon vieux," called Robidoux, lowering the rifle gently across the saddle again.

"And a reception party, no doubt," said Portugee, nodding towards a plume of white smoke that climbed swiftly up from a peak to the left. Far ahead, at another point on the skyline, a second column of smoke answered.

The strange party moved on across the vast landscape, the Indians riding silently on either side, the scouts setting a brisk pace as the sun climbed high in the clear sky. The shadows shortened beneath the horses and the horizon shimmered and danced in the heat. At length, the broken line of the ridge above Little Goose River came into sight and a row of mounted warriors, drawn directly across their line of march.

As they approached they could see the crimson pennants waving from the lances and the notched eagle feathers tossing in the breeze that flowed up from the valley floor. Away to the left was a large cluster of spindly saplings supporting row upon row of burial platforms. The carrion birds rose up in a black and ugly cloud as the riders approached.

No word of greeting was exchanged. The line of warriors opened and the war ponies preceded the scouts over the crest of the bluff. The Indians rode much closer now on the narrow trail. Portugee could study the fantastic designs of the war paint on each face, the eagle feathers and gaudy streamers of cloth interwoven into the manes and tails of the ponies— and the razor-sharp edges of the lances glinting in the sun.

To Robidoux, the sight was not unfamiliar and yet, he, too, was awed by the great encampment. It was true that a closer examination of the valley revealed empty clearings where a few months before the camps of the Arapaho and Oglalas had sprawled. But still the valley was filled with the noise and bustle and smoke of a great Indian army.

And now the details of the French scout's first ride into the valley were repeated. Down the precarious trail, surrounded by jolting war ponies and tossing lances, the two men rode to the valley floor.

A great mass of braves, women, excited children and snarling dogs rushed to meet them. Their escort reversed the lances and forced a path through the shouting crowd. The drums throbbed on all sides. Over the heads of the nearest Indians, Portugee could see more and more people streaming through the camps to meet them.

The noise was deafening. It was as if the Indians sensed victory almost within their grasp. Exultant shouts of triumph and screams of revenge were flung at the two white men, tiny specks afloat in a sea of savage dancing, sweating, jeering faces. Hands gestured in the jackal sign or made a scalping motion and pointed at the dauntless pair. At each sign a roar went up from the multitude.

The escort began to use the points of their lances to force a way through. Portugee caught sight of Jean's set face, the black pipe upside down and unlit, jutting from the corner of his mouth, the knuckles of his hands white where he grasped the rifle. Side by side they rode on, through the rows of painted totems, wheeling into the wide-open space before the three lodges, into the center of the circle where the medicine men waited.

The mob held back but they were drunk with triumph now. The drums vibrated through the hot air, the dust rose from a hundred thousand stamping feet. Danger whirled in a threatening circle, only held in check by the authority of the unseen chief.

A warrior pulled the totem from Robidoux's horse and went with it into the largest of the three lodges. He reappeared and signed to the scouts to dismount. They did so, leading their mounts close to the tepee and tethering them to a post beside the entrance.

The guard pulled back the leather flap that covered the door. Stooping, the scouts entered swiftly and stood in the dark interior. The flap dropped back. The drums and chanting seemed to recede. Blinking after the strong sunlight, Portugee and his friend waited for their eyes to become accustomed to the gloom. A weird and frightening sight slowly revealed itself to them.

A fire burned in the center of the lodge, the smoke rising in a stream and disappearing through the sunlit opening far above. The poles of the lodge leaned inwards, reaching up from semi-darkness towards the light. From every projection hung weapons of war: bows, quivers, lances, rifles and powder horns. Round the foot of the lodge the dark forms of many Indians squatted, silent, waiting.

A ball of buffalo fat was flung into the fire and instantly a bright flame leaped up, darting to the very apex of the conical lodge and illuminating every corner. The huge shadows of the seated chiefs danced black and tall on the leaning walls. The firelight gilded their features, shone on the beads and glittering vests of eagle quills.

In the center, facing the scouts, a little apart from the rest was Red Cloud.

He was arrayed in full war regalia. The flames patterned the scarlet ceremonial blanket, accentuated the hawk-like features and sparked the piercing eyes.

A hand motioned the scouts to a pile of buffalo robes before the fire. Kicking a couple of growling dogs aside, they sat down facing Red Cloud across the dying flames.

Again a ball of fat was thrown into the embers to light up the macabre scene.

Red Cloud leaned forward. The dark eyes gazed straight at Portugee. For long seconds neither moved, then the Chief spoke to someone at the back of the lodge. There was a brief conversation and then again silence.

Robidoux cleared his throat. "What was that about?" he asked.

Portugee continued to gaze unwaveringly at the Chief of the Sioux. "They recognize me," he replied.

"You mean you've talked with him before?"

"Yes, but it's not that. They've given me a name since that ride to Laramie last winter. They call me the 'Man-who-rides-alone'."

"Is that a good omen?" asked Jean.

Portugee shrugged. "I had to kill three braves on that journey."

Robidoux gave a low whistle.

The Chief sat on in silence. Periodically another ball of fat would be flung in the fire and the scene would dance with brilliant illumination. Outside the drumming throbbed without cease. At length Portugee judged it time to speak. He rose slowly, gave the Indian sign of greeting and spoke directly to the impassive figure seated the other side of the fire.

"I come in peace," he said, searching slowly for the words in the Sioux tongue. "From the white eagle of the soldiers."

Red Cloud watched him; waited, then said one word.

"Car-ring-ton?"

"No. Not Colonel Carrington," answered Portugee.

The Chief spat contemptuously in the fire.

"Little white chief," he said. Then, "Why do you come?"

Portugee took a deep breath.

"The Great Father in Washington sent me with a message for the great Chief of all the Sioux," he began. "Fourteen moons ago he called a council at Laramie to buy land from his Indian brothers and make a road through the hills. You were there; you know. The Great Father agreed not to kill the buffalo, not to drive away the game, not to make war." Portugee paused and looked round the circle of dark faces. Before he could go on Red Cloud interrupted brusquely.

"If not to make war, then why does he send soldiers to build forts?"

"He has to build forts for his people on the trail, to change horses and repair their wagons. And there must be soldiers to protect the wagons from the young braves who do not obey their chief. Red Cloud will admit that he cannot control some who rob and kill and will not let the white people travel in peace."

Red Cloud drew himself upright. "I control *all* men," he said slowly. "Different tribes—one nation. If I say 'no war,' then braves will not fight."

Portugee tried another tack.

"The Great Father gave all the land north of the shallow

river to the Sioux. All he asked is that his people be allowed to cross the land in peace."

A brave threw more fat on the fire, and as the flames rose Red Cloud sprang to his feet.

"Lies. White man's lies," he cried. "The Great Father gave us presents at Laramie and wanted us to sell him the road—but before the Indians said 'yes' or 'no,' he sent the white eagle with his soldiers to steal the land."

A chorus of agreement came from the other chiefs in the lodge. The drums seemed louder in the silence that followed. Red Cloud pressed his advantage. Pointing a long finger at Portugee, he continued.

"I spoke to Car-ring-ton. I told him, NO!" He waved his hand sideway like a scythe. "I said that I would fight for the road. I have kept my word. Fetter-man and many, many white scalps hang in our lodges. There will be many more, every mile the white eagle comes into our land."

He sat down; the chiefs nodding and grunting their agreement in the dimming light. The talk went on with question and answer, accusation and explanation going back and forth across the angry flames.

Portugee gave ground gradually. Wisely he let Red Cloud justify his cause; cunningly he argued as if to reopen the Government's case for the Bozeman Trail. At last, appearing to admit defeat against the Chief's arguments, he came to the real reason for his mission.

Rising to his feet—he spoke directly to Red Cloud but made sure that all could hear.

"The Great Father has seen his children fighting and it makes him sad. He, too, is a mighty hunter and understands the Indian's love for the land. He has seen how all the tribes have united to fight for their hunting grounds and he has seen that their cause is just."

The Indians were listening now to the scout's carefully chosen words in the Sioux tongue. Portugee paused before going on and pointed to the fire. A brave threw the buffalo fat and the light brightened. Looking across the fire directly at the Sioux chief, the scout said slowly:

"The Great Father will call his soldiers back. No more fighting. No more war. And the land north of the shallow river will be left for the Indian forever. All he asks is that his people can go back in peace."

There was complete silence in the lodge. With great deliberation Red Cloud rose, gathering the crimson blanket around him. Carefully he looked at each chief in turn. There was no perceptible sign of agreement, but when he turned back to the scout a look of triumph transformed his haughty features.

"No road? No more forts?" his voice was hard.

Portugee shook his head.

"No road. No more forts."

The Chief said nothing for a long time. When at last he spoke again it was not to Portugee but to begin a long harangue. The words came too quickly for the scout to follow in detail but it was clearly a trumphant review of the past events and justification of his leadership. Wearily Portugee sank back on the pile of buffalo robes and Jean, leaning close to him, asked whether it was all settled.

Portugee nodded. There would be long speeches and more bargaining, but he knew that Red Cloud had accepted his proposal; felt that perhaps the Chief welcomed it rather than face the difficulties of holding the tribes together through another bitter winter. He let the words flow on and noticed that the drums had taken a new and more frantic beat. The news must have spread even while they were talking.

At length Red Cloud finished and motioned towards the scouts. The medicine man drew forth a large, red clay pipe with a stem the size of a walking stick. From a pouch profusely ornamented with beads and porcupine quills he pulled a handful of kinnikinic—a tobacco made of willow bark and herbs—and proceeded with solemn ceremony to fill the bowl and then light it with a brand from the fire.

When he had finished he first pointed the long stem slowly at the four parts of the compass and then placed it in Portugee's mouth, muttering a prayer to the Great Spirit at the same time.

Portugee took a dozen slow puffs and handed the pipe back. The medicine man crossed to Red Cloud. The Chief took the pipe from him and slowly drew down the sweet tobacco smoke, watching the scouts all the time. He finished and passed the pipe to the chief on his left, who also puffed slowly.

So the ceremony went on until the pipe had been round the circle. Then there was a brief discussion to settle the time of the evacuation and at length, tired but satisfied, the scouts prepared to leave.

For the first time Red Cloud left his seat by the fire and came close to Portugee. He said no word but stood before the scout looking long and searchingly into the eyes of the "Man-who-rides-alone." Portugee returned the scrutiny. Then without a word the Chief turned away.

A brave drew back the leather flap that formed a door to the lodge and ushered them outside.

The bright light and noise hit them like a physical blow. A great shout went up from the assembled Indians as they saw the white men. There were drums and dances, bells and rattles, the sounds of victory.

Portugee and Robidoux mounted their horses. Fortune tossed his head, the whites of his eyes gleamed and his ears twitched at the din. A party of warriors on war ponies closed around them. As they moved off to begin the long trek back to Fort Phil Kearny, Red Cloud emerged from the lodge. The roar of cheering swelled up.

The paramount Chief of all the Sioux stood motionless. Whatever his feelings were they did not show. But the pride surging in his breast found its voice in a great song of triumph from a hundred thousand throats that echoed along the valley and was flung back and forth between the high bluffs on either side.

9
THE LAST
WAGON TRAIN

The bugle rang out over the fort on the Little Piney.

It was a clear bright morning in the late summer. Small white clouds moved across the sky in the southeast, heralding the end of the dry hot days.

The parade ground had been the scene of great activity since first light. The cooks were standing beside the kitchens eating a hurried breakfast; everyone else had been fed in readiness for the journey.

The bugle call was the "General," the first indication of the march. In answer, on every side, the occupants of Fort Phil Kearny prepared to move out.

As the notes of the call died away Colonel Wessells, closely followed by Major Powell and an orderly, came out of the Headquarters block and stood for a moment on the steps surveying the scene.

Portugee Phillips and Jean Robidoux were standing with their horses at the end of the long row of stables. They were equipped for the trail in their old, worn buckskin jackets that had seen so many miles of the prairie, the shining holsters and gunbelts, the kerchiefs to keep out the dust. Their horses, too, were loaded: rifles in scabbards, the bedrolls high behind the saddles, packs on either side.

To their left, the gates of the fort stood wide open. Guards walked on the banquette above the stables, but the blockhouse on Pilot Hill was already deserted. Outside the fort, drawn up in close order on the trail to the south, were the great Conestoga wagons and their teams. Loaded with care during the preceding days, each wagon carried the precious possessions of families of the garrison and, in addition, stores for the journey. Women stood in little groups, talking in subdued tones. A soldier with a rifle lounged by each wagon. The bull-whackers waited by their teams—and round and round the assembled column, oblivious to the drama of the occasion, the children played in high-spirited glee. It was a great occasion to be moving . . . old Red Cloud up there in the hills was nothing to be scared of now. The boys leaped out from behind the tall wheels with mock war whoops; the girls screamed and ran laughing into their mothers' skirts.

"It's fun for them, eh," Jean turned to his friend and laughed too. Portugee glanced through the gate and nodded but his thoughts were elsewhere.

He put a foot in Fortune's stirrups and climbed into the saddle as Colonel Wessells and his entourage began to move across the square. Jean followed suit, and the two scouts sat watching the scene before them.

The tents on the side of the parade ground were coming down. Busy soldiers moved about, dragging the canvas to the army wagons waiting by the stockade wall where Colonel Wessells had so dramatically demonstrated the power of the Springfield-Allens. The bang of mallets could be heard as the tent pegs were knocked out of the sunbaked ground. From the barracks a file of men issued, forming up along the eastern side of the parade ground.

Sergeant Hoover walked slowly up and down before the ranks, pointing here and there impatiently as the gathering fell short of his idea of discipline.

On either side of the tall flagstaff the lines of horses waited quietly in the early sunlight.

The cooks finished their meal, throwing the tin mugs and plates into the chuck wagon, kicking open the oven doors and spilling the red embers out on to the earth, to whiten and die in the cool air.

Within the fort there was little conversation. A quiet purposefulness hung over the scene. Only the rattle of army equipment and the movement of a few groups struggling with some last-minute chore broke the general hush. Sam Gibson

came by, humping a last pile of harness from the stables, and
gave the scouts a cheery greeting. The civilians had already
quitted the stockade. The wagon train, loaded and guarded
had stood beside the great walls all night and moved out on to
the trail at first light. The families passed the dark hours in
fitful sleep in the empty huts and had gone to the wagons as
soon as breakfast was over.

Fort Phil Kearny was entering its last moments as an army
post.

"John, look up there."

It was Robidoux calling, pointing to the blockhouse on Pilot
Hill. A group of dark figures had appeared on the skyline, to
be joined by others even as Portugee watched. The long spears
and pointed feathers of the Sioux moved in silhouette against
the rising sun.

"They've been on the hills all night," said the scout, turning
back to the Frenchman. "Want to make sure we keep our side
of the bargain."

Across the square, Frank Robertson stepped to the major's
side and drew his attention to the Indians. Powell spoke to
Colonel Wessells, who turned from the foot of the flagstaff
and stared for a moment at the hostiles. He turned away and
gave a brief command to the bugler.

The man brought the bugle to his lips with a flourish. "Boots
and Saddles" sang crisply across the parade ground. The children outside crowded into the gates to watch.

All along the edge of the square the soldiers moved into line;
the boards of the army wagons thudded up into place, the
infantry stood at ease before each wagon. Along the line of
horses the troopers were making the final adjustments to their
saddles.

Again the bugle sounded, "To horse." The troopers ran,
each to his mount's head.

"Prepare to mount."

Colonel Wessells himself called the command, his voice firm
and clear. Every man placed his left foot in the stirrup.

"Mount."

The troopers rose on the stirrups as one man and placed

themselves in the saddles. The infantry came to attention.
Complete silence fell on the fort.

Robidoux drew off his hat and rested it on the pommel of
the saddle. Portugee slowly lowered the battered old felt to
Fortune's side.

As the notes of the bugle fell like silver across the silent
buildings, across the great stockade and the still ranks of the
garrison, the flag sank slowly from the top of the mast.

Portugee's eyes moved over the valley, to the bright outlines
of the Sullivants, the distant purples of Lodge Trail Ridge, the
meadows running down to the Piney, the waving grass round
the white posts on the hill.

Familiar faces drifted obstinately into his vision. Lieutenant Mallory who had suffered the first attack on the wood
train . . . Grummond—and his wife holding out the golden
locket on that dark night in December. Brown and Fetterman,
faint and angry figures striding into the bloody valley beyond
the ridge . . . and Tom Haggerty, dead with a smile on his
face in the arrow-ripped wagonbox.

There were many who would not be riding back with
them, many who would stay for ever in the far hills and sweet,
bloodstained meadows.

In his heart Portugee had known it all along. Was the fighting for nothing, then? All in vain?

Fortune stamped on the hard earth. The scout patted the
lovely neck beneath him.

He answered his own unspoken question. Courage was never
worthless. It has a value of its own whatever the outcome.
Courage had marked the year in the valley and demanded respect from all.

Red Cloud had acknowledged the courage of the "Man-
who-rides-alone." Phillips in his turn respected the Indian
Chief for what he was, a brave and tenacious man holding
out for what he believed was right, fighting a losing battle
against the inevitable change that was sweeping westward
across the great continent with the advancing frontier.

Perhaps that was what came out of it all, an understanding
of the vaster picture than that which could be seen in the

Piney valley. History was in the making in this bloody and eventful year; one small step had been taken—a bitter backward one for the pioneers, a trimphant one for their foes— towards the peace that must in the end come to the prairies.

The bugle sounded "The Advance." In columns of four the troops moved across the white square. There was a sudden bustle at the gate as the children ran to the wagons, shouting in their excitement and climbing up over the wheels and tailboards to tumble inside.

With Colonel Wessells at their head, the Army moved out of Fort Phil Kearny. The howitzer teams rumbled behind, the cavalry clattered through the gate. Slowly the army wagons followed, each with its complement of marching men, moving up past the waiting bull train. The whips began to crack and with the yelling of the drivers the whole column came to life.

Portugee pulled Fortune's head round. The fort swung in swift review: the stockade wall, where the snow had piled high on the night old Jim Bridger directed the half-frozen troops to "shovel away"; the bakery chimneys, cold and smokeless; the black gaping doorways of the barracks; the tiny hospital.

An ambulance wagon rolled by, Dr. Horton sitting bolt upright on the high seat, straight as a ramrod, looking neither to the left or right. The last company marched behind.

Portugee and Robidoux were the only ones left. They looked at each other. Jean reached up and stuck his pipe into his mouth, his eyes suddenly busy with his tobacco pouch. Portugee felt a tightness in his throat. He raised an arm in brief salute at the empty square and rode out through the gate.

As they passed the last company of the Twenty-Seventh one man turned. It was the soldier of the red check shirt. He shook his fist at the hills where the Indians watched, motionless.

"We'll be comin' back!" he yelled.

Portugee rode by. In the wagons the children could be seen, clinging to the hoops, peering back. At the rear of each there were silent groups of white faces, some stern, some openly weeping.

The head of the train reached the Piney. A low thrilling sound became noticeable above the clatter of hoofs and rolling wheels, a continuous humming note that grew and throbbed on the morning air.

Everyone was looking back now, the troopers turning in the saddles, the drivers standing in the seats, their whips silent. The infantry marched with their heads over their shoulders, stumbling often into the man in front. Only Colonel Wessells rode grimly on, his eyes fixed on the trail ahead.

The hills above the fort were suddenly black with Indians. Their shouting rose up and up like the war cry of a whole nation, electrifying every man who heard it.

Suddenly they began to move. In a dark horde they streamed down the slopes, leaping over boulders, surging out on to the meadows around the fort.

The first running figures reached the stockade while the main body still poured over the hills. To the west, on a promontory overlooking the scene, a small group of horsemen watched.

"Red Cloud." Corporal Riley pulled his horse up beside Portugee. "It's Red Cloud."

The first black smoke stained the sky. Red flame licked the base of the watchtower. Swiftly the column of fire climbed, bursting outwards like some gorgeous but deadly flower. The smoke rolled across the rising sun and the terrible triumphant crying went on.

Fortune stumbled, jolting the scout's attention from the scene. Portugee smoothed his mane and leaning forward, spoke gently into the searching ears.

Straightening up, he put the horse to a canter and went flying down the column to join Colonel Wessells.

He did not look back again.

FACTS

Portugee John Phillips, Colonel Henry B. Carrington, Captain Ten Eyck and many other people in this book really lived and fought on the American frontier during the Indian wars of 1864-9. Fort Phil Kearny was built on Piney Creek, a branch of the Powder River, Wyoming, in 1866, and besieged by Red Cloud, perhaps the greatest chief that the Sioux Indians ever had. The deaths of Colonel Fetterman and his men, Portugee's epic ride, the wagon-box fight and many other incidents really happened. The Government awarded Phillips 300 dollars for his services.

How he left the service of the Army and journeyed south to start his own ranch, how once more he fought Red Cloud's warriors, is the subject of another story.

K. R. U.